HOME
FRONT
LINES

HOME FRONT LINES

A Novel

BRENDA SPARKS PRESCOTT

Bink Books

Bedazzled Ink Publishing Company • Fairfield, California

978-1-949290-53-0 paperback

Cover Design
by
Monkey C Media

Bink Books
a division of
Bedazzled Ink Publishing Company
Fairfield, California
http://www.bedazzledink.com

For my nuclear family: Arnold, Mae, and Anthony Sparks

Acknowledgements

Much respect to Joan Conner, Elizabeth Searle, and all of the teachers and mentors who helped breathe life into the beginnings of this project. A special tip o' the hat to Dennis Lehane for yang and for attention to plotting. Blessings to Eunice Scarfe, leader of The Blank Page workshop, where the first words of this story emerged. Many, many thanks to the editors of the journals in which stories and characters from this book appeared in different forms: *The Louisville Review*, "Nuclear Family," and *The Crab Orchard Review*, "The Messenger or Woman Waving to the Future." Boundless praise for the folks at Bedazzled Ink Publishing and Smith Publicity, who invited this book out into the wide world.

Deep gratitude to Paul Zernicke and Kelly Hahn for championing my writing. Much love to this book's wise and magical godmothers: Tanya Whiton, Lee Hope, Suzanne Strempek Shea, Anne Britting Oleson, Rebecca Bearden Welsh, the late Elisabeth Wilkins Lombardo, Lynn Gonsalves, Mary Archambault, Betsy Smith, and Julia Parrillo. And eternal adoration for Jim, "my knight in shiny armor."

Table of Contents

We all died during the Cuban Missile Crisis.
All of this is just an after-image.
                    —Dennis Nurske

Appointment with Mrs. H. 1

BETTY ANN JOHNSON was alone. Her two assistants wouldn't arrive at the dressmaking studio until eight. That's what she called it—her studio—although it was really just a large, open room over Paul's Vacuums in a plaza in Silver Spring. In other shops, fluorescent lights tinged the room green and errant pins stuck up from dingy, threadbare carpet. That was not Betty Ann's style. Rather than keep a dismal workroom, she had run her business from closets in her homes on Air Force posts and had saved every nickel until she could afford to open a nice studio.

She pulled an aqua Princess phone within reach, lined up a tablet of pink paper beside it, and settled on her stool. She expected the unexpected call. Tons of supplies, munitions, and personnel moved through the Maryland Air Force base where Ray, her husband, was stationed. Although the installation was undergoing rapid expansion, the current activity level outstripped its usual frenetic pace. The military does plenty of senseless things, but not at that scale. Something was up. She had to be alert.

Ray had already called earlier that morning to tell her that he was working a double shift again. It was his third in a week. When the order came to shrink the time for mandatory flight readiness down to only one hour, the wives knew something was up but the guys weren't talking. That was the disturbing part of carrying on as usual: the wives were on the inside, knew details civilians never heard about, but when the men wouldn't, couldn't tell, it was time to worry. However, Betty Ann had rules. Never worry until you know what to worry about. That was a hard one to keep, with the wall in Berlin, Castro in Cuba, missiles in Turkey, and rockets in space.

The newspapers talked about nukes and A-bombs in the abstract—how many they had, how many we had—even as American school children drilled for an emergency in the vain hope that a nuclear strike might be survivable. All of that was well and good for civilians. Her husband loaded nuclear weapons onto planes. Her son's ship was probably carrying them also. If she knew all of that, someone on the other side did also, making her home base and her son's berth big, fat targets. Fussing with pleats and sewing hidden hems seemed ludicrous when she thought like that, so she tried not to.

Clouds of taffeta and silk floated from racks of half-finished gowns for upcoming balls. Most of her clients were well-to-do Negroes who attended the Harvest Moon Ball put on by the black Shriners. She had a growing following, though, among white women who wanted more style than a department store could offer and who liked Betty Ann's reasonable prices. She kept the patterns for their gowns segregated so she could assure them that when they appeared at the Harvest Ball, no colored woman would be wearing the same dress to the Harvest Moon Ball. What she didn't tell them was that her best creations always danced with her Negro clients.

Betty Ann inspected every stitch sewed in her studio. At the end of the previous night, her assistants had left a green taffeta and a white satin on her worktable. Most of Mimi's green taffeta was fine; Betty Ann found fault only in the ruche at the back of the waist. She pinned a small square of red cloth to the spot and turned to the white satin. Terry's stitching was more problematic, as she was more likely to rush. When the hour got late and the hand and eye tired, the brain reasoned that good was good enough. Betty Ann understood, but she had her standards. The zipper would have to be redone. She shook her head as she wrote "zipper" on a piece of pink paper. She pinned the note to the offending spot and returned the gowns to her assistants' stations.

The extra worktables for her assistants, along with a serger, a steamer, a counter with a small sink, and a miniscule bathroom, made up the work area at the end of the studio furthest from the door. Ray knew a carpet layer who had patiently assembled remnants of steel gray Berber carpeting that didn't show dirt. The pearl gray walls echoed the color of a Manhattan showroom she had studied during a visit to Ray's family. The work area could be hidden by curtains that hung from ceiling to floor. Betty Ann had made them from a coral-and-salmon striped sateen she had bought on the same trip to New York. The smooth fabric had cost more than the nubs of carpeting did, but the stylish curtains lent polish to the atelier. That's what Betty Ann really called her studio, but only to herself.

Despite the seasonal jump in work, the women kept the studio clean by tidying up at the end of each day, no matter how tired they were. Betty Ann was strict with that routine, keeping it up herself as an example, and her assistants usually stayed in line with her. Even so, Betty Ann found an *Ebony* magazine on Terry's chair and returned it to the coffee table on the showroom side. Two years earlier, as 1960 headed for the World Series and its own late innings, Ray had balked at missing a late-season game to buy furniture for her studio. Despite his reluctance, though, she had gotten the pink Naugahyde and black wrought iron love seats. Then she bought the coffee table and two matching side tables from an Air Force family that had been reassigned to Japan. Ray tiled them in black, pink, and gray. Soon her lounge area, accessorized with *Good Housekeeping* and *Jet,* aqua pillows, and the aqua Princess phone with its long cord, became the nexus of a certain Negro feminine society.

After filling the percolator with water and plugging it in, Betty Ann sat at her work table in the center of the studio. An emergency repair, the fallen hem of a black wool skirt, lay in front of her. It would have to be done by hand. She decided to get it out of the way before plunging back into the froth of the ball gowns. She usually wouldn't take a routine job like the black skirt during the season of fetes and balls, but it was for Mrs. Dupont, who always paid extra. Betty Ann made an exception for her. Exceptions were good for business. Exceptions were good for life.

She had no illusions. She had grown up outside a town in Southern Illinois that was so small, folks driving south on Route 3 from Murphysboro toward Kentucky didn't notice the clapboard church and the few other buildings that reluctantly huddled down the cross road to their left. Even the outbuildings on the farms looked like strangers that had been forced into close quarters and were trying their damnedest not to touch. She knew that the Negroes in Washington who could trace their ancestry on both sides of the color line back to the 1600s could smell the dark loam settled deep in her soul. When she slipped and said "ambalance" or "su-supposed," she saw the slight flaring of the nostrils and the barely noticeable uptick of the head. Still, they came to her.

If they wanted to pretend that no one in their family tree ever picked cotton, she let them. She just charged a little more. Once, Mrs. Dupont, the owner of the skirt she was hemming and a light-skinned lady who insisted she was allergic to the sun, discovered that her neighbor paid less than she did for a suit. Betty Ann immediately offered her the same discount, saying, "Of course, for that price, you get German-inspired design, not French. It's just as good, though." She reached over to Mrs. Dupont and smoothed a nonexistent wrinkle out of her collar. "No one can tell the difference. Mrs. Kennedy, maybe. Surely, though, it won't matter to you." Not only did Mrs. Dupont refuse the discount, she told all her snooty friends to request "the French cut." Their reach for exclusivity was A-okay with Betty Ann.

The Princess phone rang.

Betty Ann lay down the wool skirt. The call couldn't be one of her regular customers; they didn't phone before nine. Ray maybe, with a request goofy enough that her heartbeat could slow and she could let exasperation creep into her voice. The phone rang again. Or perhaps it was Lonnie, her oldest, the one in the Navy, on the *Princeton* somewhere in the Pacific (he had been vague about his whereabouts in his last several letters). Perhaps he had swapped a bottle of illicit Scotch for a phone patch-through to the States. The phone rang a third time as she opened the drawer of the worktable and pulled out a man's gold ring. On its face was an eagle etched in onyx. She closed her fist around the ring and picked up the phone.

"Sonia has broken her wrist." The soft words began without introduction. "Bowling." The Southern accent and obvious frustration drew the word out long past its natural life.

"Bowling, Mrs. Hepplewhite?" Betty Ann's voice was light and clear, but the circle of the ring dented the flesh of her clenched fist. She was almost a hundred percent sure who her caller was, but if it were not the wife of the famous Brigadier General Harold "Happy" Hepplewhite, the speaker would be flattered by the mistake. Nicki Hepplewhite had a distinctive, melodious voice, familiar from her many appearances at base functions, but until now, she had never spoken directly to this particular wife. Not once.

The general's wife wasn't in the habit of calling NCO wives at seven thirty in the morning, unless, of course, they worked for her. Betty Ann didn't. She didn't even work on base, not since she had moved her dressmaking business closer to the Negro trade. She didn't consider the earliness of the call odd, the way a real civilian would. The military started before dawn and those married to it did too.

"I would not dare to bother you if this unfortunate accident had not put me in a completely desperate situation."

"Ma'am?" Betty Ann cradled the receiver with her shoulder. She dropped the ring into her pocket and picked up the black wool skirt. Her hands were steady as she worked the needle.

Mrs. H. was the Jackie Kennedy of the Maryland Air Force set, and the wives of the airmen religiously followed her Southern interpretation of the First Lady's style. Sonia K., her dressmaker, had ambition, a mutable background, and a facility with accents. Her designs flattered Mrs. H. with a natural sophistication.

"Sonia's arm will be in one of those huge, ugly plaster casts for weeks. Why can't they make them more modest? Anyway, that leaves me without a new dress for our invitation in two weeks." She assumed that the world knew about an upcoming dinner with the Kennedys. In this case, the world did know. Success at the White House would mean additional commands assigned to the base and maybe even another star for the General's shoulder. Betty Ann made it her business to know such things.

She snipped the black thread of the hem. "What may I do for you?"

"Honey, Sonia says you're the only one north of Atlanta that she'd trust. We've changed the design so much that the right pattern's not even cut yet. Think of coming here as a personal favor to me."

Betty Ann swept a look over the racks of her own colorful creations. "I can't possibly leave the studio with all the gowns to finish for the balls."

"Is it the money? I swear you people will bleed me dry."

Betty Ann's hands stopped checking the skirt's seams for breaks. What people was she referring to, exactly?

After a pause Mrs. H. said, "I'll pay you double your normal rate."

Most services were available at the right price, but a major hurdle loomed that money alone might not clear. This was the first time Mrs. H. had spoken to Betty Ann directly, but it wasn't their first meeting. That was just a few weeks before and had involved the owner of the ring in her pocket. The encounter had gone poorly. If Mrs. H. made the association, her surefire drive to engage Betty Ann might evaporate or turn vindictive. Betty Ann's casting as a generic Negress at their first meeting had humiliated her. Now the namelessness presented a grand opportunity, but accepting this commission posed a huge risk.

"You're very generous," she said, "but I was here until midnight last night, and probably will be again tonight with my existing orders."

"Then we'll come to your studio."

Betty Ann sewed for several white women, but none came to the studio. She speared white thread through the eye of the needle and started to reinforce the overstitching on the skirt pocket.

"This is a Negro shop," she said. She appreciated the quality of the silence that followed. Good. Now they were both uncomfortable.

Mrs. H. sighed and said, "Any other circumstances I should be aware of?"

Betty Ann could think of plenty. "No, ma'am."

"Then when will you be free?"

"Three thirty?"

"Three thirty it is." Mrs. Hepplewhite hung up.

Betty Ann jumped up and shook the receiver like a maraca. Its long cord waved underneath. "All right, Mrs. H.," she said, swaying her hips to her own beat. This business exception could prove deadly, her trespass too fresh to go without notice by the eagle-eyed Mrs. H. Yet. A dress worn to a White House dinner. The recognition? That would be worth the risk.

Lola
The Discretion of the Monteros 1

I AM THE sister that makes the food. I am the practical one. I have a small café named Dolores, after me, although everyone calls me Lola. It is near Plaza Valdés, not far down Calle Santa Monica. Most women in our old set would not have run a café, much less cook in their own homes, but I am a Montero, and our heritage shows no matter what we do. We have Catalonian blood from both sides. Yes, but you're showing your Versailles roots, those silly women would chide, as if that were not as good as being from old Matanzas. No matter.

We were not afraid of work and remembered well that Abuelo started in a small shack on a deserted beach. Although Mami came with more blood and money than Papi, she did not believe that women should be useless. She made sure all three of us girls learned to cook on our large stove at home. A lady needed to know how to make meals that please a man, she insisted, even if the lady is not expected to do more than supervise their preparation.

At first Chita, our middle sister, scolded me for pursuing what she called a common course. She taunted me with the venerated name of Lola Cruz, saying I was bringing shame to that gracious first lady of Matanzas (who Mami said I was named after). Then one morning, while we were drinking delicious Cubano coffee in the courtyard of our family home, Rosita, née Rosalba and our oldest, pointed out that I did what I wanted when I went to Havana with money that my José knew nothing about. That shut up Chita for a while.

What freedom my café brought. Soon my sisters wanted some too. Rosita set up a sewing room to make dresses in the back of her house. She used to be taken in private cars to Havana to fit the latest fashions on ladies who imported bolts of fabric from Paris and Madrid. Of course, due to the circumstances of the Revolution, most of her patrons went across the water. She stayed in town and let out seams and altered sleeve lengths or, on rare occasions, went to Havana about a dress to be made from a cherished piece of European cloth.

Chita, the bossy one, was also the stylish one with the beauty salon. She used to go with the very rich to Miami or the Keys to lounge and redo their hair every day because of the humidity. After the change, it was the Saturday night dancers and the Sunday morning worshippers with their twittering and little dramas that kept alive her two-dryer shop. She was a staunch comrade who never uttered a word against El Líder, but I know she missed the bright lights and fast cars she knew across the water.

Together we were known as the Sisters Montero in certain circles in the city. Our family owned a wonderful home in the Versalles neighborhood. Everyone called it the Montero House. It reflected our parents' prominence. Papi had the kind of luck in business that opened many doors and encouraged men to find new respect for a family name. Mami had the Catalonian looks, manners, and ease with money that furthered the Montero interests. We had advantages as their daughters.

My little brother, Tomás, was a lovely afterthought in our family. We had already left childhood behind when he appeared, and I had been the youngest for so long that he seemed more like my own child rather than a baby brother. We all practiced motherhood on our sweet, mischievous boy. We never squabbled with him as we did among ourselves. Rather, his injuries at our hands arose mostly from our fierce battles to take charge of him. Sometimes our poor boy was pulled in two directions by determined sister-mothers. He learned to hide until our rages were spent.

We all knew that the Russians had arrived to join in the defense of our beautiful island, but the glory of the actual revolution quickly dimmed for us. Even as most of our crowd deserted the island with only the clothes on their backs and whatever they could hide beneath their girdles and in their hair, we continued to enjoy certain privileges. Then our Tomasito was taken at the end of summer. The night it happened, Selena, his best friend since childhood and the daughter of a renowned officer of the second revolutionary war, stumbled into my café, bruised and crying. I quickly shooed out the neighbors that had lingered over coffee and dominoes and locked the door tight. She told a fractured tale of her evening with Tomasito on the Malecon and the moment when a truck full of militiamen dragged him off. It departed with Tomasito inside and Selena running and tripping behind. She blurted that Comrade Castro was no good for the Revolution. I couldn't even think such a thought without looking over my shoulder.

Immediately we launched inquiries but could learn nothing of Tomasito's whereabouts or the origins of the mysterious truckload of militiamen. Our investigation had to be discreet, as everyone knew Tomasito was indeed involved with comrades whom he called patriots but whom many others called worms. Still, we had connections, but José, my husband in the army, couldn't find any official mention of our brother's location. Neither could Ramón,

Rosita's milquetoast husband who was a deputy in the local Committee for the Defense of the Revolution. We feared the most sinister forces, since the CDRs usually trumpeted the capture of citizens whom they considered traitors. The administration went so far as to televise the executions of prisoners "against the wall" as an example to the rest of us. The week before, one of his close childhood friends starred in one of their ghastly programs.

For five days after the disappearance of Tomasito, I waited for my sisters with my back to the door of my café. Above my head was the sign that José painted in bright pink with viney green letters spelling out my name. At the top of the D was a white rose for Rosita, and underneath the S sat a conch shell for Conchita—Chita's real name. Those two are silent, or maybe not so silent, partners in my enterprise. Each day I contemplated the perfect view of the Church of Our Lady of the Sacred Heart across the plaza. Each day after my sisters arrived, we joined arms and marched over to the church to light candles and pray for the safe return of our little brother. Early on the sixth day, after setting the rice to boil, I stepped out of the café and looked through the lightening darkness at the statue of the Madonna. Her hands cupped that fickle heart. I said, "Please, Señora. You know what it's like to lose a boy. Please send our Tomasito home safely."

I couldn't see her face clearly, but she spoke from across the plaza. She used the voice only a Montero could hear, saying, "You are too demanding, my child. You must accept God's way."

"No!" I shouted, my voice bouncing off the walls and down the street. Ernesto across the road opened his second-floor shutters, and nosy Anna up the way leaned out her window. I waved at them, it is nothing. I had to continue my conversation with La Señora under my breath.

"If it is the way of God to punish us for speaking the truth about men drunk with power, then I am a crusader for the Devil!" I stopped. A silence ticked away. "I'm sorry. You know I didn't mean that."

The Madonna said, "You are upset, my dear, I understand. But now you must do penance."

Behind me the top of the big stew pot started to rattle with the escaping steam. I pointed at her church. "I will do my penance, but I will not step foot inside your useless sanctuary until our Tomasito returns."

An hour later, during breakfast, I watched through the window of my café as José approached with an unknown soldier behind him. I returned to my stove before they entered. There the kettle simmered and a pot of black beans cooled. I flipped over the frying black market eggs and turned off the fire. On the other side of the half-wall, six of the eight tables were filled with neighbors who had come together to keep each other company. Some ordered nothing, but I gave them a small plate anyway.

My José rushed in the front door carrying a large crate and made with the big important swagger in the five steps it took to cross the floor. He lifted the crate onto the counter beside the stove. Another language marched across the side of the box in angry red letters. The soldier who followed was a big blond man, muy guapo, a full head taller than my José. He wore a uniform different from that of our local comrades. His walk was precise and forceful, much too large for my small space.

José introduced me to this Captain B., who said, "It's a pleasure to meet you, Señora. I've heard many compliments of your cooking." He spoke continental Spanish with a Russian accent.

"The pleasure is mine." I know this Russian accent, this way of moving. I had a Russian lover during the heady days of the revolution, while my husband was stationed across the island and it was too dangerous to travel. At the time I believed José's letters that said Comrade Castro and his Revolution would make a better life for all of us. My affair was full of patriotic fervor, but I was glad that I had no blond baby to explain to dark José. When the promises evaporated, I became suspicious of anything the Russians brought.

"Please, Señora," the captain continued. "We have some men who are doing important work in the field. We need a cook. Might you do us the favor of helping out?"

This was not a mere invitation. I had just been enlisted. "Of course."

He glanced back at the full tables. Everyone, from old Pablo down to baby Trini, had stopped eating and had an ear turned to our conversation. The captain stepped closer and bent toward me with a confidential air. I smelled the acrid tang of last night's vodka and the sweet sweat of a pig eater. This one would like my pork sandwiches. Since the rationing, I'd missed the aroma of roasting meat. "Your husband assures me of your discretion," he said in a low voice.

"Claro que sí." Of course José made these assurances. Did he know about the Russian lover? No! You see how discreet I was even with my own family? "And perhaps you could help me with one small matter. My customers need strength to serve our country and would appreciate fresh pork. I'm famous for my pork sandwiches."

José's eyes grew wide at my request, but the captain never blinked. He merely smiled. "Of course, Señora. I'll see what I can do, especially if you would do me the personal favor of making one of your famous sandwiches for me." I nodded my agreement, and our contract was complete.

Lola
The Discretion of the Monteros 2

IN THE DAYS following my enlistment as a cook for the Russians, I discovered how Cuban I could make my Soviet-Cuban dishes. By the following week, I knew which spices to pack and which to leave at the café. One afternoon, I waited in the shade of a dump truck for a ride back to the city from the Russian work camp. Although clouds were building all over the sky, they had not yet obscured the hot sun. I was anxious to get home. My days had been longer than usual, and I had many new things to learn in a short time. The Russian crew chief approached with a boy whose uniform was covered in grease. I stood up. The chief introduced me to Karl, this boy who would drive me home, then said, "No Spanish, this one."

He turned to the boy and spoke rapidly in Russian, gesturing turns and curves in his directions. Karl nodded. "*Da, da,*" he kept repeating. When the chief stopped him with a hand on his arm and an urgent tone in his voice, the boy shrugged him off and started toward the truck.

We loaded my supplies into a small flatbed truck and drove away. Most of the Russian phrases I knew implied intimacy, but I tried a few of the more formal ones on Karl. He just flicked his flat gray eyes at me as if I was not good enough to touch the greasy pocket of his overalls. Ah, the arrogance of youth and dominance. I wondered if he concealed his contempt with charm when giving the soap to the girls on the beaches. Perhaps he didn't bother, knowing that they would eagerly follow his light skin into the darkness.

Despite the jolting from the pockmarked roads, I soon fell asleep. I dreamed of Captain B., his first taste of my plantains, his easy movements among the men he commanded, his smiles in my direction. I awoke, thinking surely by now we had reached the coastal road and soon would be enjoying the ocean breezes. Instead, we were creeping along a narrow dirt road that was flanked by Royal palms and hemmed in by aggressive bushes and vines. In several places the roadside vegetation had a flattened, scarred look, as if it had been trampled by a monster. Further on there was a new clearing in the jungle. For a moment, I wondered about Karl's intentions, but I could read only fear in his hunched shoulders and scowling face. He tapped on the steering wheel as he stared straight ahead. He had every right to be scared, for the island landscape had become so complicated. Too many secret operations advanced under the cover of foliage and silence. Whispers reached me (I cannot say from whom) that told of Soviet sites deep in the jungle that would scare the devil out of our Northern neighbors. Lost travelers, even the most innocent and patriotic, were not welcome at such installations.

"Comrade?" I said. The boy twitched. "Where are we?" I didn't know the Russian words.

He shrugged. Was he answering me, or was he simply abandoning responsibility? He stopped the truck and shrugged again, taking his hands off the wheel. I waved to indicate he should drive into the clearing, but before he could move, a horn blasted behind us. I whipped around and saw the grille of a giant truck as it crashed into us. The crash threw me against the dashboard. Karl grabbed the twisting steering wheel and slammed on the brake, but we were no match for the force behind us. We skidded into the clearing, and I crawled back into my seat with a throbbing shoulder. Men swarmed near sleek tubes that were on the beds of other gigantic vehicles.

Rockets.

Missiles.

Dios mio!

Could they be the kind that will end the world? I wished I had not seen!

We finally came to a stop halfway into the clearing. The truck behind us rumbled, as if it was catching its breath to assault us again. In front of us, men pulled tarps over the obscene weapons, and a figure stalked toward us with a flank of soldiers armed with machine guns. As the group neared I recognized the leader. Captain B. Of course. He was no innocent, and I was now at his mercy because of the bumbling of a young ally. My frustration at Karl exploded, and I shoved hard at him. His arrogance dissolved. He hunkered down like a puppy awaiting punishment.

A soldier opened the door and yanked Karl out of the cab. I huddled as far away from them as I could and wedged my heels against the shift box. The captain's contorted face came looming into the truck. Please let him remember his humanity, I prayed. He took one step back and held out a hand for me. "Señora."

I didn't move. "The driver made a terrible mistake."

"We cannot afford such mistakes." He flicked his hand once. The command to exit was clear.

"Unfortunately, I can't see out of this windshield and don't know where we are or what's out there." Karl and his armed guards retreated toward the far end of the clearing. He suddenly dodged backward, but the guards on either side of him grabbed him tight before he could get away. The pulled him along.

Captain B. dropped his hand into a ball and rested it on his hip. A hot breeze rippled his clothes, and I thought for the first time of his flanks where he would run to fat with all the drinking. A dump truck drove by with an entire bush caught behind its front tire, the branches waving as if it were calling for help. It left a trench in the churned up soil. The whole area went from light, to dark, to light again as a cloud's shadow passed overhead. Thunder rumbled in the distance. Captain B. grabbed a fistful of my hair and wrenched me closer.

No one knew where I was.

A thrill ran through me and left me panting along with the huffing of the truck's engine. The child that Tomasito had been came to me, his face upturned and trusting. I hadn't been able to protect him, either. Then I saw him as a man, alive, laughing, his deep brown eyes sparkling in the sun. I drew courage.

"Let me go."

"I don't have time for this," Captain B. said.

"Nor I." I lifted my head as far as I could in his grasp. "Send me home with one of your trusted men." His arm flexed, ready to pull me from the cab. That would be my end. "A man you can trust as much as you can me."

He drew me closer. I could feel his breath, alcohol-free, on my cheek. "You owe me," he whispered. I nodded as much as his grip would allow. "A warning, Señora. I have never met your lovely children." He glanced at Karl and his guards. The boy struggled in their grip. "You breathe a word of this . . . no one in your family is safe."

"You have my word, Captain."

His fingers still clutched my hair.

"I am in your debt."

With that he shoved my head away and straightened up and turned away.

The sound of rapid-fired shots spurted from the other side of the clearing. I turned toward the sound. Most of Karl's guards were already walking away, while one nudged his body with his boot.

Captain B. turned back toward me and shut the truck's door. "His family has to be notified. He died a hero."

No one was immune from danger on this island of secrets and lies. *We must save our children from this evil.*

I don't know how long I sat in a daze before a grim older Russian slipped into the driver's seat and turned the flatbed around. It was such a hot day, yet I couldn't keep warm on the drive back to the city. The only words that passed between us were my simple directions to the café.

When we arrived, I hurried inside and locked the door tight before a nosy neighbor could rush over to hear the latest. I called the Montero House, but Chita wasn't home. Her maid said she and Rosita had gone to our favorite spot on Varadero Beach. I couldn't hold this horrible mess in my arms alone, so I asked Ernesto across the street for a ride to the beach in his ancient Ford truck. His reply was made easier when I settled a small sack of vegetable patties in his hands. Despite the usual oppressive heat, I wore a light jacket. Even under its sleeves, my skin prickled from my chill. Every time I closed my eyes, even for a second, I heard the sharp reports and saw Karl's slumped body.

I passed through the usual hotel to gain entrance to the beach where I would find my sisters. I kicked off my shoes and trudged along the hot, white sand. The damp traces of high tide would've made walking easier, but the warmth on the soles of my feet and the burn in my calves as I churned through the sand kept my mind from flying off in a complete panic. Even so, when I found my sisters on their striped blankets beneath the palms, I couldn't open my mouth for several minutes. How to tell them about this latest danger to our future? What could we do to release our children from its menace? Like so many of our compatriots, our family had discussed the possibility of escape across the water. Now Captain B.'s threat of harm may have closed off less drastic options. Whatever we decided, we would act together.

Appointment with Mrs. H. 2

BETTY ANN SAT down with the tablet of pink paper and jotted a list. *Move racks by window & stagger.* That would get the unfinished gowns out of the way but would create a pleasing display of autumnal colors. *Flowers. Music. Arrange magazines. Ebony* and *Jet* would be relegated to the second shelf of the coffee table. *Finger sandwiches.* No time to do them properly. She lined it out. *Cookies. Dust. Vacuum. New dress on mannequin. Sweep stairs. WH fashions.* She clipped pictures and kept notes on the clothing Mrs. Kennedy and her guests wore. They may not look at the notebook, but having it out would show Mrs. H. that Betty Ann had the style and know-how to complete this commission. *Portfolio.* That's what she called the scrapbook where she kept photos and sketches of her own designs. *Grayson House.* Too bad she couldn't include it in her portfolio.

That would be suicide. Her hand sought out the man's ring in her pocket. She had originally slipped it into the lost-and-found so no one would think it special. Terry speculated about it when it first appeared, but neither girl had commented when Betty Ann sometimes wore it on her index finger. The frequency of the ring's appearance increased as the tensions on base heightened.

The percolator ceased its husky pops. Coffee was ready and the girls would be in soon. The Hepplewhite commission, added to the orders for ball gowns, would mean many late nights for them all. She also had orders for winter suits, complete with plackets, darts, and pads, for regulars like Mrs. Dupont and Mrs. Neville. Betty Ann poured herself a cup and turned on the radio on the counter. A Maytag commercial gave way to a weather report. A slight chance of rain. It was followed by the ninety-second spot that regularly featured the man with the nasal voice who had all the answers. That day he was demanding that the president send an invasion into Cuba to "get rid of those Ruskies on our back door step." Sure, Betty Ann thought, that's easy for you to say from the safety of your soundproof booth. But it's my husband, and my son, and our friends out there on the planes and ships that will have to go. Jump on Cuba and you touch off Turkey and Berlin and who knows what else. No thanks. She settled with her coffee cup at her worktable. She didn't allow the girls to have drinks at their stations for fear that a spill would ruin the delicate fabrics they worked, but Betty Ann knew what she was doing.

She slid the notepaper closer and reviewed her list. Yes, Mrs. H. conjured up the Grayson House, and that always led straight to the captain. Betty Ann thought of her usual flirtations as harmless. Her attraction to the captain was not. Each breach of a rule felt innocuous at first, but together they led to a dangerous territory. She had it under control though, and this new risk only served to recall the thrill of her moments with the captain. She first saw him late in the spring as he jotted notes at a table in the library on base.

The mustiness of public books mixed not unpleasantly with the sweet-sharp smell of buffed floors. A gridded square of sunshine from the window opposite lit his long, straight lashes and glinted off his pen and the bars on his shoulder. Books about historic homes littered the table. Few scars marred the surface of this study table tucked behind the home and garden stacks.

It was unusual for such a young Air Force base to have a well-stocked library, complete with an auditorium, in a two-story brick building. This random fortune arose from the installation's proximity to Washington and the ease with which national and foreign dignitaries could be steered there for both scheduled and unplanned visits. The brass wanted to showcase American might and know-how, hence the rocket and jet monuments on the parade ground, as well as this brick shrine to knowledge imbedded across the street from the movie house.

"We don't get many officers in this corner of the library," Betty Ann had said.

The captain's pen stilled as he looked at her. He ran a hand up over his short, blond hair. "I'd never hear the end of it if I brought these books to the office."

"I bet," she said. "Sir," she added.

"No need for that." A hint of a smile and crinkles at the corner of his eyes reinforced his words. "You probably outrank me when it comes to all this." He waved a hand over the books piled on the table. A gold wedding band flashed in the sunlight.

"Most men leave decorating to women," Betty Ann said.

"So do I usually, but I'm doing something for the general." On this base, the general was Hepplewhite, the base commander; all other generals had names.

"Why don't you ask your wife to help?"

The captain glanced out the window. "She's in Nebraska. There's no room on Officer's Row right now. She's waiting until that new development on the north side is finished."

"Then maybe I can help. I have lots of experience."

He laid down his pen. "Thanks, but I have to keep this quiet."

The need for confidentiality allowed Betty Ann to slip into the chair beside him. Her boldness with a white officer surprised her, but not much. "I'm a dressmaker. My clients depend on my discretion."

"Your husband?"

"Master sergeant, loads planes. I don't bother him with my business affairs."

He sat forward and considered her. "He—the general—doesn't want Mrs. H. to know."

"Of course," she said. She smelled something other than Old Spice, something muskier.

He covered his mouth with a loose fist and rubbed the black stone of a ring on his bottom lip. He introduced himself, and after she did the same and they shook hands, he paused again, ring to lip. Finally, he told her that the general wanted to pre-empt his wife's plans to make an old homestead known as the Grayson House into a wives' club. The general wanted to do an end run by turning it into a VIP club while she was in Germany over the summer with their daughter and new grandson.

"That old place would be perfect with a little updating," Betty Ann said. "The dining room could be turned into a large conference room, and you could tear down a wall upstairs and make a smaller meeting area."

"Exactly. How do you know the Grayson place so well?"

She smiled. "Why couldn't it be for both wives and VIPs?"

"The men won't want wives anywhere near it."

"That kind of place?"

"Yes, ma'am. Can't imagine it'll get too bad, though." He capped his pen and flipped his notebook closed. "It'll be quite a challenge to pull this off before Mrs. H. gets back. I don't suppose you'd be interested in going out there with me to take a look. Strictly professional, Scout's honor." He held up three fingers and grinned.

The grin said that although he was an officer, he was no scout. That suited Betty Ann just fine. She had an instinct for men. This one wouldn't get too obnoxious and looking at the house would be fun.

"Sure," she said.

He shut the book and piled it with the others in front of him. "I can't use regular channels on this. You know Mrs. H."

Everyone knew about her far reach. "I have sources Mrs. H. doesn't know anything about. Guaranteed," Betty Ann said. Several Negro tradesmen would benefit from this connection.

At home later that afternoon, Betty Ann gloated over the stipend Captain Bledsoe had offered for her expertise and discretion. She would've done it for free, just to spend more time with a man who paid attention to her decorating ideas. She smoothed her hand over a piece of maroon damask she had pulled from the hall closet. Most people would pair gold with it, but she would argue for silver. She tried to tell Ray about the decorating project when he got home, but he was too intent on an early season baseball game to listen. She didn't mention the captain that first night, and later it just seemed better not to.

Betty Ann had rules. No white men. No officers. No one she might like as much as Ray. But with Martin, she always followed her favorite rule: exceptions were good for life. The next several weeks were filled with consultations late in the day and necking sessions in the empty rooms of the Grayson House or in his car, hidden behind warehouses in the industrial parks they visited. Then on a summer Friday, her husband called to say that their plans for dinner and a movie were off because he had to work a double shift. She had been looking forward to some adult fun since their youngest boys were going to be out of the house at sleepovers. When Martin called about inspecting the installation of her draperies at the Grayson House, she had no reason not to go. She told him she wouldn't be free until early evening, which was long after the installers would depart. When Martin spoke again, his voice had dropped a notch. They both knew what the timing meant.

The early evening sunlight glowed burnt orange in the back of the house, leaving the front parlor cool and dim in its maroon and silver dressing. Her damask sample had given way to a lush velvet chosen by Martin. The dark wood floor had just received a new polish, so they took off their shoes and glided in stocking feet to the front window. Betty Ann ran her hand up the curve of silver fringe and down the soft maroon. She turned to him.

"Good choice, Captain. Very good choice, sir."

Martin answered her with a kiss. He closed the drapes, then left her at the window and pulled a plaid car blanket out of a duffel bag. Like the Boy Scout he wasn't, he was prepared. He spread the blanket on the new Oriental rug in front of the fireplace, then pulled out a transistor radio and put it on the mantle. He twirled its small opalescent dial. Snatches of songs and deep, confident voices jumbled out until he settled on Bobby Darin's "Mack the Knife." He reached into his bag one more time and liberated a brown leather portable bar set, which he stood on the coffee table.

Betty Ann trailed behind him but stopped at the radio. Darin was trying too hard to swing. She rotated the dial, moving down in megahertz.

"Do you mind?" she asked.

"Of course not." Martin knelt before the bar set, which he splayed open like an upright book. He poured amber liquid into two gold-rimmed glasses.

Betty Ann stopped on Billy Eckstine's fluid voice singing "My Foolish Heart." The radio's dial recalled the mother-of-pearl ground of a silver Nefertiti brooch her mother wore to church. Her mother had always said that white men see only one thing when they look at us.

What did Martin see when he looked at her? She wanted him to see the woman who had conjured the luxury of this parlor room. Every time a white man sat down in this room, it would be on a chair or a couch she had chosen. Every party girl who gazed out the window while being sweet-talked from behind would caress silver fringe that Betty Ann had sewn onto maroon velvet. She took the glass of bourbon that Martin offered and let herself be kissed by the thin, hard lips that had said "yes" to maroon and silver.

He would see a woman whose name could never be associated with the success of the Grayson House, but who could christen it with her essence, right now, before it opened. Ray could never have given her this, but would Martin have given it to her without the assumption of the act to come? She slipped away from him. Martin watched her, drink in hand.

She took a healthy gulp of bourbon. Its warm cascade ran straight down toward her true desire. The rest of her world disappeared into the tingle of her pelvis. She stepped onto the blanket and sank down, first to her knees, then to her hips, with her bare feet tucked beside her. She held Martin's gaze the whole time. She knew what she was doing.

Soon, a last rule was about to fall—no going all the way—when Martin shifted his hips away from hers and said, "I can't do this."

Betty Ann didn't understand. All indications were that he could. "Baby, everything's okay."

"Jesus, I don't deserve you," he whispered. He scrunched his eyes closed, as if that were the only way he could speak. "I wouldn't do this with a white woman. With a lady, like you are. I'm not like that. We'd go to a fine restaurant, check into a fancy hotel." He smiled, eyes still closed. "Mr. and Mrs. Jones."

Betty Ann allowed herself the same fantasy. It was interrupted by the hotel clerk's lascivious stare that was guaranteed, even if they were actually married. She sat up and surveyed her room: the tufted leather club chairs, the silver leaf frame on the mirror over the fireplace. "This is better than any hotel that would have the two of us." She clasped her hands behind his neck and drew him close again.

Betty Ann had another rule: never bring it home. Those floozies that got caught in their own beds were just plain stupid. Not like her.

She was back in her car, alone, by ten.

At home, a thorough washing dampened the sensations of her skin, and by eleven she was ready for her own bed. She slipped into the smooth coolness of freshly ironed sheets and fell right to sleep. She awoke momentarily when she turned over to embrace Ray's solid bulk and her hand fell to the flatness of the empty side of the bed. She pinched one of his pillows under her cheek and went back to sleep.

BETTY ANN WAS wide awake to the dangers those memories held now that Mrs. H. was coming into her life. She crossed out *Grayson House* repeatedly until the paper tore, then dropped the pen and picked up the black skirt. The news came on the radio. A double tractor trailer had jackknifed on the new highway circling the District and was snarling traffic. The initial excitement of a White House dress faded, and Betty Ann was left with the weight of possible disaster. She had trained her mind to skip away from the moments of humiliation at the hands of Mrs. H., but in light of the upcoming meeting, she had to revisit them.

It was just before Labor Day and the Grayson House was finished. On a last visit, Betty Ann and Martin had kicked off their shoes and were smooching on the new sofa in the parlor when they heard voices in the front hall. They jumped up and straightened their clothes but didn't have time to retrieve their shoes before General Hepplewhite and his wife appeared in the doorway.

Betty Ann scooped up her clipboard and pencil. "I'll make a note of that, Captain."

General H. touched his wife's arm. "Honey, this is Bledsoe, the captain I was telling you about."

No one introduced Betty Ann. Mrs. H. stared at Bledsoe's shoeless feet but didn't broaden her glare to take in Betty Ann's.

"We didn't want to soil the new Oriental," the captain said.

Mrs. H. stepped into the room and surveyed its furnishings: the plush curtains, the deep, tufted leather sofa and chairs, the mahogany cabinets, the portraits of early Air Corps heroes, the beveled mirror and its silver-leaf frame over the fireplace. She turned in profile to her husband behind her. "You two men couldn't have done this well on your own."

"Cap'n Bledsoe is very good with these things," he said.

"Actually, ma'am, I had a lot of help." Bledsoe pointed at Betty Ann, but when Hepplewhite shook his head behind his wife's back, the captain's hand continued upward into a pass over his brush cut and down to rub the back of his neck.

Mrs. H. followed the altered gesture. She caressed a brass reading lamp with a gloved hand. "You're not telling me a little colored gal is responsible for this elegance."

Behind her, General H. narrowed his eyes at the captain.

"No, ma'am," Captain Bledsoe said.

She turned her back on the room and said, "Congratulations, Happy. You seem to have won this one." As she left she said, "Come on, boys, show me the rest."

The captain slipped on his shoes and followed the general and his wife without once glancing at Betty Ann. She carefully set the clipboard on the table.

After that incident and the end of the project, Betty Ann had no real excuse to see the captain again. No useless phone conversations or suggestions of unsavory rendezvous followed. Even so, one day a few weeks later, Martin appeared early in the morning at Betty Ann's studio, before the girls came in. She leaned against her worktable and he stood near a bare dress form. He touched it lightly on the shoulder and said, "I wish . . ." Betty Ann moved closer. After a moment he took off the onyx ring and slipped it on her index finger. He cupped one of her cheeks and gave her a long, slow kiss on the other. He strode to the door and went out without looking back. She had leaned into the kiss but didn't follow him to the door. After all, letting him go was for the best.

Chita
The Discretion of the Monteros: 3

MY SISTER LOLA will tell you she's important because of this or she's important because of that. Sure, she has the café, but whom did she marry? What is the Santos name in this city? That José is a loyal soldier but he has no imagination. He conducts life by the book, even when everyone knows that the people who write the rules are the last ones to follow them. Not so long ago, his family lived in the fields and no one bothered to learn their last name. Lola saw something in him, though, and convinced Papi that they should wed. I've said more than once that José should've taken the Montero name. Instead, Lola took the Santos name. Thanks be to God that she had enough sense to train her children to always use Montero Santos and never let anyone shorten it to the nondescript surname of their bland father.

Of course I was much more sensible than headstrong Lola. I married a La Luz. And our oldest, romantic Rosita, well, her husband was completely useless. Ramón was one of those anemic boys who finished school in the States and returned with nothing more than bad habits. The only way he managed the tannery was through the ready fists of that drunkard brother of his. Theirs was another last name not worth remembering.

The La Luz dynasty ruled an important aspect of life: mechanics. Their name was synonymous with the best of the sugar mill shops, and my Diego's grandfather worked on the first cars to land here. He was among the first to cross the island by auto when the trip involved hacking out a path across the mountains. Diego was known for his expertise with any type of engine, but particularly with those in luxury American cars. The Revolution curtailed the imports from the North, but it never diminished the Cuban appetite for magnificent wheels. Diego continued to be in demand. He put in long hours but always came home with hands clean enough for a judge, as he would say. He even cleaned around his fingernails, unlike the men who worked for him.

If Lola hadn't married a Santos, everything would be different now. He was the one that brought the Russians into our lives. The day that Lola came to tell me about her enlistment to cook for them, she stayed until the evening birds chattered and squawked. Then she took her officious air away from the Montero House.

Yes, I, Chita Montero de La Luz, the middle sister, lived in the family home. It had a grand inner court and large guest house; it also was a mishmash of styles that an early sea merchant originally from New England had acquired a taste for on his travels around the world. He had copied the wrap-around front porch and the widow's walk on the roof of a whaling captain's house he visited on the island of Nantucket in his native Massachusetts. However, instead of using the North's wood clapboarding and shale shingles, he covered the house with island stucco and the humps of red Spanish roof tiles.

Wings flew off behind the staid front of our house and formed the Mediterranean-style courtyard. A windowless wall of the guest house enclosed its fourth side. A fountain in the shape of a lion's head hung in the center of the wall and was smothered by the grape vines growing along the wall. Legend had it that the original owner kept his mistress in the guest house, which was why its back faced the main house with no access to the courtyard. Family lore claimed that the merchant's wife, ensconced in what was one of the finest houses in Versalles, didn't bother to be jealous of anyone she couldn't see.

The house had been in our family for years, and we Sisters Montero and Tomasito enjoyed busy, gay childhoods in it. After we started families of our own, our parents moved into a smaller but still stylish home and gave the main house to Diego and me. Before the Revolution, the wags at the tobacco shops debated whether Tomasito deserved the house more than I did since he was the only male heir, or whether perhaps Rosita did as the oldest of the Montero offspring. Papi hadn't given her husband the tannery, just the job of running it. Was a job as a factory manager for that useless Ramón the equal of a fancy house near the river?

I heard that Rosita laughed when confronted with such impudence. Despite myself, I admired her reported aplomb in sidestepping the intrusive curiosity. Even though the busybodies reported she implied she could've had the house if she wanted it, I wouldn't give those meddling gossips the satisfaction of a public feud. Then, post-Revolution, with Ramón's appointment as a deputy in the local CDR, no one broached the subject, even in jest, for fear that their own house deeds would be scrutinized.

The La Luz name was well respected, but everyone, even Diego and me, continued to refer to our home as the Montero House. It perched on a slight rise in the middle of the block, guarded by a black, scrolled, wrought-ironed fence with a wooden gate guarding the end of the driveway and giving privacy to the side yard. The house stood out as a popular neighborhood landmark—east or west of the Montero House, one would say. No one in the family thought anything of speaking in such a manner. "Seven blocks west of our house," Lola said when pinpointing the location of her precious café. She never meant the house that peasant of a husband bought for her.

I sat alone in the courtyard until Diego arrived home with his immaculate hands.

"Where are my boys?" he asked, standing in the doorway. I sat at the wrought-iron table drinking a papaya milkshake. The light shade of early evening had already overtaken the yard.

"In their room."

I could barely see Diego through the striving branches of the mamey sapote. It had become uncivilized and needed pruning. I often dreamed of this tree laden with fruit, which he and I had planted together when the house had become ours to run. That was before the furrow between his eyes had become permanent.

He slipped past the tree and came to me for a kiss. After taking a sip of my drink, he leaned toward the kitchen window. "Lupe," he called.

Our maid appeared in the window, her dark face blank above the yellow blossoms in the window box. "Please," Diego said, raising my glass. He put it down in front of me and Lupe disappeared.

"But their set's out here," he said. He moved the box filled with chessmen from a seat and sat down.

Miguelito and Beto had three chess sets, one carved in ivory, but the blocky wooden warriors in this box were their favorites. Miguelito, at twelve years, reigned as the best junior at the Matanzas Chess Club. His brother, although two years younger and more easily distracted by baseball and girls, ranked close behind at the fourth spot. If they maintained their standings, they would be part of the Club's junior team to compete in the national tournament at the Capablanca Club in Havana in late October. Diego, a junior champion himself in his day, gave instruction to the boys and harangued them to practice for two hours each day before dinner. At that moment, they should have been hunched over the set that Diego had just put aside.

"They left such a stew of books and dirty clothes and stale food in their room," I said. "They're old enough to know better." Lupe had been grumbling about the duty of the domestic worker to resist the slothfulness of the upper classes. We were not of the top class, but we could afford her, so her resistance was well-placed, I guess. I shifted in my seat and brushed a foot across Diego's. "So they're cleaning up their own mess."

He pulled his foot out of my reach and raised a hand to smooth back his thinning hair. He needed a haircut. "Chita, the tourney is only a month away." Plenty of time for them to finish tidying up, I thought, but I said nothing.

Lupe sauntered into the courtyard, pushed aside the tree branches, and banged Diego's glass on the table. Dealing with her had been such an ordeal since the start of the Revolution, but by that fall, she had gotten openly hostile, even to my husband.

"Many thanks," Diego said with his best smile. He wasn't a classically handsome man, but women found his confident ways attractive. When he raised an eyebrow, he charmed the proletarian righteousness out of our maid. She nodded once and returned to the doorway.

"Señora Peña," Diego said. Lupe stopped and stood taller in her small frame. She loved the formal address. "Tell the boys to come out here, please. And to bring the board." He flipped his hand toward the chess set.

"But they're not finished with their room yet," I said.

Diego turned his back on Lupe, as if she were already gone. "Señora Peña can finish for them."

Lupe hissed something and slammed the screen shut behind her. I'd told Diego about Lupe's knowledge of Santeria, and how I'd seen her pocket clumps of his hair from the tub drain, but he remained unconcerned. I can't believe the bad luck that visited our family was Lupe's doing. She wouldn't have wanted to put the children in danger, but then, you never know. In any case, misfortune first splattered Lola and soon drenched the rest of us.

Appointment with Mrs. H. 3

BETTY ANN WORRIED as she planned for the afternoon's VIP visit. Word of a White House dress would fill her appointment book for months to come, but then, no dice if Mrs. H. acted up. Betty Ann had to think of something, but she couldn't sit idle. She picked up her tablet and ran through her list. *Dust.* The studio was spotless, tabletops and cabinets clear, but she tied a blue scarf over her French-curl hairdo, got a feather duster from the closet, and began the rounds.

A picture painted by Lucy Saunders, another NCO's wife, hung above the hi-fi set Ray had bought secondhand. Betty Ann flicked the duster over the frame of the oil painting, which captured the romanticism of a real Parisian atelier. Warm light refracted across half-sewn dresses and played in a spill of royal blue velvet. Betty Ann liked to think that her studio was as genteel as this imaginary room, but she might have a real cat fight in it if the general's wife turned nasty. Mrs. H. could call her out in front of everyone and threaten Ray's livelihood, or even force her to do the dress for free! She needed reinforcements, someone who could stand with her against the clout of Mrs. H., if she was going to go through with this meeting. She tapped the handle of the duster against her chin.

Betty Ann had few true women friends, since she preferred the company of men, but Lucy was quiet, didn't ask too many questions, and she listened when you wanted her to. Lucy was about as good a friend a military wife could have. They lived on the same block and their husbands worked together, but they hadn't really gotten to know each other until they had both been volunteered by their husbands for the Air Force Fifteenth Anniversary Committee. Betty Ann felt comfortable with Lucy to the point that she had almost told her about Martin as they made flag place card holders for the anniversary gala on Armed Forces Day. Yes, Lucy was the right choice.

Betty Ann propped the feather duster on a straight chair and went to her work table. She took a deep breath. She knew Lucy's number by heart.

A young voice answered. "Master Sergeant Saunder's residence, Erica speaking."

In the background Betty Ann heard, "Erica, give me that phone and get ready for school." A moment passed before Lucy's voice came in more clearly.

"What are you doing around three this afternoon?" Betty Ann said.

"God, I thought you were Sonny."

"Come on, what are you doing?"

"Minding my own business—I said NOW, little miss—if I know what's good for me."

"I need you down at the studio. Mrs. Hepplewhite's dressmaker can't finish the gown for her White House invitation, so she called me."

"No, sir!"

"Yes, ma'am."

"You're kidding me. How'd that happen?"

"Fill you in later. Bring your portfolio—this will be great for you too."

"You don't need me there," Lucy said.

"Yes, I do. I've had a little run-in with Mrs. H. before and . . . it'll just be easier if you're here."

"What happened?"

This was not a story to tell over the phone while her friend was urging her daughter to get ready for school. And Betty Ann's assistants could arrive at any moment. This was certainly not a tale she wanted them to overhear.

"I'll tell you when you get here. About two thirty. And Lucy?"

"What?"

The resigned tone of that one word told Betty Ann that her friend would show. Her dimples deepened. "Wear something nice, hear?" Lucy was an artist. Nothing wrong with that, but sometimes she forgot she was going out into polite society and showed up in an old, paint-smudged man's shirt half-tucked into her dungarees.

The studio's door swung open, and Terry and Mimi clipped in with waxed brown bags from the plaza's coffee shop. Betty Ann felt hopeful again about the appointment with Mrs. H. and greeted her assistants with a smile.

"Morning, Miz Johnson," they replied in unison. They both wore regulation black skirts. Above these, Mimi's flat front was covered by a conservative button-down white blouse, while Terry's curves rounded out a yellow angora sweater. The girls knew each other from junior college. Betty Ann had hired tall spare Mimi first, but soon after, the quiet girl's more vivacious friend had talked her way into the shop.

"Hurry up with your coffee," Betty Ann said. "We have a lot of gowns to do and Mrs. Hepplewhite's coming today."

"Here? Mrs. H.?" Mimi said.

Neither of the girls were Air Force, but they lived within Betty Ann's world and knew all about General Hepplewhite and his Southern belle wife.

Betty Ann recounted the early morning phone call. When she paused, Terry said, "Lord have mercy." She twirled and snapped her fingers.

Mimi shook out the doughnuts and arranged them on a plate. She claimed to love them but usually ate only half of one each day. She had potential but starved herself like that in so many ways. Betty Ann decided to take her on as a serious project once this Hepplewhite affair was over.

The two young women complained about Betty Ann's strict dress code and fussy neatness, but it was idle chat. They both adored their boss and the worlds they glimpsed through her. She also taught them things that none of their gal pals were learning. Things like how to make all the yardage of a full five-foot diameter circle skirt lie flat at a twenty-three-inch waist, or how to shake their hips under a demure, black wool skirt until men came crawling on their elbows. Useful things.

"Come on, girls, we have work to do and customers coming," Betty Ann said.

"Yes, ma'am." They moved off toward their workstations.

Mimi settled behind her sewing machine. "Why didn't Miss Sonia take Mrs. Hepplewhite to one of her white friends?"

"You mean to one of her competitors?" Betty Ann asked.

"But why here?" Terry asked. She hung a pink satin number on a rack and turned on the steamer.

Betty Ann perched on a stool at the cutting table. She picked up a microscopic piece of thread with the pad of her ring finger. "She owes me. I told you about the white major's wife that blew in from North Carolina a while ago. The one I decided not to work with and sent along to Miss Sonia."

"The one you said had a ridiculous bouffant and called the studio filthy?" Mimi asked.

"Um hmm." Betty Ann deposited the speck of thread in the wastebasket. "I found out later she left the major for a Congressman from her home state and wanted an entirely new wardrobe. Miss Sonia made enough money to take a Caribbean cruise."

Mimi slid a length of pinned chiffon under the presser foot of her sewing machine. "Guess that major's ex-wife was lucky for you. Even if she was mean."

Indeed, thought Betty Ann. She blessed Sonia for returning the favor.

"The Loco-Motion" played on the radio while Betty Ann spread out a champagne satin and overlaid it with the pattern for the skirt of Mrs. Neville's gown. She concentrated on aligning the pattern for the optimum drape of the slippery fabric but couldn't keep her mind away from her first non-meeting with Mrs. Hepplewhite. She pinned the paper and fabric along one seam but soon pricked her finger. She needed to move more than just her hands. The janitor did an adequate job of sweeping the stairs, but it wasn't good enough for Betty Ann. Mimi usually swept after he did, but today's agitation sent Betty Ann into the closet for the broom and dust pan.

She opened the glass door to the stairway and squinted into the sunlight. She swept with strong, swift strokes. Near the bottom of the stairs her broom stuttered over a curled edge of the rubber mat. No one else would notice it until it had lifted far enough to slip a finger under, but Betty Ann believed in catching trouble early. She made a note to bring it to Mr. Paul's attention.

She returned upstairs and put away the broom. Despite the interlude, her mind again flashed to that moment when she stood barefoot beside the captain. She had been stupid to think good could result from that relationship. She slid the ring out of her pocket and wondered if she should hock it. It had been her talisman during the base buildup, but she had treated it casually on purpose. No sense in getting attached to a thing if you weren't really attached to the man that gave it to you. She angled her body so the girls couldn't see what she was doing as she unearthed the magnifying glass she used when sewing on sequins. She checked the ring's gold stamp. Eighteen karats. Not bad. It would bring in more than enough for a new steamer, maybe a down payment for a serger. She noticed another inscription. *To BA with love.* What?

That poor fool. He hadn't been practical like Betty Ann. There were rules, even when you played out-of-bounds. Love had never entered into the equation. It couldn't. Betty Ann hadn't allowed it to. She couldn't afford it. Now she definitely would have to get rid of the ring. What if someone else saw the inscription? They might get the wrong idea. She was not in love with him. Not really. She dropped the ring back into her pocket and settled down to work on the satin gown as she waited for her first clients to arrive.

Appointment with Mrs. H. 4

THE LAST REGULAR customer cleared out of the BA Johnson Studio at two fifteen. As soon as the door closed, Betty Ann went into overdrive. Everything had to be perfect for Mrs. H. Betty Ann dusted again. She went to the plaza's bakery and personally chose every one of two dozen assorted cookies. She sent Terry out for the latest edition of *Look*. She sent her back for *Life*. She ordered Mimi to sweep the stairs and their part of the sidewalk. She fretted through the pile of phonograph records until she settled on Mozart. She threw out the coffee and made another pot. She told Mimi to sweep the stairs again after the postman came in with the day's packages. She caught Terry rolling her eyes at this request to clean an area that was already spotless.

"Any attitude can walk out the door right this minute. Do you hear me?" Betty Ann said.

"Yes, ma'am." Terry ducked down over her work.

Betty Ann decided against bringing out the feather duster again just as Lucy arrived. Her friend laid her portfolio on the cutting table and hugged Betty Ann. She opened her arms for inspection. She, too, wore a black skirt and white blouse but had added a black cardigan and had tied a red and black scarf around her neck. Very smart. Betty Ann nodded her approval.

"Where do you want me to stand?" Lucy said. "What do you want me to say?"

Terry giggled and Mimi smiled at the pieces of plaid cloth she was matching.

"Can I help it if I want everything to be perfect?" Betty Ann moved the portfolio a smidgen to line it up with the edge of the table.

"Of course you do. What do want to say about me being here?" Lucy asked.

"You can wait down in the coffee shop, and about ten minutes after they get here you can come up and say you just dropped by . . ."

"Whoa, slow down," Lucy said. "I know you like drama, but I thought about this on the way over just in case you came up with something like that." Betty Ann reached over and fussed with her scarf. Lucy pulled out of her reach. "Oleg Cassini sketches Mrs. Kennedy in his studio. You'd like to extend the same service to Mrs. H. How about that?"

"Brilliant." Betty Ann patted herself on the chest. "I'm glad you're here."

Lucy took out a large sketch pad and arranged her pencils on the table. "So?"

Time for the truth. "Come sit on the couch," Betty Ann said. "You girls go on with your sewing until Mrs. Hepplewhite arrives."

Mimi and Terry scrambled back to work as Betty Ann put three Mozart records on the hi-fi and Lucy sank into one of the love seats. *Look, Life,* and *Vogue* formed a precise arc beside the picture-perfect plate of cookies on the coffee table.

Lucy pulled an *Ebony* off the table's bottom shelf and leafed through it. "What's the big secret?"

Betty Ann sat and pitched her voice low so the girls couldn't hear her over the music. "This isn't the first time I've met Mrs. H., but I don't think she knows it." She glanced over at the girls and scooched closer to her friend. "Remember the renovation of the Grayson House? How angry she was because she had to wait for new construction for her officers' wives club?"

"I thought some captain had done that." Lucy stopped turning pages.

Betty Ann again made sure that the girls were intent on their humming machines. She pulled the onyx ring from her pocket and held it out on her palm. Lucy was intelligent, an artist. She would figure it out.

Lucy's brow furrowed for a moment, then smoothed as she cocked her head. "No."

Betty Ann nodded.

"No. Not with a white officer."

At one time Betty Ann would've confided in Lucy with guilty pleasure. Now all she felt was a burn beneath her breastbone.

"You haven't told anybody."

"Of course not," Betty Ann said.

"So what about Mrs. H.?"

Betty Ann recounted the Grayson House scene with the general and his wife. She left out the smooching but included the bare feet. Again, she knew her friend would get the picture.

"You still seeing him?" Lucy asked.

Betty Ann shrugged and shook her head.

Lucy leaned back. "Girl, you sure take the cake. I always thought you just liked to flirt."

"I swear this is the only time that it's gotten this far."

"Um hmm." Lucy's eyes narrowed. She must be thinking about the threat of leaving her own husband alone with her friend. Betty Ann would have to be extra careful with him from now on. No more casual touches or flirty remarks. This friendship now meant more than those fleeting satisfactions.

"He must be awfully special," Lucy said.

Betty Ann bowed her head.

"You ever throw him in Ray's face?"

Betty Ann pursed her lips. Her dimples appeared, but there was no mirth in her look. She shook her head. "Never."

"Better not. He's a *good* man."

"This whole thing might land on him anyway. What if Mrs. H. recognizes me and winds up sending him to Iceland or something?"

Her husband could be exiled with a mere flick of a pen without the commander's involvement. The husbands wouldn't know the significance of the orders, but the wives would.

"Wait a minute. Now you're dragging me and Sonny into it," Lucy said. Betty Ann hadn't thought about that. Lucy snatched a nonpareil cookie from the plate and popped it into her mouth.

The coffee table picture was no longer perfect, but Betty Ann couldn't chide the friend she had just imperiled. "Maybe this wasn't such a good idea." She looked at her watch. "You still have time to make a getaway."

Lucy glanced around the studio as if she were taking stock of the worth of everything in it. Her gaze paused on each of the girls at work at their stations and lingered on her own portfolio on the table. At last she turned to Betty Ann and took the ring. She rubbed its onyx face and peered into its inner circle. She paused without expression before shaking her head and letting out a bemused hum.

"Ah hell. With everything going on, both our men could be sent to Timbuktu or worse, with or without Mrs. H." Lucy flipped the ring back to Betty Ann, who automatically put it on her finger. "Besides, we can't let the old biddy act up in your shop."

"No, ma'am." Betty Ann smiled for the first time in their conversation.

"Every good fighter needs a wingman. Guess I'm it." Lucy tossed the *Ebony* on top of the carefully positioned mainstream magazines. "Battle stations," she said as she got up. She crossed the studio and sat on the stool nearest to her portfolio. Betty Ann left the *Ebony* on top of the other magazines but couldn't resist turning it so it fell in line with the fanned display.

She moved to a vantage point near the door and listened as Lucy chatted with the girls about a coat sale. The light in the stairwell wasn't on, and now that the afternoon shadows had moved across the entrance, the stairs were dark. Betty Ann opened the door and flicked on the lights and let the door fall back into place. A man in an Air Force uniform grabbed the handle of the glass door downstairs and pulled. A flash of mushroom gray skirt swept past him.

Betty Ann briefly touched the black eagle to her lips, then said, "It's show time." Terry and Mimi stood and smoothed their skirts with identical motions. Lucy leaned on the cutting table and raised her eyebrows. Betty Ann smiled, making sure her upper teeth rested just so on her bottom lip, and opened the door.

Mrs. Hepplewhite led her group up the stairs. The full skirt of her greige dress floated over what must have been several layers of crinoline petticoats. It was too elaborate for an afternoon visit to a Negro dressmaker's shop. After the tall, auburn-haired general's wife came Sonia K., her arm and cast cradled in a deep purple scarf that complemented her lavender blouse. She carried a carpetbag, which had a bolt of blue cloth sticking out. The soldier, who must have been Mrs. H.'s driver, trailed them and stopped at the top of the stairs. After the women entered, the driver executed a smart about-face and descended the stairs. Betty Ann let the glass door swing to a close.

Sonia introduced Betty Ann as they stood just inside the door. Mrs. Hepplewhite smiled with a slight squint. "Have we met before?"

"No, ma'am," Betty Ann said. The true answer itched in her throat. She ushered her guests into the lounge area, where she made introductions to Lucy and her assistants and served coffee. Mimi and Terry returned to their workstations while the older women chatted for several minutes.

Being close to the action, their talk naturally lit on the day's editorials about Berlin and Castro. Betty Ann asked whether the United States would invade Cuba. Mrs. Hepplewhite replied, "The general thinks we might have to, but he doesn't want to dog fight the Russians. We'd lose too many boys, and for what?"

Lucy turned to Betty Ann. "With this invasion talk, you must be glad your son's still in the Pacific."

"You have a boy in uniform also?" Mrs. Hepplewhite asked.

Betty Ann nodded. "Yes, ma'am. Lonnie's in the Navy. On the *Princeton*."

"Why Betty Ann, you don't look old enough to have a son in the Navy," Mrs. Hepplewhite said.

Betty Ann laughed, but it was true. She'd had him when she was a baby herself, when Ray was her ticket out of town, long before a career as a military wife clashed with her aspirations as a businesswoman and owner of a dress studio.

"Our oldest is in the Pacific also." Mrs. Hepplewhite set her coffee cup on its saucer. "At least I think so. Marines. They get moved around. A lot. Of course, I would be much happier if he were behind a desk somewhere, but you know how it is." She looked from Lucy to Betty Ann. They both nodded. "And of course the general wouldn't dream of pulling strings for him."

Betty Ann doubted that, but as she watched her guest's pale hands caress each other, she felt the mother memory of the time when your boy fit into the safety of the curve of your arms. Even rank and privilege couldn't keep your boy as safe as he had been then, and for a moment Mrs. H. was just another mother hoping that her love was enough to bring that boy home again.

Eventually the talk turned to Mrs. Hepplewhite's style. "I'm moving her into slender two pieces," Sonia said. "But she just loves her petticoats."

"I do." Mrs. Hepplewhite smiled and patted the fluff of her skirt.

Betty Ann leaned over to examine the fabric. "Such an elegant dress for your visit here."

"I'm meeting the general at a reception in the District immediately after this. Otherwise . . ." She surveyed the room but didn't continue.

Betty Ann sat up straight. Her hands tightened in her lap. That look, just on the polite side of a sneer, reminded her of the only other white lady who had come to her studio. When the major's wife had realized who had sat on the couch before her, she leapt off of it as if it were covered with the smallpox blankets the Army had given the Indians on the frontier. The association proved to be too much for Betty Ann. "You and Mrs. Kennedy. First her wedding dress, made by a Negro dressmaker who sews for the society ladies up in New York, and now your White House dress."

"You do flatter me with your comparison to the First Lady." Mrs. H.'s stretched smile did not reach her eyes.

Of course, you do have Miss Sonia." Sonia's murky background was clearer to some than to others, but Betty Ann woke from her momentary lapse and scolded herself for skating so near the color line before the commission was hers. Lucy looked away, intent on the hi-fi as the first record finished and the second one dropped.

"Let's look at the design, shall we?" Sonia stood, and the moment passed. "We don't want Mrs. H. to be late for her reception." The group moved to the worktable so Sonia could lay out her designs and unfold the icy blue silk she had brought. Lucy sketched as the women discussed lines and darts, buttons and necklines.

Sonia pulled out a listing of Mrs. Hepplewhite's measurements, but Betty Ann asked if she could take her own. The general's wife looked at Sonia, who nodded her encouragement. One woman's thirty-eight-inch bust curved differently than another's, and if Betty Ann were going to cut this outfit perfectly, she would need her own sense of the body to be fitted. She directed her guest to the triple-mirrored changing booth. Betty Ann draped her measuring tape around her neck and waited outside the booth.

Sonia skirted the table to look at Lucy's sketch. "That's very good."

"It's not finished," Lucy said. She lay down her shading pencil and picked up a beige stick.

"I can tell from what you already have. You've obviously had good training."

"That oil is hers, also," Betty Ann called from her post outside of the changing booth. She pointed across the room.

Sonia went to examine the painting more closely, then turned to Lucy. "Did you work from a photograph?"

"No. Miss Betty Ann told me what she wanted and I imagined the rest."

"That's great. I have an idea for a show but can't do a thing while this monster is on my arm." She tapped the cast. "Maybe you could help me out?"

"What did you have in mind?" Lucy asked as Sonia sat beside her. Betty Ann beamed. This was the kind of connection she was hoping for when she invited Lucy. Now if she could just banish the shadows of Martin and the Grayson House, the appointment would be perfect.

"Come on in," Mrs. Hepplewhite said.

Sonia looked up from the sketch pad. "Mrs. H., do you want me too?" she asked in a raised voice.

"Beg pardon?" Mrs. Hepplewhite peeped out as Sonia stood. "Oh, no, sugar. I'm fine here with Miss Betty Ann."

Sonia sat again and Betty Ann stepped up into the booth. She gave the curtain a firm tug to close it completely. Not a sliver of daylight was to be seen. Of course only women occupied the studio, but each client deserved her privacy. Mrs. Hepplewhite's rosewater eau de toilette infused the booth with the light scent of an English tea garden. Her dress hung on a satin padded hanger on a hook above a stool. She faced the mirrors in her bra, girdle, and stocking feet in the middle of the platform. Her pale skin glowed against the plain maroon velvet that lined the inside of the curtain. Her lacy petticoat mounded like snow in the multiple reflections of the triple mirrors.

Betty Ann dropped her clipboard on the small stool in the corner and stepped in front of her client. She flipped her tape from around her neck and snapped it taut. "We'll start with your bust."

Mrs. Hepplewhite raised her arms. Her gaze became more intent as she watched dark hands wield the tape measure. She then whipped her head up and stared into the mirror over Betty Ann's shoulder. Her whole body stiffened. Some white women didn't like to be touched by blacks, but Betty Ann had assumed that Mrs. Hepplewhite's Southern upbringing had included Negro maids. Her client's reaction puzzled her, but she had a job to do. She slipped the tape under Mrs. Hepplewhite's arms and around her back. With a deft touch, she quickly completed the circles around the bust, chest, waist, and hips. She made notes on her clipboard, then dropped it on the floor and knelt to measure skirt lengths.

She searched for a topic to distract Mrs. Hepplewhite and to soften her stiffness. "What type of shoes are you thinking of wearing?"

"Did you think I wouldn't recognize you?" Mrs. Hepplewhite's words were crisp and distinct, but she spoke too softly to be heard by the others.

Betty Ann felt a brief relief that the other woman's problem wasn't her touch, but as her situation became clear, the warmth in her limbs rushed to her center. A burst of angry self-survival rushed her blood out again. She wanted to rise and stare her tormentor in the face, but that would have aborted the commission. She could not afford to be impetuous. Not again. She swiveled on her knees and confronted the other woman's multiple mirror images. A few strands escaped from Mrs. Hepplewhite's otherwise perfectly smooth bun. Betty Ann appeared darker than usual against the frost of the petticoat behind her.

"Ma'am?"

"Captain Bledsoe. The Grayson House," Mrs. Hepplewhite said.

Maybe Betty Ann could bluff. She'd been in worse fixes. She cupped her chin and shook her head with a polite smile, as if a stranger had just stopped her on the street. "I'm afraid I don't know what you're talking about."

"The curtains." Mrs. Hepplewhite pointed into the mirror at the curtains behind her. "Maroon with silver fringe. Did you sew them yourself?" She stooped over and pointed the same slender finger at Betty Ann's hand. "Maybe there was a sale on maroon velvet, but that's his ring. From Germany. I admired it that day. He let me try it on."

Oh, Jesus. She had worn it so often, and when Lucy had flipped it to her, she automatically slipped it on her finger, and it felt natural there. She'd forgotten all about it. She covered the ring with her other hand and sank back onto her heels. "So you don't want me working on your dress."

"Oh please. I'm not going to let some officer's indiscretion ruin my chance to wear a dress that Jackie Kennedy herself will envy." Mrs. Hepplewhite picked up her petticoat and gave it to Betty Ann, who, after a moment's hesitation, got up onto her knees and stretched open its waist.

"You two okay in there?" Both women flinched, as Sonia sounded close enough to be just on the other side of the curtain.

"Right as rain." Mrs. Hepplewhite's voice was clear and bright. She steadied herself with a light hand on Betty Ann's shoulder while she stepped into and pulled up the petticoat. Betty Ann rose and retrieved the gray dress and helped Mrs. Hepplewhite slip its smooth fabric over her head and down into place. Mrs. Hepplewhite watched herself in the mirror as she brushed her hand over her dress. Betty Ann looked down at her clipboard on the floor; picking it up now would be too much of a reminder of their earlier encounter.

"Here's my card," Sonia said from the other side of the studio.

Mrs. Hepplewhite nailed Betty Ann with a look and stabbed a finger at her. "Sonia says you're the best," she said with the hiss of a whisper. "That's what I deserve. The best. That's what you're going to give me. Understand?"

"Yes, ma'am." Betty Ann put on her beauty pageant smile and left the booth to join the other women at the table.

When Mrs. Hepplewhite emerged from the booth, she had her gloves in hand and her purse over her arm. Sonia quickly gathered her notes and pens and dumped them into her carpetbag. Mrs. Hepplewhite shook hands with Mimi and Terry and exclaimed over the sketch. Lucy rolled it up and handed it to Sonia, who nestled it in her bag. After a final round of pleasantries, Betty Ann escorted her guests to the door and opened it.

Mrs. Hepplewhite waved Sonia into the stairwell but paused before entering it herself. Her driver waited outside with his back to them, but at the sound of Sonia's low heels clattering down the stairs, he turned and opened the door.

Mrs. Hepplewhite offered Betty Ann a gloved hand. "Get rid of the ring," she said with a smile, her lips barely moving. "I'm not the only one who knows where it came from." She swept through the door and down the stairs. Betty Ann watched until Mrs. H.'s skirt floated from sight. Only then did she return to the others clumped around her work table.

"That went well," Lucy said. An upswing at the end of her sentence asked for confirmation.

Betty Ann's body felt heavy and uncomfortable as she lit on the familiar perch of her work chair. "She knows."

"Knows what?" Terry asked.

"You girls pick up the lounge," Betty Ann replied.

"Yes, ma'am." Terry threw a look at Mimi but held her tongue. They moved off to their chores.

"She say something?" Lucy asked.

Betty Ann nodded. A real conversation would have to wait. Until then Betty Ann was alone with her troubles. She dropped the ring into her pocket and rubbed her bare finger over the icy blue silk that Sonia had left. She picked up her notes from the meeting. They had work to do.

Chita
The Discretion of the Monteros 4

ROSITA AND I lounged on our striped beach blankets in the shade of the palm trees. It was past the heat of the day but before the clouds on the horizon grew large enough to cover the sun and deliver the daily showers. Rosita was boring me with the details of the quinceañera she was planning for her daughter.

Although the sun didn't beat down with the strength of summer, it still was fierce on skin, fair and dark. All the Cubans hugged the choppy sand beneath the palms. Only a few beach umbrellas, shading visitors on lounge chairs from the nearby hotel, dotted the white expanse of beach. No one splashed in the rippling waters beyond. Besides the ever-present waves lapping lower on the shore, not much movement intruded on the afternoon's repose, so the figure at the curve of the beach immediately caught my eye. Even from that distance, I could see that it was Lola. She knew the hard, damp sand at the water's edge made walking easier, so I wondered at her laboring steps across the brow of the beach.

Lola ended her trek across the sand by plopping down in the middle of my blanket, forcing me to the edge. I asked what was the matter, but she just shook her head. Although her drawn face concerned me, I wasn't in the mood for her games. Our other sister continued on about the party for Virginia, her oldest, who was becoming a young lady. Rosita was determined to celebrate her all-important fifteenth birthday in pre-Revolutionary style. She described the amount of black market food served at a recent quinceañera. Two cold-water lobsters had set on ice in front of the birthday girl. Rosita didn't want to be a copycat, so instead she wondered if she could get enough salmon so all of the guests could have a taste.

"Almost anything could be had for the right price," I said.

That one hogging my blanket, the one that tells you she is the one to make the food, merely nodded. She closed her eyes and shivered. Rosita patted at her but turned her attention back down the beach. A man sprawled near the water's edge. "Shouldn't we wake that man with the fiery back?"

I sat up to get a better look. "What a Yanqui. Can't he see that all sane people have protection?"

"He's certainly not a Yanqui." Rosita stood. She retied the bow on her wrap and walked across the glaring sand. Lola would say that our sister is a kind soul and is always watching out for others. Please. She was just jumping at the chance to meet a new man. As she knelt beside him, I lost interest in her goings on. I crawled around Lola to lay back on the empty blanket and closed my eyes.

Rosita nudged me a few minutes later. I sat up again and scooted back toward Lola. Here I was, in the middle as always, this time between her brooding hunch and Rosita's satisfied smile. I knew she wanted us to ask about the gentleman, but I for one refused. No matter.

"He's English," she said. She waggled in her content until she took another look at our baby sis. "Chica, what's wrong with you?"

"There are A-bombs right here on our island," Lola said, barely above a whisper.

"So everyone says." Rosita rummaged in her beach bag for a brush and stroked it through her hair.

"I saw them. Sleek tubes the length of a yacht. With my own eyes. The driver got lost . . . I saw them."

Rosita stopped brushing and huddled closer.

Lola rushed on. "I wasn't supposed to, but I did. Deep in the bush. I woke up thinking to see the ocean, but instead all I saw were palms and a fresh clearing."

I felt her breath as she hesitated again and blew sighs louder than her words. "Everything could end with the push of a button." Her histrionics over nothing as usual.

Such drama. I folded my arms and pretended to yawn. "Find a new phrase, chica. That one's old already."

Lola's loose hair whipped my arm as she twisted around to face us squarely. "I saw rockets. Missiles." Her voice had sudden strength.

Rosita grabbed her arm. "Are you sure? That they're A-bombs, I mean?"
Lola nodded.

"The Russians are here. So it's with powerful weapons. Good," I said. "What does that have to do with us?"

"They shot him."

"Shot who?" Rosita asked.

"The boy. My driver." Lola stared past up as if seeing another scene. "He made a mistake and they shot him. Right then. Took him to the edge of the bush. I heard the shots and saw his body. I was next."

"Oh my God." Rosita crossed herself.

"The captain said . . . he let me go but said . . . he brought up the children . . . he said no one was safe." She looked at us with wonder, as if she couldn't believe it herself. She clutched both of us with her strong hands. "That boy was younger than Tomasito."

Rosita moaned. Is that what happened to our boy? Shot by the Russians? No. Please God, no. As our world turned upside down with each of Lola's words, the beach around us seemed to go on as normal. Countless times we had sat there with no more pressing conversation than whose child refused to eat which delicacy. Now what?

Along with our compañeros, the three of us had pledged loyalty to family and Cuba, but who in the family came first? And what was best for the country? The Revolution was still a baby, barely three years old, and the line between danger and safety was uncertain. The Sisters Montero would have to stick together, that was certain.

Movement near the water caught my attention. The tourist stretched and pressed the crimson skin on his shoulder before putting on a shirt covered with parrots. Rosita also watched for a moment, then dragged her beach bag over and started rummaging in it. "It's time," she said without looking up. "The children must go across the water."

My boys. No. We had spoken many times of getting the children out, but I couldn't imagine going with them someplace else, or worse, living without them. But now the Russians were executing their own without a thought, and Lola had gotten us mixed up in it. I argued, but Lola's fright made the possibility real, and I knew I would have to go along with the wretched idea.

"Maybe the men know someone we don't, who could help," I said.

Lola jerked her head and gave me that demonic stare of hers. By then I was out of the reach of the lash of her hair. The wind had picked up and small salvos of sand skimmed across the beach and needled my bare arms. Away to our left, a beach attendant furled the umbrellas and carried the lounge chairs back to the hotel's fenced yard. It was almost time to go.

"No men," Lola said.

"What?" Rosita and I exclaimed together.

Now I shifted around so I could clearly see the faces of both of my sisters. This plan for treason and betrayal was much too important to leave to lazy eye contact. "I can't whisk Diego's boys away from him without warning."

"Would he let them go? His precious chess players? The future of the La Luz dynasty?" Lola said. Such a dig. Despite the La Luz fame as mechanics and the supposed equalization of the Revolution, they were still in a class different from our own.

"Of course not at first, but—"

"But. But. By the time that dog gets off the porch it will be too late."

"And there's all the talk about the government assuming guardianship of all Cuban children. We'll have to do something before that happens," Rosita said. "But wouldn't it be better if—"

"If my José knows, the plan will be sunk." José the rule follower. Lola was right on that point. "No. Men."

We talked some more but Rosita finally agreed. Me too. In the end, I had to believe it would only be for a while, hoping the crazy wobble of Cuban politics would soon come to a rest.

Once we agreed on sending away the children without telling their fathers, we had to figure out how. The Pedro Pan airlift was too public for our ties with the army and the CDR, so it would have to be by boat. As soon as we decided that, though, complications mushroomed. Before, always, we had assumed the trip would be with Quique, but he was gone now, betrayed by some friend and shot out of the water. Who could tell would be next best? We went back and forth, finally settling on Carlos, the brother of outspoken Selena. Perhaps we could persuade her to go along to watch after the children and to save her own resistant heart.

Rosita gathered up her brush and her true romance novel and such. She picked up the notebook she was using to plan Virginia's party. She suddenly crumpled into a heap.

"What is it?" Lola asked.

With tears in her eyes, Rosita offered us the notebook, turned to a list of guests. "Can we wait until after the party?"

Our dear sister. Our world was certainly ending, but still she had to celebrate her debutante. Of course, it maybe would be the last thing that she'd be able to do for her daughter.

Lola smiled and patted her hand. "Of course, little dove."

Woman Waving to the Future 1

LUCY SAUNDERS SWIRLED her brushes in the jelly jar of turpentine, as she did at the end of every oil painting session. This ritual caressed her. The only problem was the abrupt ending, which cut off its soothing rhythms from her domestic duties as wife and mother. Her younger self dreamed of the bold gestures and unconventional postures of an artist's life in Greenwich Village. She tried not to leave that artistic self behind as she reentered her other life but found her vision and ambitions dulled by the sight of stark white kitchen cupboards and the scatter of dolls, books, and model car parts every day.

Routine could kill a girl.

She painted in the living room, the only viable work space for her. She delighted in the diffuse light but didn't like being on display in the front room when unexpected guests dropped in. They often thought they had the right to comment on a painting in progress, so she kept a cloth ready to drop over her easel at a moment's notice and at the end of her work sessions. She left the brushes to soak and draped the cloth over her latest canvas, hiding the overlapping splotches of blues and lavenders of a cityscape blurred by a sudden downpour. Dinah Washington had purred along with the quick blue strokes of the street scene and still crooned from the hi-fi.

Lucy stared through the picture window into the afternoon calm of a still October day. This was her third Air Force base. The first was Biggs in West Texas, the second Edwards in Southern California. The kids had known cold in those high desert abodes, but they had never seen snow before this place that cycled through all four seasons. In El Paso, the maples and oaks kept green leaves through the warm autumn, then dropped them—desiccated but still green—in the dry season of winter.

Right here and now, though, the sycamores and oaks that lined her street fluttered and flashed their fancy autumn colors in front of the rows of boxy duplexes. The street Lucy and Betty Ann lived on followed the usual plan— flat-topped ranch duplexes lined both sides of the street. The two friends lived on the same side of that street at opposite ends, Lucy in an "A" unit and Betty Ann in a "B" unit. Their homes were mirror images of each other.

Lucy found the relentless sameness of American military base housing stunning in its monotony, but even she could appreciate its benefits. A wife could close up her home, drive her kids a thousand miles away, and have them sleeping on sheets and pillows the night they arrive at their new home base. She could set up her couch and easy chairs with the same orientation to the living room window and the television. Light would fall on the pages of a book at the same slant (give or take a few degrees for latitude), and the kids could settle into their usual spots to watch after-dinner TV. Point an experienced wife toward the center of base, and she would find the commissary, the PX, the hospital, and the parade grounds on her own, if necessary. Not that she would be on her own. A base veteran would take the newbie under her wing, tell her about the liverwurst there or the fresh crabs here, which beauty shop to patronize, and who always brings the potato salad (not you) to the potluck picnics and cookouts.

Despite the tranquil scene in front of Lucy, peace was an illusion, since the airfield at the end of their neighborhood crackled with the comings and goings of personnel from all the military branches, not just the Air Force. Somewhere someone banged a hammer, each blow echoing from an unidentified direction. The sound cracked four times and stopped. A lone, scruffy white mutt trotted down the sidewalk as if he had an appointment to keep.

Sonny often complained about the cloying, pungent odor of her oil paints, although she wondered how he could detect it through a nose deafened by tobacco smoke. Erica thought it was how mommies smelled, and Tony never mentioned it. Out of habit, she cranked open a long window flanking the picture window, even though her husband was working a double shift again and wouldn't be home with his sensitive nose until after she'd had another go at the street scene. Now her last task was to turn the easel to the wall.

Lucy glanced at her watch and scurried into the kitchen. Dinah would turn herself off at the end of the record, and Betty Ann would be over soon for a rare afternoon cup of tea. Lucy opened the cupboard and inspected the jumble of coffee cups and mugs. If she lived alone, they would be in neat rows. If she lived alone, she wouldn't have to leave behind her artist self for most of the day. Of course, if she lived alone, her silences might grow into a fence too thick for anyone to penetrate. She took down two cups and saucers and put the kettle on.

Her friend was a sass who usually got away with her saucy behavior. Lucy liked her—she would say what you were thinking but wouldn't dare utter—but some of the wives didn't. They had to worry about their husbands' wandering eyes. For those women, her curves, dimpled smile, and full-on gaze added up to trouble. Those and her martini habit. She offered husbands a wide-mouthed treat instead of their usual Pabst Blue Ribbon. Yes, trouble.

When Betty Ann arrived she said, "Let's have gin."

"I don't know, I usually wait for Sonny." His double shift meant waiting for a cocktail until tomorrow at the earliest.

"This is serious: we're preparing to be attacked." Betty Ann hauled a bottle out of the liquor cabinet.

"What are you talking about? We're always preparing. Look at those everlasting exercises." Lucy pushed aside the cups and took down glass tumblers.

"No, I mean a real attack." Betty Ann opened the gin. "Missiles. A-bombs."

Lucy's forearms prickled. "What makes you think that?"

"Two things the guys said last night." Betty Ann and Ray had brought the kids over for hot dogs and beans. "One. As I stood right there with the coffee," she pointed to the swing door leading into the dining room, "Sonny said that there were no dummies this time. Everything's live. Everything." As Lucy reached for the knob on the stove to turn off the flame under the kettle, she remembered Betty Ann's silence, the swing door held open a crack by her elbow.

Betty Ann dropped ice into the glasses and filled them with gin and tonic. "Two," she continued as she poured. "When I passed by on my way to the bathroom, Ray said everything is steaming south. Why south? Why not over to Germany, where they're building that wall?"

"The only thing south of here we're interested in is Cuba." Lucy took a sip, then went to her fridge and took out a lime. She deftly sliced out two wedges, squeezed them, and dropped them into the drinks. "But we wouldn't attack them now. That would be like a direct hit on Mother Russia."

"Exactly. Despite all the demands for action, Kennedy's already been burned once there. I bet he wouldn't make these kinds of moves unless a real threat existed."

"Any other possibilities?" Lucy asked.

They debated as they sipped. News about Berlin dominated the papers, but they were on the front lines with their Air Force husbands and knew other hotspots were brewing. Lucy didn't mean to finish her drink but kept slurping as they speculated. Could they survive a nuclear war? If America launched, Russia would too.

"A-bombs," Betty Ann said.

Lucy glanced at the clock. "Oh my God, the children." Tony and Erica would be home any second.

"Yes, the children." Betty Ann slumped in her chair. After a moment she said, "We have to plan. We have to." She banged her fist on the counter. "We have to plan for the children."

"What do you mean?"

Betty Ann swept up the glasses and dumped the dregs into the sink. "First, we have to stop drinking gin in the afternoon. Lord, it's only three o'clock." She grimaced, dimpling her face. "Second, we're going to call a bunch of gals for a meeting tomorrow morning to decide what to do."

"What to do about what?" Lucy didn't quite follow Betty Ann, but she had caught her mood. In her agitation, she bumped her friend away from the sink and started to wash the glasses.

"You know we're a first-strike target." Betty Ann grabbed the dishtowel off the hook to dry.

"But we're just wives." Lucy was plenty scared.

"Exactly, no one will suspect anything we plan, as long as no one blabs."

Action steadied them. They made a list of mothers, all Negro Air Force wives like themselves. Neither of them mentioned the scarcity of air raid shelters on base. They lived in Maryland; they assumed that the few spots in the shelters would not be offered to anyone who drank at the colored fountain. They were on their own, expected to leave thinking and non-domestic action to others. Lucy was tempted to withdraw into a terrified silence, but she knew that was not Betty Ann's style, and most importantly, her own absence would do nothing to protect Tony and Erica.

Betty Ann mentioned Clara.

"Not Clara, we need allies," Lucy said.

Clara Menendez and her husband were Mexican, but the crew thought of them as colored. She was mostly a housewife but had taken some accounting courses and kept books for a few small businesses. Her husband, Manny, though, posed a problem. Several times, when Betty Ann's husband was on second shift, Manny escorted her home from a party and returned far later than he should have. His petite wife was no fan of Betty Ann.

"Oh, come on. She loves her kids more than she hates me. Besides, we need her. Manny's in the supply depot." They plotted until Erica tumbled in with her usual demands for attention.

You couldn't invite that many women over and not offer them something to eat, so the next morning both Lucy and Betty Ann got up early to make coffee cakes. Lucy marveled at all the affirmatives they'd gotten on short notice of an urgent matter that couldn't be discussed on the phone. As the women arrived at her house, they chatted and fussed over Betty Ann's lemon ice cake, but didn't ask questions. Perhaps they sought some last carefree moments before the "urgent matter" reared up. All of the invitees attended: Dorothy, Gladys, Debbie, Shirley, Linda, the other Gladys, Peggy, Pepper, Judy, May, and

Lavonia. Most sat on the folding chairs Lucy used for canasta nights. Dorothy, feet planted wide, watched the youngest kids in the back yard through the dining room window. She was formidable. Even an MP would think twice about tangling with her. Clara was there too, tucked beside the television and with her knees pressed firmly together. Although short Gladys had light skin, she still looked black, unlike Clara, whose dark, thick hair and broad face proclaimed her Mexican origins.

Lucy leaned against the wall between her clean worktable and the hi-fi and chatted with the women closest to her. As a last napkin passed down a row, Betty Ann squeezed into the space in front of the hi-fi. Lucy hopped onto her worktable to make room for her.

Lavonia, seated right up against the television, rested a piece of iced-lemon coffee cake over a saucer under her chin. "Lord, here's Miss Betty Ann and her White House *co-miss-shun*. I'm surprised Miss Betty Ann would have time for us little folk."

Pepper, sitting beside her, scratched the inside of her elbow. Everyone knew the wiry mother of two got hives when she was anxious, but her big alto voice fluttered with amusement. "What you mean, Lavonia? I do believe Miss Betty Ann is here to take your dress order. Just add a couple of zeros onto the price of the last one." As with one of her solos at the church on base, the chorus responded.

"Um hmm."

"I know that's right."

"Said she's only sewing with gold thread from now on."

"Real gold, I heard."

"Ladies." Lucy leaned forward from her perch on the table, her hands gripping its edge. "We can order our gold lamé dresses later. The kindergartners have an eleven thirty pick-up time." Several women glanced at their watches and most straightened to attention. Time for the urgent matter, their postures said. "Betty Ann?"

Betty Ann clasped her hands and held her pointer fingers to her lips. Her smile settled into a more somber look as she waited a moment before speaking. She then recapped their conversation from the day before. Tall Gladys gasped when Betty Ann said, "Everything's live." Twice jets roared overhead as if to underscore the urgency of her talk. When she finished, there was silence.

The sideboard clock tocked four beats. On the fifth, as if released by a starter's gun, the women all nattered at once. Betty Ann let the sound crest, then held up a hand. The room quieted. "Dorothy, what does Mac hear in the officers' mess?" Her husband was a cook.

"He does *not* speak out of turn," Dorothy said.

"Of course not," Betty Ann said.

Dorothy rapped on the window to get some child's attention. She wagged her finger, *no.* "I did, however, happen to overhear him comparing notes with another cook. The other guy said we've lost a plane over Cuba."

"Oh sweet Jesus," someone said.

"Maybe it's just a rumor," Clara said.

"Don't count on it," Betty Ann said.

Clara ducked her head.

"Okay, there are a couple of things we can do," Betty Ann continued. "First, we must show faith in our husbands and our country. Agreed?"

"Agreed," the women said in unison.

"However, we must be prepared to act if the situation becomes dire. Agreed?"

"Act how?" The crook of Pepper's arm was scored red. "We're just wives," she said, echoing Lucy.

"And mothers," Betty Ann said. "Anything happens, we're our children's only line of defense, right?" Voices murmured. "Agreed?"

"Agreed." The word staggered into the air from many mouths.

Betty Ann waited for a dissenting voice, but none rose. "So what are we going to do?"

"How long would it take a missile to get here?" Dorothy asked.

They all knew the answer: not long enough. But they had to hold onto something. They had to believe that their smart, beautiful president had learned the right Cuban lessons from the Bay of Pigs. They had to hope that if he couldn't avert a nuclear launch, they still could do something to save their children, and so they planned.

"We need some kind of early warning system," Lucy said.

"Does anyone have radio equipment?" Betty Ann asked.

No one answered.

"Even if we did, we wouldn't know what to listen for," Dorothy said.

Heads nodded.

Then Clara came through for them, in her way. She sat up straighter. "Manny supplies the specialty aircraft."

"Yes, we know." Lucy spoke to keep Betty Ann from asking what that had to do with warning systems.

"He always stocks the copters for the foreign ministers that visit the White House," Clara went on. "He had to find special bottled water for that official from Algeria."

Betty Ann rustled. Lucy put a hand on her arm to still her. Clara could be easily derailed, and the women couldn't afford a loss of focus. They needed every bit of intelligence on the table, relevant or not.

"Anyway, have you noticed the Sea Kings on the apron of runway 31L, you know, at the end of Cedar Street?" Most of the women nodded. "Manny said that he had to put diapers and baby formula in one of them. 'Diapers, are you sure?' I asked. 'Sure,' he said. 'Why?' I asked." She swung a look around the room and then took a sip from her coffee.

Lord, help the poor, that girl could milk the spotlight, Lucy thought. She hoped her impatience didn't show.

"The supplies are for families of White House personnel if . . . you know." Clara's voice trailed off.

"Wait a minute," Lucy said. Betty Ann cocked her head and waited a minute. At first Lucy imagined a mad dash of police cars and limousines through their neighborhoods. Then she realized that the copters would just take off for the White House lawn. "They'd fly over to the District."

Clara nodded.

Lucy remembered Mr. Gorale's Ford Coupe that she had passed every morning on the way into school when she was a kid. He was her dreamy fifth grade teacher who drove a fast car and had a pretty new wife. One day no Coupe sat at the end of the row where the teachers parked. Mr. Gorale never missed a day of school, but then his new wife was eight months pregnant. Lucy ran around the far corner of the school to peer across the river at the big brick pile of a hospital perched on the opposite hillside. Sure enough, she could just barely trace the outline of a Coupe through the winter-bare trees. It was parked at the end of the row on the side of the building that meant you were going to be there awhile. Other people must've owned black Ford Coupes, but observation met intuition and she guessed that the baby had arrived early.

She gathered coins from the girls that loved Mr. Gorale as much as she did, and even from some of the boys who wanted to drive a car like his, and persuaded Mrs. Nelson to give her a discount on a cute little knit coverlet for the baby. When the Coupe was back in its customary place on Monday, she had the blanket all wrapped up and ready to give to him when he told the class about the unexpected arrival. She made her best friend take the present up to his desk, but the handwriting was hers, and he looked directly at her as he thanked them. Plus everyone said it had been her idea, but she never told anyone how she knew. Still, she knew before everyone else did, and all because she noticed a missing car.

"So if those copters stay put . . ." A grin tugged at her lips as she slipped off her perch and waved a prompting hand in the air.

" . . . We stay put," Pepper sang out. She rested her hand in the crook of her elbow.

"We stay put," others echoed. They had discovered a simple warning system, courtesy of the government.

"Clara, you're a genius." Betty Ann sliced a cymbal-splash clap through the air. "Yes, ma'am." She threaded a path to the dining table and slid the last piece of her coffee cake onto a saucer. She sidestepped around knees and stopped in front of Clara. "Sugar, I do believe you haven't had any of my world famous iced-lemon coffee cake."

Closed lipped, Clara smiled, but she giggled when the other women clapped and cheered. Betty Ann curtsied as far as she could in the tight quarters and laid the saucer in Clara's lap.

The wives set up a schedule of patrols down Cedar Street and devised simple signals. The logistics came easily to them—the husbands would have been proud—but it was harder for them to decide what to do in case they discovered an empty apron at 31L.

"Who'll go with the children?" Dorothy asked from her post by the window. No one volunteered.

Gladys, the tall one, stood. "I'd rather be with Ted, if I knew the children were safe, or at least in good hands." The other women nodded.

"My mom lives in Cincinnati," Lucy said. "I know she'd take in anybody who had her grandbabies in tow."

It was also Dorothy's hometown. "Yeah, and who would bother to bomb Cincinnati?" she said.

Soon the women were all talking at once:

"How many cars do we need to fit all the kids?"

"Should they all go to one place?"

"My family has a farm in West Virginia."

"We have a bunch of those big water jugs from when we were stationed out at Alamogordo."

"What do we tell our husbands?" Clara asked.

Lucy and Betty Ann looked at each other as the room quieted.

"Nothing," Betty Ann said.

"But—"

"They have too much to worry about already, right? They take care of the world, we take care of the kids," Lucy said.

The women murmured.

"Why bother them with plans for something that may never happen?" Lucy crossed the fingers of both hands.

"We say nothing. Agreed?" Betty Ann asked.

"Agreed." The chorus was loud.

Dorothy wanted to run a practice drill for getting the kids out of school. The guys always said that practice eliminates mistakes in combat. "Naw, wait a minute," she said. She seesawed her head and folded her stout arms across her ample chest. "Someone might notice that all of the colored kids were gone and think we were about to riot. Won't work."

The wives continued to make concrete plans for evacuation. It came naturally as they and their families were all veterans of military moves. Even the youngest children playing in the yard sensed that they shouldn't get too attached to anything or anyone that didn't fit in the family car. They had all learned to make friends quickly but not to love too deeply. Meanwhile, training dictated that thorough task identification and assignment and absolute trust in your comrades increased the chance of a successful mission.

"How many of us drive?" Dorothy asked. She counted the raised hands. Lucy's was not among them. "Six. Sure would make assignments easier if we had an even seven—each one could take a day of the week."

Betty Ann stared at Lucy, her face dimpled into a puzzled smile. "Hon, you didn't raise your hand."

"I can't."

"Yeah." Clara touched the edge of her napkin to the corner of her mouth. "I just learned to drive last year and I'm doing it."

They all turned their faces to Lucy, waiting, but she could say nothing.

"Dorothy, you go ahead while we get that other coffee cake." Betty Ann nudged Lucy and then picked her way through the gathering. She accepted the empty cake platter that was passed to her while Lucy trailed her into the kitchen and felt the slight push of air as the door swung closed. She uncovered her cinnamon and walnut coffee cake and carefully folded the crinkled foil. Betty Ann rinsed and dried the knife before dropping it next to the cake. She backed up to lean a shoulder on the fridge. "So what gives?"

How could Lucy tell her about her silent days? About not being sure she could keep her own two safe on her own, let alone shoulder the responsibility for other women's children? She just wasn't up to it.

"Your husband," Betty Ann said. "He came to me."

First Betty Ann ropes her into a scheme with Mrs. H. and risks her husband's career because of an affair, then Betty Ann convinces her that they may be bombed out of existence at any moment, then Betty Ann expects her to blithely accept responsibility for taking a brood of children across state lines, and in the middle of it all, she brings up Sonny. The nerve. She trusted him, but Betty Ann could always take what she wanted. Lucy slid the cake onto the platter and attacked it with the knife. Each stroke ended with a dull thud against the dish, but the slices broke cleanly and stayed in a perfect circle.

Betty Ann straightened and turned to examine the pictures and alphabet magnets stuck to the fridge. She touched a photo of Lucy and the kids in front of a rocket monument. "He wanted to talk," she said.

"Sure. That's how it starts." Lucy dropped the knife, which clattered into the sink.

"I know, believe me, but not this time. He just asked me to keep an eye on you. Never said why."

Look at what happened between Betty Ann and that white officer. Quiet Lucy knew a thing or two about cutting, but this wasn't the right blade. At most, its rounded tip and serrated edge would leave only a small, pretty scar and a good cocktail party anecdote. Some distant part of her was amused with herself for thinking in such crude terms. No, she needed a much more subtle weapon.

"I'll be there," Betty Ann said. "You know I will. And if by some crazy chance I'm not, you'll do what you have to. I know it."

Why did women have to be so complicated? In the midst of Lucy's righteous anger, her friend had zeroed in on her darkness and had offered the one condition that could make it bearable. Besides, with each step, Betty Ann's desires had left her vulnerable to betrayal, by the officer, by Mrs. H., and now by Lucy. Her best weapon was trust.

"These women are counting on us. What do you say?" Betty Ann asked.

Lucy picked up the platter. "Okay. Yes. For now."

"Now is all we have." Her ally swung open the door and held it.

Lucy followed through the opening. She bent to offer cake to tall Gladys, who took a piece and then took the plate to pass it to her right. Lucy returned to her perch before saying, "I'm in."

"Good," Dorothy said. "An even seven."

Before wrapping up, the wives devised a rotating scheduled that ensured no one mother got stuck with a high target day like Sunday. Any woman could be chosen purely by circumstance to evacuate. During the entire meeting, not one comment or question came near to wondering about another woman's ability to take care of the children. In the end, they even planned for a return.

The Man with the Spanish Shoes 1

RAMÓN DIDN'T WORK well with his hands. He had finished school in the States but returned with more interest in comfort than in hard work. "What will he do?" the Monteros wondered back when Rosita accepted his proposal. He knew numbers, Rosita said, and that was that. They gave him a job as manager at one of their tanneries. He kept the books and rode herd on the workers. Though he never bared his arms or stirred the stinking potions, he learned to thwart the tricks men tried to make factory life easier. He understood, but he didn't let his tender feelings get in the way of production. The Monteros thought he managed well. What their employees thought didn't matter. At first, more experienced workers threatened him, but Guillermo, his older brother whom he hired as soon as he could, planted his feet and balled his fists. Soon the workers sulked but left Ramón alone.

Lucky for him, the Revolution rewarded his skill in curtailing unacceptable behavior by giving him a prominent position in the local Committee for the Defense of the Revolution. Neighbors grew to fear his knock on the door, as fellow citizens suffered dire consequences from his reports. He sighed and apologized while he crushed dreams and splintered families. He came to be known as the Velvet Enforcer. No one called him that to his face, but when he found out, he was pleased with the respect (non-existent) he assumed was for one considered a ruthless man. Meanwhile, his friends and family continued with clandestine activities to move valuables and eventually themselves out of the country. Even he had possible plans. Or rather, the Monteros did, and he was one of them. He saw no irony in the punishment of the less privileged for activities his own people pursued. Things had always been done that way.

The business about Tomasito was too bad, but his hot-headed brother-in-law had been about to make trouble for the whole family. Yes, Ramón had arranged his disappearance, but it was only to prevent the ultimate disappearance against the wall if he hadn't interfered. He made sure Tomasito was sent to a work farm in the province of Sancti Spiritus that had a better reputation than most. It was the one thing he couldn't tell Rosita about. He hated to see her so forlorn when he told her there was no word from his CDR connections, but if he had told her the truth she would've blabbed to those sisters of hers, and then no telling what they would do. He was thinking only of her in his silence, but he missed her full-throated laugh.

The days crept by as Ramón attended the repetitions of summing figures and yelling at the workers. Then he received terrible news. A typed envelope from Sancti Spíritus arrived for him at the office. He closed the door and sat at his neat desk to open it. Inside, a terse letter informed him that Tomasito had died from an infection that set in after he injured himself through his carelessness with a farm machine. There were no words of apology or condolences, just the fact that his body had already been buried. He panicked at first, wondering what he would tell the family now. And what awful deeds had been shoveled under with a quick burial? Were there bullet holes in the body? He shuddered and rummaged in this desk for a bottle of clear liquid he had taken from a tanner. His eyes watered as he drank, but the sear of homemade liquor helped him to focus on this latest catastrophe.

Slowly he calmed as he reasoned that he couldn't possibly feel responsibility for Tomasito's death—that boy had brought it on himself with his unpatriotic activities and careless ways. Perhaps his hasty burial was for the best, as he had now truly disappeared. Another gulp of fire decided him. One day he might relieve Rosita of the burden of uncertainty, but for the time being he would keep quiet. And he would find her a treat, maybe some perfume he'd confiscated from a smuggler and had been selling at a good price. He could spare a bottle for his wife. Yes, that's what he'd do.

Once he made the decision, he busied himself with work details and put all the unpleasantness out of his mind. Early that evening, when his crisp white shirt had long gone gray, he made his customary rounds of hidden spots where workers relaxed for a snooze. Behind the big boiler, in the cool pocket of air beneath the grueling heat, Ramón found Guillermo curled around a bottle. Not much rum was left, and he could tell from his brother's bloodshot eyes where most of it had gone.

Ramón slumped down against the cinderblock wall and shook his head. His brother roused to flick his eyes at him, then went back to staring at nothing. His mouth worked, spittle at the corner, but he said nothing. Even in this recess, the stench of dead flesh and sharp chemical odors assaulted the nostrils. Ramón noticed his drunk brother's shoes. Fine brown leather, Spanish, not from the factories down the street or the cardboard fakes the Russians passed off as footwear. Only a large wad of cash could secure such a luxury on the black market. An illegal transaction, or an even darker crime had bought those shoes.

He looked down at his own shoes. American, not new, but not too worn. They were like the pair he'd had on recently when a woman down in old Matanzas had beseeched him for help. No money, he had said. She peered at his shoes and made a suggestion. He followed her into an alley, leaned back against a wall, and unzipped. She knelt and put her mouth on him. He emerged from the alley barefoot a few minutes later. When he got home, he told his wife he had been robbed. He felt guilty about the lie. What stories footwear could tell. He nudged his brother's leg. "Where'd you get the shoes?"

Guillermo stirred and drew the empty bottle closer. "These days one shouldn't ask too many questions, hermanito." He slurped spit back into his mouth and pushed up to a sitting position. "You might follow your precious Quique to the bottom of the sea."

Guillermo's venom was no surprise. He should have been the shining light of the Fernandez family, but he was eclipsed in their youth by Quique Mendoza. The three of them had been holed up in the brothers' bedroom when their juvenile experiment with matches and rum had gotten out of hand and set one of the beds afire. Guillermo, at ten, the oldest, was nearest to the door and ran out screaming for their mother. The room rapidly filled with black smoke. Ramón, only five years old, was trapped by the scorching heat of the fire, so he crawled into the closet and pulled the door closed. Seconds later Quique flung open the closet door, grabbed him by the shirt, and dragged him toward the fire. He pulled Ramón's shirt up over his head and rushed him through the line of flames and into his mother's arms. Ramón had burns on his arms and legs, but he healed well. Quique had more extensive injuries and a long convalescence. He emerged from the ordeal with tight bands of scars pulling at the features of his face and restricting the swing of his left arm.

Ramón's mother always treated Quique as one of her own after that. She called him her favorite son, and often cited his bravery while giving him a piece of candy first, or later, when carving out a choice piece of pork for him. Those moments remained clear in Ramón's memory, the ones clotted with smoke and compressed with heat, when his brother had run away and their best friend had stayed to save him.

Quique grew into a man of daring. Until the previous week, he had been the only Cuban who Ramón would trust to make the run to the Florida Keys, away from the madness engulfing the island. In only a short time, unthinkable by the hopeful supporters of Batista's overthrow three years before, sons had betrayed fathers and husbands had stolen away with their children without a word to their wives. Quique had navigated the treachery of the post-revolutionary period and the Caribbean waters equally with the sureness of God's chosen ones. He knew the waters better than any of Castro's boys and had made dozens of trips under their very noses. Ramón added to his friend's mystique by mangling tips about him from tattletale neighbors before he passed the information on to his CDR comrades. Quique was known to the authorities, but he was known to be invincible.

Then God chose someone else. Quique made a run to the North during a moonless night, even though he, along with everyone else, knew the patrols were tripled then. Somewhere at sea, soldiers strafed his trawler, no questions asked. Most of the bodies were recovered, but not Quique's. At first, Ramón joined in his mother's hope that his boyhood savior had survived and swum to safety. Not anymore. The most he hoped now was that Quique had regained his smooth skin and joyous smile as an angel.

Some of the patrol boasted that a good source had led them straight to that worm's boat. Ramón stared at his brother's feet, shod in shoes that would be excellent pay for an informer. Sure, you turned people in, but not your own, at least not for profit. Would his brother stoop so low? He forced the question from his mind, banishing it to the same far corner as Tomasito's demise, and looked at his watch.

"Lucky for you it's after six," he said. "You're too drunk to go back to work."

His men took a nip now and then but knew better than to drink too much. The tannery was a stern mistress with many evil tricks. She was full of poisonous gases, boiling vats, sharp edges, and greasy floors. A man had to keep his wits about him or risk becoming a victim of her murderous ways.

They stood and headed for the exit. Guillermo palmed the rum bottle against his leg, hiding it from no one. As they passed a container of sulphuric acid, he looked around, then lifted the lid. Ramón whispered a warning, but his brother ignored him and slipped the bottle into the drum. Despite the rules, many of life's little irritants disappeared this way. It was routine to strain the acid to catch the few materials, like the glass bottle, that didn't dissolve to keep them from clogging the hoses.

They passed a vat set in the floor where Guillermo spent many of his days. A catwalk stretched above the steaming surface of saltwater and lime, its one rail high enough to let a worker hang over the grated floor and reach the hides below. A man wouldn't last long if he were completely submerged in the caustic solution, but Guillermo and his comrades thought nothing of reaching down from the catwalk, barehanded, and plunging in an arm up to the elbow to untangle a stubborn clump of hides. Working without protection earned them boils on their hands and arms, which, along with a characteristic raspy cough, distinguished the tanners from their compañeros.

The factory's stench followed them outside, but the wind was blowing in from the bay and within a block, Ramón inhaled the fresh sea breeze. They came to the corner where they parted to go to their own homes, Guillermo to the two-room apartment of a man whose wife had left him, and Ramón to the tidy home, bought with Montero money, near the bay. Ramón grabbed his brother's large bicep.

"Enough of the drinking at work," he said, separating the words into a distinct command.

Guillermo easily threw off Ramón's grasp. "What will stop," he said, thumping Ramón twice on the chest, "is me going to that stinking factory. You'll see, hermanito." He turned and walked away.

Ramón watched his brother weave down the sidewalk, his feet tapping out an uneven rhythm. The failing light dimmed the rich tan of the shoes but didn't obscure their possible connection to Quique's fate. Ramón tried to remember anything he may have said in front of Guillermo about wanting to leave the island. He had to tell Rosita his suspicions.

The Pattern Man 1

RAY JOHNSON WAS a pattern man. When his black man's dream to be an architect smashed into a whitewashed wall, he moved on to improvise to the rhythms of the newly birthed Air Force. His training as a draftsman housed visionary talents. He could look at a plan in two dimensions and walk through the building as if it had been built in three. He could see in a thickened line the snafus it would cause as if it were an actual cinder block wall in front of him. He claimed he heard a wrong note and immediately knew the frequency of the right one. Move that one there, he would say, stabbing at the plans. His instant insight met with suspicion at first, but when he pulled over an adding machine and talked through the savings in time, money, and effort, even the most entrenched lard butt rushed to agree.

Ray read purchase orders and schedules and saw the storage, movement, and use of supplies as if he were watching a Technicolor movie. Shipments arrived at destinations before they were needed via means that were dismissed as impossible by lesser minds. A miracle worker, more than one CO called him. A few years before, back in the fifties, when Ray and Betty Ann arrived at his assignment on the outskirts of Washington, the base was rapidly expanding. Major Hamilton "Ham" Stone was in charge of doing it right. Ray was a pattern man, always was, but the major didn't believe in his patterns at first. He had commanded too many airmen who wrote their own copy. And Ray talked crazy. Talked about hearing with his eyes. Answered "why" questions that way. Stone barked out strings of curses impressive in their crudeness, even for a soldier. Only then would Ray explain in proper logistics speak, in dimensions and distances and quantities per box.

Besides, Stone was a Dodgers fan who still grieved over their traitorous move from Brooklyn to Los Angeles. Ray was a Yankees man, proud of his Bronx Bombers, with little sympathy for a fellow New Yorker who backed the wrong team. As the two sought a working groove, the 53rd Wing was dropped into their laps. They had to execute plans to house the incoming group at the southern end of the base. Pronto. Neither of them had any say in said plans. They were drawn upstream by someone given a terrain map and a deadline. Someone who had never visited the actual site. The drawings of the south side arrived crisp and clean, the two required hangars set near the hills and the location of two more suggested by dotted line footprints.

Ray and the Major drove out there for the first time, out to the point where the air strips outran the last buildings and stretched past the scrub that foretold the rise of the surrounding hills. Ray sensed trouble right away in the steady buzz of the drawings, but he had no words yet to tell exactly what needed to change. So he yanked off his boots and socks and left them in the Jeep. *One, two, unbuckle my shoe.* His feet needed to see, he said. Stone strode away, his boots leaving a line of heel marks. Ray followed. He left no footprints at all. The crunch of Stone's impatient step outranked the snick of his bare feet.

They traced a wide arc up to the base of the hills and returned to the Jeep to roll out the plans. *Three, four, bomb the Corps.*

That was it.

"Don't build the hangars up against the hills," Ray said. "Leave some space, I'll tell you how much. Some will be like quarter rests; others will be whole bars of silence."

"Nonsense," Stone said. "You're speaking in tongues again. The hills—"

"Are regular. So it's not a straight line like Pearl Harbor. So what? Any pilot able to take off could hit every last one of them in one run. Take me up and I'll show you if you don't believe me."

Stone pressed down on the plans laid out on the Jeep's hood. Chances were that any attack that reached this base would be by nuclear missile—it wouldn't matter how far apart they spaced the hangars since the whole installation could be destroyed in one strike. Even so, the military's cumbersome logic always fought the last war. And plenty of people had lost friends or family at Pearl Harbor. It was just too fresh not to be a political force, even at the scrub end of the Maryland countryside. Stone turned his face upward, his gaze rising high and then swooping down over the field. Ray was right, he always was.

Stone conceded the point with a quick nod. "Okay. What do we do about it?"

"A little syncopation is all we need. Leave it to me."

Ray devised, and the major fought. The higher ups, that is. Usually, he would be sloughed off as a pain in the ass. Couldn't he see the box marked complete with permanent ink? But he knew how to play in the big leagues. "Don't want another Pearl Harbor," he remarked more than once while stalled in some outer office. Somehow the message got passed along, a door opened, and he carefully steered the ensuing conversation to the point where he was congratulating the desk jockey for catching the subtle flaw. The duo worked this out-of-date danger well and wound up slipping in extra storage space and a south-side field station for their own use. When the installation was complete, even General Hepplewhite could see that the modifications, while utilitarian, had a spare logic that rivaled that of Ellington's "Sophisticated Lady."

Ray received his due, even got a promotion to master sergeant, and Stone soon depended on him to see motifs that no one else did. As they dug into other projects and bonded over their favorite sport, Stone found creative means of compensating him for his unusual talents. It was a time when an enterprising Air Force officer could find military business near most Major League Baseball cities. The officer, if shrewd, would develop these opportunities in such a way that he would practically be commanded to take along an NCO as an assistant, and not just a tag-along but a logistical expert.

Stone took him to Cuba once, to Havana and out into the countryside. They went to a local baseball stadium where every single fan seemed to have a passion that reached infinitely deeper than his, and he a man hopelessly in love with the game. But that was an eon ago. Before the Revolution.

Stone's roving schemes and fixation on baseball meant that for several seasons Ray left Betty Ann alone many a night to attend urgent "duty" near Los Angeles, Chicago, or Houston. She pouted, pretty dimples ringing her full lips and pocking her apple-round cheeks, when he announced the latest off-base excursion.

"You have plenty of gentlemen friends to keep you company," Ray said, as if she had voiced a complaint.

The Pattern Man 2

A MAN HAD to be confident to stay married to a woman like Betty Ann. To let her out of his sight. To sit deathly still in the face of a petty informant until the waspish report of a party disappearance dwindled away. To watch another man's gaze follow her backside until she and it disappeared into the kitchen. To fend off the sloppy kisses of a drunk wife who claimed she was only doing what Betty Ann always did, given half a chance. To believe her when she said she was working late in her studio with the girls.

Ray wasn't always that man, but he was a pattern man, ever since he was a child.

As a teenager he stood on the rubble of an ancient office building, gone before he was born. Up there, a story above level ground, he found tough plants that grew only in the cracks of pavement and abandoned buildings. Some called them weeds. He called them homeboys. He imagined the broken granite blocks beneath his feet when they were upright and whole, somber in their austerity, ten stories high. His uncle had worked in this building, riding an elevator up and down all day long. Ray imagined the columns of broad windows his uncle knew only from the outside and the men in dark suits who strode through the tall lobby. They formed a rough circle that squared off when it pushed into his uncle's elevator. A gaunt man with quick eyes and mobile lips greeted his uncle, called him "Jack," even though that wasn't his name. Not even close. Ray heard the bells of the passing floors.

Uncle Alonzo never visited the site of his former job. Said he had already spent far too much time there in a small cab or idling in an underground room, which since then had become the repository for wrecked file cabinets, disintegrating folders, and other debris of past glories. Ray asked once if a colored man had ever had an office above the basement. Uncle Alonzo had not answered.

High above ground, Ray rocked a granite jag with his foot while he dreamed of developing this plot of land. He loved the open sky, and a garden would go, right here, but it would never be. A young lady clipped toward him on the broken sidewalk below, her dark, slender legs slipping in and out of the kick-pleat of her gray wool skirt as she walked. He thought of the bare steel legs of a carport. Wondered how big they would have to be to hold up ten stories, if they could tilt like that girl's legs now beneath him. "Hey, baby," he said, but the girl never noticed him up on his heap of rubble. Only a plant had caught his line, and it wasn't impressed. *You gots to speak up if you wants to be heard.* Ray looked down on the only greenery this lot would ever grow. "You'll never get out of the Bronx talking like that," he told the plant.

At tech school, he drew his building with its bare legs of steel. It had diamond windows and an entrance set back under a second-story overhang.

"Nice drawing," his drafting teacher said.

"What about the design?" Ray asked.

"Boys like you don't have to worry about design," the teacher said.

"Architects do," Ray said.

His teacher moved on to the next drafting table as he pushed the rolled up sleeves of his white shirt further up his skinny arms.

"Architects do," Ray said louder. In fact, it was the loudest he had ever spoken in class. Heads popped up while hands held circle and triangle templates in place against T-squares.

The teacher turned to stare at Ray. "Who here is going to architecture school?" he asked. He didn't bother to look around as heads dropped and mechanical pencils continued their arrested movement.

Ray's tablemate nudged him in the back. "Better get back to work," he whispered.

Ray did. Kept his grades up for the rest of the year too. But something worked itself to the surface. It started with smokes. His older brothers had always told him not to take them up. "Don't do as I do," Phinn, the oldest said, cigarette arrowed at him between index and middle fingers. Then, about two weeks after the architecture knockdown, Ray ran into his brother outside the printing company where he worked. Phinn, coatless in the late winter gloom, hunched over a cigarette in his ink-stained hand. After a "What's up?" Ray plucked the lit stick from his brother's fist and took a drag. Didn't even cough. Inhaled as if he had been smoking since he was five. Looked at Phinn straight in the eye—he had grown tall enough to do so—and asked, "How do you blow it out your nose?"

His brother pulled back and crossed his arms, then rubbed his shoulder, as if to warm it up. He started to say something but stopped when he looked Ray full in the face. "Baby boy's growing up." He shook his head and reached into his shirt pocket for another cig. He lit up and exhaled smoke through his nose. When Ray tried it, his eyes watered, but he shed the tears of a young man grown unhappy with the meager rewards of being good.

Next it was an encounter with the doll with the inspirational legs. He was the quiet one, but still a Johnson boy. He had absorbed more from his brothers than anyone thought. When the girl next hurried past his favorite pile of rubble, he was balanced at eye height. "Say, Miss." The two syllables intoned as if by a respectable customer at a perfume counter. She turned her head without slowing. He jumped from his perch, smooth and agile, and landed near her.

"Care for a cigarette?" he asked. He held out a pack.

"Why would I—?"She had automatically swerved away from him, but perhaps his relaxed stance or maybe it was his wispy try at a moustache that pulled an easy laugh out of her. "Why not?" Her fingers glanced off his as she drew a cigarette. As he replaced the pack and offered a lighter, she leaned into it and then squinted at him as smoke rose. "Your mother know you're out?"

"No, Miss," he said with solemn face.

She laughed again. She was older than he, but it didn't matter. She introduced him to the party circuit, and when that route brought him face-to-face with Phinn in a darkened, smoky living room, the girl was snuggled up to Ray and drinking from his highball glass. He was a Johnson, after all.

It took a while for his new behavior to catch up with him, but near the end of the school year, when a knife fight tumbled down the stairs at another late-night gathering, the police arrived at the Johnson home. His mother called for Phinn, angry resignation drawing down the corners of her mouth and leaving teeth marks on her lower lip. The cop stopped her with an abrupt palm and the name of her youngest child. Afterwards, when the cops had left him with stern words and a promise his mother had been forced to repeat too many times for her sons, they sat at the kitchen table. He couldn't look at her as she spoke softly of her disappointment in him. Her words laid a hot poker across the knuckles of his clasped hands. "Why?" she asked over and over. All he could do was shake his head.

That summer, for the first time, he took a ride familiar to many black sons of the North. He went back home to his mother's side of the family, back to a home he had never visited before. His journey took him to southern Illinois, which he thought of as going out West, but no cowboys greeted him when he stepped off the Greyhound Bus. He did meet the clenched mouth vowels of his mother's people, who lived on the banks of the Mississippi River. His grandmother ran a small restaurant with the help of his aunt, and any child sent back home was expected to work in it. He started with clearing tables, filling salt and pepper shakers, washing dishes, slicing potatoes, and tipping and tailing long string beans. In the early mornings, before the heat shimmered the hills and bluffs, he hoed the rows of a garden his grandfather had planted along the railroad right-of-way. He swung the sharp blade with care, mindful of the gleeful tales echoed about his middle brother's summer residency when he mistakenly chopped up young potato plants.

In the restaurant, Ray was swift, quiet, and courteous, and offered to do more than he was asked. In idle moments, he rearranged the shelves in the kitchen so the dishes and pans came off of them in the order in which they were needed. His organizing ways cut down on collisions and heated exchanges during the busiest parts of the day. His grandmamma was quick to correct but slow to praise, but after only a matter of days, she brought in a younger cousin of his to clear and wash dishes. Then she took it upon herself to teach Ray how to cook to her satisfaction. He learned how to cut a whole chicken into parts, dip the pieces in buttermilk, and dredge them through flour laced with salt and pepper and fresh herbs from the kitchen garden. He fried them in the big cast-iron skillet at a heat that crisped the outside and seared the sweet juices of freshly slaughtered meat inside. He learned to turn the furthest pieces first and not to jerk his hand away when the oil popped and landed in burning drops on his forearm. She made him eat his entire first batch. Too much salt scalded his tongue and left sores in his mouth. After that he was much more careful to add in smaller measures and taste even the dry flour mixture for the right balance.

Grandmama never did say how good he was to his face, but one day he heard a customer say, "Miss Frances, your chicken is extra good today."

"Should be," Grandmama said. "Nita's youngest made it. Had him practice 'til he got it right."

"Nita's youngest," the woman's voice repeated. "The one that was out here picking up dishes a while back?"

"Hm hmm."

By now Ray was leaning in the kitchen doorway. He cradled the peach pie—one slice gone—in his hands, ready to offer it if Grandmama asked him what he was doing standing idle.

"Now why she send all these hard-headed boys back here but she don't come herself?" the woman complained. She was a big, tall woman whose pressed hair had gone scraggly and dull in the heat. She sat facing Ray on the window side of the middle table.

Grandmama shook her head. "Just wish she'd had more like this one." She whipped her dish towel in the direction of the kitchen. Ray leaned back, as if the cloth had brushed him. "He takes after us. Not at all like that Johnson boy Nita married. Remember when he almost burned this place down?" That was his father she was talking about. Everyone said the oldest three took after him, but Ray wanted to shout that half of his blood was Johnson blood, too.

Across from the customer sat a much younger woman with her back to the kitchen. Her hair was pulled back into a neat bun and her beige top was crisply pressed. Ray noticed her calm, straight posture, but her caramel-colored hands floated around the table, straightening her napkin, re-aligning her knife, switching the pepper to the other side of the salt. She turned her head to watch a crowd of teenagers saunter past the cafe and waved when one of the boys cupped his eyes to peer in the window. The quick glimpse of her profile spoke of both a woman in bloom and one that had not yet left all of childhood behind.

In New York, a desirable young lady like that would be out of his league, Ray thought as he faded back into the kitchen. But he wasn't in New York, and neither was she. They'll be talking about this Johnson boy, too, he vowed. He deftly cut and plated two pieces of the peach pie and scooped vanilla ice cream onto the dishes. He swept out of the kitchen and over to the young lady's table and placed the desserts in front of her and her older companion.

"We didn't order this," the older lady said, but she plucked her fork from her dinner plate.

"Compliments of the chef," Ray said with a slight bow.

They all glanced at his Grandmama. She'd been known to snatch away a fork poised before an open mouth if she didn't like what was going on in her cafe. Yes, she was persnickety, but everyone—black and white—agreed she served the best food in town. She inspected the desserts while Ray remained stooped with his hands behind his back. "I swear you're going to drive us all into the poor house," she said. That was her favorite prediction to levy against any relative who dared to work in the cafe. Meanwhile, Ray and the girl were pretending not to look at each other. Grandmama's face softened into an almost smile before settling back into its usual frown. "Boy, the least you can do is clear those dinner plates."

"Yes, ma'am." Ray skimmed the older woman's plate onto his forearm as he was taught and turned to her companion, who had picked up her plate in both hands. None of his furtive glances had prepared him for the fullness of her beauty. All thoughts ceased. His fingers pinched thin air two inches above the plate and remained like a crab claw stranded over the table. A New York woman would've laughed straight into his bewildered face. This one. He saw the making of a decision in the settling of her shoulders. No one else saw because they were all too busy guffawing at his school boy freeze. He saw, and though he didn't understand why, his Johnson blood understood what.

She calmly lifted the plate until it met the back of his outstretched hand. "Roessel's." Her gaze met his before traveling on to her companion.

"What?" The word indistinct around a mouthful of pie.

"You asked me where we got that good beef we had last Sunday. We got it at Roessel's." She was actually answering a question that Ray was too scared to ask: can I see you again? Yes, he heard her say, at Roessel's, where the crowd gathered in the parking lot after hours. He worked later than most of his peers who quit when the sun went down, and until now he had no good reason to hang out there.

Later, after the girl had gone, the afternoon lull meant that his cousin cleaned and set the tables and his aunt did paperwork and ordered food for the next day while Ray and his Grandmama worked side-by-side on prep for the dinner hour. He cut up chickens and she chopped eggs he had boiled and peeled for the potato salad.

"What's her name?" Ray asked.

"Who?" Grandmama threw the chopped eggs into a large ceramic bowl. Her upper arm jiggled as she stirred its contents with a wooden spoon. The sharp odor of fried foods lingered in the air around them.

"The girl with the peach pie," Ray said.

"Oh her. That's coming out of your pay." She turned back to the chopping board and spilled out a number of pimento olives. Most folks thought that olives were the sign of a sophisticated potato salad. She rolled them into a line to be chopped, but suddenly took a full gander at her grandson. He felt her silence and scrutiny. He kept whacking at the chicken, but he wondered if she might be thinking about the time that another Johnson boy had come to town and had asked the same question about her daughter. Did she wish no one had answered?

She turned back to the salad. "Betty Ann McBride. We don't know her people."

Understood.

The cafe's routine continued, and the dining room filled with customers and emptied out again as the evening crept toward his Roessel's debut. Grandmama still opened the cafe in the morning but no longer stayed until closing at night. By the time he wiped down the sink and turned out the kitchen light, only his aunt was left, counting the day's take, to make him promise not to stay out too late. He checked his reflection for flour smudges in the broadside of the chrome toaster before pushing through the back door into the hazy, buzzing night. He zipped across the open field behind the cafe but paused in his rush when the ground dipped into an unexpected cool spot. Fireflies hovered, the centers of small halos of light. The most natural moments, a refuge in a slight change in topography, reminded him the most of the pleasures of a city summer night, of the heat held by the sidewalks suddenly left behind as you entered the park, drawn by the bursts of laughter as friends played the dozens and called each other's parentage into question with ever more far-fetched claims.

Roessel's was a low-slung wooden building at the southern end of Main Street. With a different store front, it could've been a truck repair shop or a warehouse, but instead it was the "big" market in town that stayed open late and always had a well-stocked cooler of soda pops. The street lamp out front afforded enough light for a passing adult to see who had gathered at one end of the building, but not enough to keep the kids from slipping liquor into their sodas and other clandestine activities. Whites and Negroes hung together, but didn't mix as couples. Not in the light, anyway. As Ray approached the den of loungers he sought out Betty Ann. She didn't turn away; nor did she beckon. Not at first. Much later, when he had travelled more in the adult world, he realized that Betty Ann must have known how to work a roomful of males since she could pull herself up by the bars of her crib and make eye contact while sucking from her bottle.

If she had taken him up right away, at least one local boy may have wanted to stab him in the neck and dump him in some cornfield to become a speed bump for a harvester that fall. Because Betty Ann had rules. More than half the young men lounging against fenders or propped up against the store's wall knew her major one by heart: No going all the way. Ray could see them slit their eyes at her even as they laughed and joked. He also met Jessie, her brother, that night. Jessie offered him a cigarette, extended a lit match, said, "There's me, Norbert, Howard, and Tom. Then there's our sisters' husbands—Freddie and Elmer." He shook out the match and tossed it past Ray's shoulder into the night. "Just me and little Norbert here right now, rest of them's in the Army. But they will all go AWOL for family."

Understood.

But Betty Ann also had plans. And when a well-built New York boy showed up he fit right into them. It took her two weeks to work him into her regular rotation and another couple to work the other fellows out. By then, the crowd looked forward to his stories about rent parties and train rides to Harlem to sneak into clubs. She played him and he let her. There was nothing else to do. He arranged the spices alphabetically and the knives by size. He wrote letters home about picnics among the bees on the banks of the Mississippi and the violent storms that shook the ends of the earth.

And he fried chicken.

He saw boiling oil when he closed his eyes. He no longer noticed its hot speckles on his forearm. He learned Betty Ann's various rules and how they all had exceptions. He assumed a girl as popular as she had already made an exception to her major rule. He wasn't surprised that August night in the cemetery on the hill when she didn't stop him at the usual time. They lay on a blanket they had used earlier for a picnic by the river. Heat lightning flashed over Missouri to the west and lit up tall columns of thunderheads. He slipped into her but was surprised by a current of resistance he didn't know existed. She grunted as he pushed past. He froze.

She moved first, rocking her hips. He matched her. Those New York women had an itch he had learned to scratch, but none of that compared to this. This falling, falling, and never wanting to stop. Wanting it to always be now, never wanting it to be after. Later, she straightened her clothes as fat raindrops fell. He thought he glimpsed blood on her handkerchief as she folded it away in her pocketbook. They never spoke about that. They didn't have to. They were one.

End of summer and he wanted to cry. She didn't, so he couldn't. She had a plan, and certain things happened in a certain order. In her plan, love came first. The only certain thing that happened to be out of order was Lonnie. He was on his way to being born by the time Betty Ann arrived in New York that fall.

The Man with the Spanish Shoes 2

AFTER DINNER, ROSITA said, "Let's sit inside tonight." It was stuffy inside, cooler out, so Ramón knew she wanted to discuss a topic not for the neighbors' big ears. He was tired after another day of fighting the inertia of unhappy workers and worrying about his brother's loyalty, but he stayed up until all their girls had gone to bed. He, too, had sensitive thoughts to voice. He followed his wife into the kitchen. Most of the house was furnished with the history and tastes of the Monteros, but the Formica-topped kitchen table where they now sat had been his mother's. Rosita bent over to sweep up two small barrettes from the tile floor and dropped them on the table beside the day's newspaper. No matter how much she scolded the girls, the small things still escaped her control. Her skin glowed with perspiration. She wiped a drop away from her cheek with the back of her thumb.

"Our children will go without us for now," she said.

Quique was gone. What could she be thinking? "How? Why now?"

"The Sisters Montero have pledged to get all of our children off the island." Rosita lifted her dark, wavy hair from her neck and let it fall again.

Ramón felt a familiar stir, despite the serious conversation, or maybe because of it. He folded the newspaper and pushed it aside. "What happened?"

Rosita settled her elbows on the table. "Lola saw missiles, the worst ones. With her own eyes. She was coming home after cooking for the Soviet soldiers and was asleep when the Russian driver took a wrong turn. Such a little mistake. But then the Russian captain . . ." She covered her mouth with both hands, as if she were praying into her fingers.

"What happened?" Ramón said again, softer. He reached across the table and spread his slender hands flat in front of his wife.

She spoke from behind her steepled fingers, her eyes wide and brimming. "They shot him—the boy—the driver—just like that. He was just a boy, Lola said."

Ramón shook his head slowly. He turned his palms up and Rosita clasped his fingers.

"If they have so little regard for Russians," Rosita said. She squeezed harder. "They'll think nothing of taking Cuban lives." She sniffed. Her nose had reddened with her tears.

He loved her at that moment, not the he didn't love her most of the time. But this. If he were dying far from home while defending a cause he wasn't sure of, he would want some unknown local woman to mourn him simply because he was a mother's son. For this he could almost forgive the flirtations on the beach and at the club, the new shoes instead of meat from the black market, the insane loyalty to her sisters.

"The Sisters have a plan?"

She drew her chair closer. "I'm not supposed to tell. Even you."

He sat back and threw his hands into the air. Those goddamn Sisters, thick as thieves. His moment with Rosita was ruined. "Then don't." Maybe he shouldn't say anything about his brother. And he certainly couldn't say anything about her brother's disappearance.

"Ramón, no."

He went to the cupboard and took down a red juice glass and a bottle of rum. He poured himself three fingers' worth.

"Mami!" Margo's voice floated down the hall. She was their youngest, sensitive to the appearance of saints and the psychic noise of arguments.

"You see? You're upsetting her," Rosita said, rising from the table.

"How do you know? Maybe it's the Madonna again. She seems to like your family."

Rosita skirted the table and strode out, leaving Ramón to his rum. He sipped the warm drink and thought for the first time what their evenings would be like without that small voice to interrupt them. He wanted to wait until the whole family could leave together, he, Rosita, Virginia, Alma, and Margo, moving as one. But it was not to be. He had gotten used to the idea of movement, but not of separation. Well, he would have to see exactly what the plan was. Rosita returned and sank into her seat. He slid his glass across to her and she took a sip.

"Which boat?" he asked.

"Carlos—"

"Figueroa? Never."

"He's family." A distant cousin on her mother's side.

A whole other clan he had to deal with. "So what? That lizard takes advantage of young girls whose parents pay good money for safe passage. Then he gets sloshed at the Bohio and brags about it. No, I'm not letting Virginia near him."

"How do you know this? You don't go to the Bohio, do you?"

"Of course not, but I have it on good authority." Guillermo was a regular at the rowdy bar.

"But surely he wouldn't take advantage of family." Rosita wrapped her arms around herself. "They'll be okay," she said, perhaps more for herself than for him.

If he wanted to go alone, he would stow away on one of the big freighters that left port for Mexico or Brazil. He knew a few dock workers who would look the other way for a reasonable price, but he couldn't bear the thought of freedom without his girls, or them without him on this island of uncertainty.

"There must be some other way," he said.

Rosita tilted her head, jutted out her chin, and threw a mocking glare that he had seen more frequently in recent weeks. "Name one. Oh yes. Big-shot Quique. Where is he now? In the belly of a shark?"

Ramón's mouth went dry. Sweet Rosita had learned to be nasty. He couldn't say anything about his suspicions about his brother, and now she was mocking his lost savior. It was too much. He swiped his drink off the table with the back of his hand. The glass hit the wall. Shards of red and golden drops of rum rained down on the clean tiles. The sting of her and Guillermo's mockeries gathered in his hands. His brother was out range, but his wife wasn't. He shoved the table hard into her and followed with another backhand, this time across her cheek.

"Ay!" she yelped.

He had never hit his wife before. It felt so good he didn't want to stop.

"Mami!" Margo shrieked from the bedroom, loud enough, it seemed, to wake the whole country. Their old mutt stuttered out barks from the front room, starting a chorus of strays and outside dogs.

Rosita's fists trembled on the table. His mother's hands had clenched the same way on this yellow Formica. He had wanted those hands to caress his face, to let him know that everything was all right. Now he wanted to pound them flat. He raised his arm again.

"*Ramón.*" Rosita's high, fierce voice rang out in a tone he'd never heard before.

He paused in his back swing.

She was trapped behind the table, but her eyes glittered as she lifted her chin into that haughty Montero pose. "You think *this* will make you a man?"

He landed another blow to her face. Just then he noticed Virginia's tousled head in the doorway. Did she see? Her lithe teenaged body tensed under a pink night gown. Alma, their middle daughter, peered around her. A second later, Margo, her face wet with tears, crowded in on Virginia's other side. The mutt's grizzled snout poked in between the two oldest girls.

Rosita eased the table away. She dipped her head and mustered a crumpled smile. Her multiple dimples had been known to disarm the most skeptical of government officials, even the female ones.

"We've had a little accident," she said. "The drink fell off the table."

Virginia followed the long arc the glass would have to travel to make the mess across the room, then stared at her mother's swelling face. Ramón saw his wife's lie register in his daughter's eyes. Virginia left him at that moment. Nothing would ever be the same with her.

"Mother," she said, choosing a formality she almost never used. "Help me put Margo back to bed."

"Of course, hija." Rosita winced as she stood but didn't stop moving before joining her girls in the doorway. They all turned their backs on Ramón.

"Rosita," he said.

She gathered in her girls but didn't turn around. A man from work had said to always punch them where the bruises wouldn't show in church. He saw the man's black teeth and the boils on the finger he used to punctuate this bit of wisdom. Ramón could dismiss this mofeta whose stink rivaled that of a rotten hide, but he had finally joined the brotherhood that nodded and laughed along with him. It defeated him, this country, with its secrecy and betrayals and violence.

"Rosita, my life," he said.

She looked over one shoulder. Virginia peered over her other. The twin set of dark eyes, so alike in the gloom of the hall, decided him.

"Do what you must," he said.

Rosita nodded once and turned away. Virginia held his gaze until her eyes were lost in the shadows.

The Pattern Man 3

RAY SAT AT his desk and counted. He counted the number of minutes until midnight. *Seven.* He counted the number of cigarettes he had left. *Nine.* He counted the number of voices arguing over a box of scuffed and nicked O-rings. *Three, now four.* He went back to the paperwork on his desk. The hours between eleven at night and seven in the morning could stretch into eternity, but not when flight readiness had dropped to an hour. Each day, papers stacked in his in-box while he trailed Stone to catch changing orders or harangued men to get faster without the carelessness of being in a hurry. He flipped through a stack of blue carbon copies and counted the cartons of O-rings they had. *Four.* Not counting the disputed case. Okay, that would get them through a couple of days, but the next order would have to go on the fast-track list. Seemed as if everything went on the fast-track list these days.

"Owens," he yelled. An airman leaned across the doorless entrance to his office, his hand braced on the frame. Ray looked into coal-black eyes. "Tell them to take that box back to the depot and pick up another one."

"Yes, sir."

"And for Chrissakes be careful this time."

"You got it, Sarge." Formalities were for day shifts and one shift at a time and for men you barely knew. Still, he had gotten the "Sarge." Men around here always gave him that.

Owens disappeared and Ray went back to counting. The phone rang, its jangle surely suggesting another dropped delivery or misplaced pallet. He lifted the phone and heard big band music and a mix of male voices. Here was a disaster of another sort. What did Ham want now?

"Grayson House. On the double," his CO said. The words were crisp and low. Someone who didn't know him would think that he were sober.

"Ham, we have a whole convoy—"

"Now." The line went dead.

Ray threw the stack of invoices back into his in-box and shouted.

This time Owens appeared with O-rings in his hands as if he were about to juggle them. The ones in his right hand could be salvaged, Ray noticed. Good thinking. Owens was an asset.

"Take over here. I gotta go to Stone." He slipped on his jacket. "Keep them moving. We're going to get more tomorrow."

"I'm on it, Sarge." He backed up to let Ray pass. "Good luck."

Ray snorted and went out to the Galaxy 500 he had gotten when the youngest was finally out of a booster seat. Betty Ann drove the new Pontiac, but that was all right. Ray had this baby painted a cream color, and some people assumed it was a Thunderbird before they got a good look at it. That was cool with Ray. It hadn't been washed in a week—a long time for him—but he had been pulling double duty and the only time the car was home, it seemed, was when the boys were fast asleep or gone to school and he was too tired to keep his eyes open. He emptied the ashtray and the small trash box that sat with weighted flaps on the hump, just in case his CO needed a ride home.

What in devil did Ham want with him? It was bad enough that he bartered parts off the books. And that he called Ray off of duty when things were slow. But not now. Not with the Russians in Cuba. It was no longer amusing. Both of their butts would be in a sling if they were caught now. Of course, the men who would do the catching were probably the same ones Ham was playing poker with or whatever they were doing at the Grayson House. He had been past there plenty of times but hadn't been inside. Not yet. He pulled into the parking area shadowed by a circle of trees. Several cars skewed this way and that, all squeaky-clean and reflective even though the dark muted their colors. He sought out Ham's car but didn't see its distinctive two-tone paint job. No wonder he called.

Ray approached the porch, which was dimly lit by an electric lantern swaying in the wind. His first thumps of the brass lion knocker went unanswered, and the doorknob didn't turn when he tried it. No sounds escaped from the interior, although a sliver of light seeped from the large window to his right. He finally located the rectangle of a doorbell and pushed. Almost immediately the door opened and a young black man in a waiter's coat stared out at him.

"Major Ham Stone," he said.

The waiter opened the door wider and Ray slipped inside. He hadn't realized how cool the night had gotten until he inhaled the warm air of the foyer. The waiter turned to lead him deeper into the house. He glanced into the front room as he passed without breaking stride or appearing to snoop. The errant light had come from a table lamp beside a leather chair near the window. It was the only illumination in the room, as if the master of the house had sat down to read a chapter in a history book as the rest of the household slept. Nice fantasy, Ray thought. He could almost believe it if it were not for the woman's sling back shoes kicked beside the chair.

This glimpse lasted all of two seconds and it took in something else. Something that meant much more to him. Red velvet curtains with silver fringes arrested his inner motion even as he kept a steady cadence down the hall. He'd seen them before—not here—he'd never been here before. It was at Betty Ann's dress shop. When she created a combination she liked, she tended to repeat it. He loved that about her. It let him track her riffs across social landscapes on lines that no one else saw. But what was her pattern doing here in the officers' clubhouse? The waiter stepped aside and allowed him to continue into a room where two tables of poker were in steady action and where a couple of officers lounged in chairs in front of the fireplace. Neither officer occupied his chair alone. One girl's stockinged leg swung lazily over the chair's arm, her foot bobbing up and down. Those slingbacks go with her, he thought as he flashed back to the red velvet curtains.

The color scheme in this room continued in the spectrum of rich reds, but different materials and livelier patterns suggested a more casual use. Maybe his brain wouldn't work this way if he had never met Betty Ann, but he had, and it did.

"Johnson." Ham's voice rose up from a couch opposite the club chairs. He pushed a striped pillow onto the floor as he propped himself up into a slouch. More of Betty Ann. Not the same fabric but he could almost smell the musk of her hand. But how? Why didn't he know? He might have been imagining things, but he wasn't. He knew Betty Ann's phrasing the way you knew it was Dexter Gordon and not Sonny Stitt blowing that horn. Did Stone know? And if he did, why hadn't he clued him in? Stone launched himself off the couch and swayed into Ray before putting an arm around his shoulders and turning him to face the nearest poker table.

General Hepplewhite, sitting in profile to them, looked up at the commotion. "You can't leave yet." Hepplewhite dropped his fanned cards face down on the table. "Give me a chance to win them back."

Stone leaned on the chair of the nearest player and peered over his shoulder. The man shoved back with his shoulder while cupping his cards away. Chips seemed largely distributed away from Hepplewhite, which might cause a man to be belligerent at this point in the night, but he rolled the ash off his cigar in the cut glass ash tray and relaxed back with it cocked between his fingers as he re-fanned his cards.

"General, sir." Stone steadied himself on the high back of the wooden chair in front of him. He pulled two tickets out of his breast pocket and held them high in the air. "I'm giving these," he shook his raised fist, "to Johnson here. And I'm instructing him . . ." He paused and raised his index finger. "No. I'm *ordering* him not to surrender them while we're in this building." He passed the tickets back to Ray.

Ray glanced at them as he palmed them and slipped them into his coat pocket. He didn't get a full look but saw two words he didn't think he'd see on a ticket this year: "World Series." No wonder Hepplewhite wanted them back. On the other hand, how could anyone justify a trip with everything going on?

Hepplewhite jammed the cigar in his mouth and gave Ray the once over. "Sergeant, play poker?"

The general knew the answer. No man worth his salt on this base would answer no. What he meant was, do you play poker badly enough for me to win back my baseball tickets? Ray knew how these places could get. This was a tame night. Sometimes the ricocheting energy of a build-up ignited a delirium from which airmen woke up with pregnant girls they hardly knew or stripes stripped from their shoulders. In the other direction, a kind of pall could fall over the base as double duty sputtered into a dull throb of listless card games and half-hearted jousts over steins of beer. Tonight was like that, so far anyway. He knew any night could turn on a dime, especially with his CO involved. He was itching to look at the pair of tickets but kept perfectly still.

The player facing them held the deck as the current dealer. He leaned toward Hepplewhite and said something that Ray couldn't hear.

"The rules. Of course I know the goddamn rules," Hepplewhite said. "I made them. I can break them." He discarded three cards and swept up the new ones into the stack of his hand without looking at them. He tossed two blue chips into the pot.

Stone leaned in as if to look at the hand of the closest player, but the guy just threw the cards on the table. Stone stood up as straight as his condition allowed. "Rules are rules."

Ray assumed they were referring to some kind of ban on having an NCO at the table, which meant the stakes were higher than a master sergeant could afford. Of course, the World Series tickets were enough evidence of that. He wondered what his CO had put on the table.

Stone reached back and grabbed him by the shoulder. "Come on before I change my mind." He threw a half-hearted salute at the general, who flipped him the finger. Stone chuckled and circled behind Hepplewhite on his way to the hallway. Ray followed.

The red curtains stood silent watch as they passed the entrance to the front room. "Ham." He slowed to a stop. "How'd this place get to looking so fancy?"

Ham had reached the front door. At that moment no one else was in the hallway, and the front room was still occupied only by the shoes. "Yee haw!"

someone shouted and a hubbub rose from the game room behind them. The sounds of a big pot being raked in followed.

Stone raised his hand as if to open the door but instead swiped his forehead with the heel of his palm. He turned and walked back to stand in front of Ray. His face sported a light sheen of sweat but no hint of emotion. Even so, there was something in the almost imperceptible squint of his eyes, something hard but not unkind.

"Need to know basis," he said.

Ray stood his ground. "I need to know. Now."

"Okay." Stone shrugged. "Ask you wife," he said and turned away.

The Pattern Man 4

THEN IT WAS the next Saturday night at the NCO Club. Ray took it all in. He had been to clubs like this across the globe, each one had its local flavor, but they all felt the same on Saturday nights. They were filled with energy, stacked up behind the fences of routine and let loose in controlled bursts of laughter and unrestrained drinking. He had been to Berlin before the wall became concrete. As if on autopilot, his mind traced the plan of German airstrips and overlaid them with his runways in the Maryland countryside. Blue lights lined the runways at night. He knew the exact distance between the blue bulbs dotting flat land, knew where you got two hundred of them at a time and where to stow them when they arrived.

Red vinyl booths lined the south and east walls of the club, and four-top tables marched right up to the plate glass windows on the western wall. The sun had just set behind the rolling hills beyond, leaving a rim of bright sky over the shadowed trees. It sparked the underside of stray clouds, turning them pale pink and deepening them by the minute as Ray watched. Instruments would rule flight by 2100 hours, he thought. They were out with Sonny and Lucy and sitting almost dead center of the action in the dining room.

Betty Ann was over at the jukebox, sliding her quarter into the slot, pushing B-29, and swaying in time to "Blueberry Hill." He hadn't said a word to her, not a word, about the Grayson House. One moment he vowed to have it out with her, the next his throat itched at the thought of where else she might have gotten her thrill. He took a swig from his whiskey-rocks to soothe it and piled bacon bits on top of his lettuce and bleu cheese as Betty Ann settled back into her chair.

"My birthday's coming up," she said. She stabbed a cherry tomato in his salad. It erupted with the piercing of her fork, pulp and seeds dripping, just once, onto her own salad as she ferried it to her lips.

"Big shindig?" Sonny asked.

"I want it to be. He doesn't," Betty Ann said. She reached for Ray's salad but he pulled his bowl out of reach. He hated it when she pretended she wasn't that hungry but then ate most of his food.

"Don't feel like it this year. Too much going on."

"Maybe that's exactly why we should get everyone together," Sonny said.

"Sure," Betty Ann agreed. "Lots of new folks coming in, too. Have you met the Wilsons yet? They seem fun."

Who were the Wilsons? Ray wondered as the conversation ran along like that, names of couples spilling across the table. He listened, placing its ebb and flow within the rising hubbub in the restaurant. He picked out the patrons who were laughing through their second drinks, noted the ones that wouldn't be cutting into their steaks until he and his party had moved on to the lounge. The waitress cleared the empty salad bowls while a voice at the next table said, "Tis-sue, I don't even know you." A spray of laughter followed, larger than the joke. The man must be mugging it up, Ray thought, not looking. He zeroed in on the day's special, recited for the fourth time by the waitress with the gum-chomping punctuation as a counterpoint to Sonny's bass rumble and Betty Ann's swinging melody.

He looked at Lucy, who hadn't said anything. "What do you think?" he asked.

She gazed at the beer clock on the wall. He didn't know if she were sliding down the cool, clear water that trickled mechanically in the clock's mountain scene, or if she were wishing that the second hand would sweep faster around the backlit face. She was a good one, but too quiet for Ray. He bet Sonny found her perfect, though, with her narrow face, her smooth charcoal-dark skin, and her track star thighs that did more talking than her mouth ever would.

Lucy brought her gaze back to the dinner table. "Let's have a dinner party."

"Who'll cook?" Sonny asked.

"C'mon. Let's dance. More people, more fun." Betty Ann pouted. Most times that was all she needed to do to get her way. Not this time, not with maroon velvet curtains shrouding Ray's mind.

"Dinner party would be okay." Ray picked up his glass to signal another drink to the waitress, then circled it to order another round. "We can have it here. Four, five couples? I could cover that. It'll be the first of the month—I'll be flush."

Their waitress arrived with a tray full of their main courses. Sonny leaned back to let her slide his steak, cooked rare with onion rings, in front of him. "Of course we'll help pay."

"Then we can have ten or twelve couples," Betty Ann said. "First Saturday in October."

Lucy sent a look to her husband, one that said, "She's doing it again." Ray caught it, but Betty Ann was busy guiding her plate of roast beef to a safe landing. She was roping them in, assuming they wanted to spend that much on a party just because it was for her. He used to just accept that was her way.

Now he was embarrassed by it. He didn't know what he was going to say until he opened his mouth.

"That many people, maybe I should see if Ham could slip us into the Grayson House."

Sonny swallowed a mouthful of food. "Ham's good, but no way José. It would take special dispensation from the pope before a bunch of us would be allowed to party there."

Betty Ann kept her gaze on her plate a second too long before looking up as the waitress handed her empty tray to a passing bus boy and continued on to the next table.

"You ever been there?" Lucy asked.

"Just once, when Ham was in his cups." He watched his wife, expecting her to play innocent by asking him what it was like, but she was better than that.

"How many times has she said it?" she asked.

She was very good, indeed. The dessert special was Nuclear Pie, but the waitress kept saying "nu-cu-lar."

"Four," he said, smiling despite himself.

Lucy doctored her baked potato without looking up. "How many times has who said what?"

She missed Ray's glance at the sharp-boned waitress in the lime-green uniform, but Sonny caught it. He leaned back to listen. "Five," they said together. Sonny was a good guy, he knew, even if he didn't know everything.

Lucy finally looked up. "Six?" she said. Ray felt a distant affection for her. She wanted to play, even if she didn't really care what the rules were. She made up her own; that was the artist in her.

"Wait a minute. What about the Series?" Betty Ann asked. She had lost birthday celebrations to the World Series before. Sometimes she won. She was batting average so far.

Ray felt the weight of the game tickets press against his chest, even though they were tucked in the jacket hung on his office chair. "They won't have a Saturday game early in the Series," he lied. "I promise." He was good too.

THE MEN DISCUSSED what they could tell the girls about the situation in Cuba. Not every detail made it into the newspaper. Ray had a map of all of the air raid shelters. Knew exactly how many minutes it would take his family to get to the nearest one. Still, they didn't want their wives to worry. Meanwhile, amidst the quiet clamor on base, his wife worked with the situation to plan her birthday dinner at the NCO Club. She and Lucy invited Mac and Dorothy, Ted and Gladys, John and Debbie, Todd and Shirley, and the Wilsons. They'd take over the back end of the main room—cozy but still in on the action. Ray didn't stop her.

The week before the big event, Ray and Betty Ann finished the day by watching *The Late Show*. As usual, he slouched in the recliner and Betty Ann lounged on the couch, her feet tucked beneath her. She had just finished hemming one of her own skirts. Ray thought he would face the Grayson House situation head on, would bring it up calmly and give his wife a chance to set him straight. He sustained this image of himself and his wife right up until he lowered the sound on the television and slipped the tickets onto the coffee table in front of her. She looked at them, flicked a glance at him, and went back to her sewing.

"We'll be gone Saturday night."

Betty Ann brought the new hem up closer to her eyes. Suddenly she ripped it apart. "How do you get to go to the World Series with all of this other"—she waved the needle around, clearly searching for a word—"commotion going on? Is this what you call combat readiness?"

"He finagled it so it's part of our duty."

"Your patriotic duty to uphold American institutions or your duty-duty."

"We're inspecting a base or something."

"Jesus, God, I'm glad he's on our side." She folded the skirt and slipped the needle and thread into her sewing basket. She carried her glass into the kitchen. Sid Caesar came on the TV, and though the sound was muted, Ray smiled at his grin and not so innocent eyes.

Betty Ann reappeared at the corner of the dining room. "How long have you known about this?"

Before he could land on an answer, one that wouldn't break them apart, she crossed in front of the TV and stopped at the entrance to the hallway.

"You owe me," she said.

He owed her nothing. "Since the Grayson House." There, he had said it. He half expected the lights to flicker or the floor to drop away. Or at the very least for his wife to catch her breath.

"Oh." She came back into the room far enough to pick up her sewing basket. She clasped the handles and shielded herself with her folded arms. She turned toward the TV but didn't seem to be registering the men sitting on the talk show set. "What do you want to do?" Not defiant, not contrite, seemingly relaxed except for her grip on the basket. A stranger might have thought she was waiting for a bus rather than to hear the fate of her marriage.

Ray remembered the first time he saw her and how much he knew about her from the set of her shoulders. He realized he knew this moment would be in the future, and maybe not even just once. That was the time to make a decision to walk away, not now. Guys always said they wanted to know, but for what? As long as this thing lay dormant, they could continue on. Not exactly the same way, but also not as shattered pieces.

"You owe me," he said.

She relaxed her grip and settled her shoulders, the way she had the day they first met. But this time, he had chosen her.

"Enjoy the game," she said.

Betty Ann turned and went up the hall. Ray wondered what rhythms had just changed. He had time to discover them. He was a pattern man, he would figure this out. He turned up the sound on the TV.

The Man with the Spanish Shoes 3

THE NEW MOON came and went without the disappearance of Ramón's daughters. He heard nothing about the preparations for what he hoped would be a temporary separation. During the day everything seemed normal, but Rosita was cold to him at night. She either slept in Margo's bed all night, to the satisfaction of their youngest, or rolled to the edge of their bed with her back to him. As the moon waxed to a quarter full, Rosita asked him to withdraw a large sum of cash from the bank. Although most of the money came from her family, the bank officials would question a woman acting without her husband's approval. He did as Rosita asked.

At the end of that week, Ramón and Rosita hosted the quinceañera for Virginia at the family's beach house. Everyone was there, including Carlos Figueroa. Guillermo also attended, and even Guillermo's ex-wife and their two kids were welcomed. Ramón's girls flocked around Guillermo as soon as he arrived. He was an alluring uncle with his flaunting of convention and reputation for late nights out. He often had something for the kids, dispensing gifts such as firecrackers and small, soft leather pouches he made from the trim of hides at work. Soon a horde of kids piled into his Chevy for a ride along the beach.

While they were gone, Ramón smoked with the other men in rocking chairs on the veranda of the big house. The family's original cabin still stood at the bottom of the hill, but as the Monteros prospered in tanneries and shoe factories, they had built a grand two-story house with tall, shuttered windows and a wraparound porch at the top of a bluff. Set back from the shore, it caught the fresh ocean breezes but was protected from the full force of northern storms. For years the family had used it as a vacation house, but recently the older Monteros had to move in to keep it from appropriation by the officials (for the People, of course). On the porch, Carlos's night business was an open secret among the men, but even within the safety of the Montero property lines, no one spoke of it directly.

Ramón realized that he and Carlos were the only two men at the gathering who knew about Lola's encounter with the missiles and the Sisters' plans to send away their children. He looked around the veranda at faces wrinkled and smooth, light and dark, and wished he could somehow prepare this extended brotherhood for the pending separations. If he breathed one word, though, the men's wrath would be enough to scrub the plans, at the very least. He couldn't be the cause of a delay or even a cancellation. He would remain silent.

Chita, the hairdresser with the quick mouth, swished through the screen door and onto the veranda. Her hair was piled high on her head and her many silver bracelets jangled. She picked up her husband's glass, which needed a refill. He smiled at her, eyes trusting.

"Come around back," she said to the men. "The table is set up in the garden."

"About time," someone said, and a laugh rippled through the group. The men got up, leaving their empty glasses among the chairs. Someone's child would be sent to collect them later. They ambled in twos and threes through the house or down the stairs and around on the path. Ramón leaned against the railing to finish his drink and cigarette. He watched Guillermo's Chevy return along the beach road as it splashed through the spray of high tide or disappeared behind rises in the land.

Carlos stopped beside Ramón and followed his gaze. "Guillermo needs to fix that junky car," he said.

Ramón had said that very thing to his brother, but Carlos was only a relative by circumstance, and even though Ramón now suspected his brother's disparaging reports on him, he still was not one to agree with too quickly. "It runs all right."

"Sure," Carlos said with an easy shrug. "I've been meaning to ask you something. I'm looking for a man who's available for some night work and knows the shoreline around here. Selena and Rosita said to ask you. Interested?"

"Any travel involved?"

"No." Carlos shook his head with vigor. "Nothing like that." He glanced at Ramón, as if to judge how much he could say to the Velvet Enforcer. "Just some signaling. That's all."

The lives of Ramón's daughters would depend on the choice of the right collaborator, but he wasn't supposed to know that. He looked back at the vacated chairs guarded by empty glasses. The children's disappearance would blindside the other fathers.

"After curfew?"

Carlos nodded.

"You ask a lot, my friend."

"Not so much," Carlos said. "A few hours, a man with balls, and a good story for the patrols."

At times like this Ramón tried to put himself in Quique's shoes. His friend would've thought this tame for himself, but would've cautioned Ramón.

"Careful," he had said more than once. "You're not made for excitement." Right before Ramón's wedding ceremony, Quique had stopped him when he blindly walked from the church and had propped him up near the altar until Rosita's beautiful glow drew him to stand unassisted.

"I wish I could, compañero," Ramón said. "But a man in my position . . ." He traded on his status in the CDR.

"Of course."

Ramón clapped the other man on the shoulder and gave him a rueful smile. "No hard feelings?"

"No, no problem."

Guillermo's Chevy topped the drive in front of the house.

"Come on," Carlos said. "We'd better get to the table before those hungry kids wolf down all the food."

Later, in the deepening night, after the salmon and the cake and the toasts and the speeches, and just as the mosquitoes began to bite in earnest, Ramón took some empty baskets and clean plates out to their car parked in the field next to the house. Rosita and the girls were staying out at the house for the night, but he had to get back to the city for a Sunday morning shift. As he returned, he spied his brother and Carlos conferring under a tree at the far corner of the yard. They finished with a handshake and Guillermo swaggered back toward the house as Ramón took a seat on the porch stairs. Guillermo claimed he despised Carlos, but here he was whispering and shaking hands with him. As his brother neared, Ramon said, "I thought you hated him. Carlos."

"Hermanito, Matanzans too often let feelings get in the way of business." He winked, scrunching the entire right side of his face, and went into the house.

Ramón returned his attention to Carlos, who lingered under the tree, and wondered anew about his brother's wild claims. Would the Sisters trust him if all the stories were true? Carlos finished his cigarette and flicked it away. The curve of its red tip disappeared down the hill. He strolled back toward the house, and when he reached the stairs, Ramón asked, "Did you find what you need?"

"Yeah, even more than I had hoped." He leaned closer. "An experienced man."

"Good," Ramón said. Carlos continued into the house.

Ramón should have felt relief at his own brother's part in his children's planned escape, but Guillermo wouldn't know that children of his own blood would be in the boat. Even if he did, would it matter to him? He always protected his own, but too often that meant only his own skin. Fear shot up through Ramón and pressed behind his eyes and into his temples. Something must be done.

Rosita came out and sat beside him on the steps. "You should be going."

"Yes."

"I just spoke with Carlos."

He could feel the film of damp air between them. Could he tell her about Guillermo's shoes? "About that—"

"Everything's fixed," she said firmly. "Nothing for you to do."

They used to tell each other everything. "Of course." He rubbed his forehead.

"Come say goodbye to your daughters."

"I already told them I'm going."

She stood up. "Come kiss them."

He smoothed his hair back with both hands, stood with a squint against the pressure behind his eyes, and followed her into the house. Children sprawled around the living room and parlor, many of them dozing after the excitement of the day. Virginia reclined among several cousins on a sofa in the living room.

"Say goodbye to your father," Rosita said.

"Bye, Papa." His daughter yawned. He pulled her up and hugged her, trying to transfer strength to the woman she would become. She groaned but didn't resist his embrace. When he let her go, she flopped down again, wiggling to regain her place on the sofa. He found his other two among a tangle of arms and legs and pillows on the parlor rug. They were fast asleep. He wanted to wake them, to see their bright eyes again, but couldn't. He squatted and kissed them. Surely not for the last time.

He rubbed his eyes as he listened to the slow breaths and soft sighs of the children around him. Adult voices and laughter washed in from the back rooms. Guillermo's rumble punched through the convivial sounds. He must be stopped.

That night Ramón dreamed of the Spanish shoes. They grew in size as they slid toward each other on the slippery tannery floor. When they met, they sprouted human arms and shook hands. As they touched, the left shoe palmed a folded piece of paper to the right. The right shoe lifted money from under its tongue and, again in a handshake, passed it to the left.

Ramón woke with a chill in the hot morning. Quique had trusted Guillermo as he would a brother, and look what happened to him. Now Carlos trusted Guillermo. Ramón bathed but couldn't wash those handshakes from his mind. He could warn Rosita not to send the girls, but that wouldn't stop his brother's betrayals, and the next one might be of someone else Ramón cared about. Or he could tell Carlos, who certainly had friends who took care of traitors. That's what he would do.

He paused in the front room. A photo of Rosita on their wedding day gazed past his shoulder at the man he could have been. He went on to the kitchen and brewed a cup of coffee. He popped holes in a rare can of condensed milk as he thought back to the last time he sat with Quique at his house, smoking cigars. Ramón had fretted about betrayals, but Quique wouldn't speak of them. People do what they must, he said. Not everyone shared his view. Ramón had agreed when it came to Tomasito, although he had tried his best to cushion his brother-in-law's exile. Now he stewed over the tortures men like Carlos reserved for rats. Did he want to leave his brother to such a nasty fate? Did he want to run away like Guillermo had on the day of the fire? No.

Guillermo was his brother. He was Ramón's responsibility.

He tried to eat biscuits as he sipped his coffee. He was not a man of action, but he was a man of feeling. He forced himself to see his girls in the escape boat on the murky waves. He focused his gaze on the little ones' eyes as the searchlight of a government boat swept over them. That was enough.

He retrieved a packet of Rosita's sleeping potion from the bathroom. On the way back to the kitchen, he raised the packet for her portrait to see. "This will make me a man," he said aloud. He continued into the kitchen.

He took down the bottle of cheap rum kept for his brother's visits and poured the sleeping powder into a small pan. He doused it with the rum and mixed it well, then put it on the burner until the liquid turned clear. He let it cool as he finished getting ready for work. His hands were unsteady, but he poured enough of his concoction back into the bottle to do the job.

At work, he investigated his brother's favorite hiding place between the fence and vat he usually worked. As he expected, he found the same brand of rum. He switched the two bottles and went off to his office. He passed Guillermo several times during the day, but it wasn't until early afternoon that he saw his brother lying on the catwalk, one arm flopped down toward the vat. His brother was in the same position the next time he sauntered by. Ramón mounted the catwalk and surveyed the building as he stood over his still brother. The Sunday shift was often lighter, so no other workers were near.

Forgive me, he thought.

He nudged his brother with his foot but got no response. He pushed harder, keeping an eye on the main door. His brother rolled over the edge and splashed face-up into the caustic solution.

"Help me," Ramón said softly. He waited.

It took his brother a while to sink, the toes of his ordinary work boots the last of him to disappear.

"Help!" Ramón cried. He ran toward the rescue kit.

Lonnie Takes It to the Bridge 1

SAM DOG ASKED Lonnie Johnson did his mother ever complain about having to give birth to him with that goddamn toolbox welded to his hands. Lonnie didn't mind the ribbing. He had learned a few things from his mama. One. A good servant and his tools of trade are admitted into realms both physical and emotional that the most privileged of guests can never enter. Two. Once you're there, keep your eyes and ears open. Three. Don't worry until you have something to worry about.

Lonnie had broken ranks with his dad and had joined the Navy. He liked the constant movement of a ship, he said. You didn't have to qualify for anything above scraping paint to be able to travel. He had set about making himself a good servant as soon as he received his rating as an interior communications man on the USS Princeton. This job took him everywhere that there was a need for communications equipment, which was everywhere on the ship.

His rating was higher than those who did straight maintenance, but a good communications guy knew how to repair way more than just electronics. He worked out of the main machine shop. It was littered with metal flanges, tubs of solvents, pneumatic nail guns, and jury-rigged gadgets. Littered wasn't exactly the right word. No place on an aircraft carrier should be littered. In heavy seas, you don't want to be clocked upside the head by a hammer as it flew from starboard to port. Everything had its proper secured place, although a few of the guys got messy in the middle of a job. Not Lonnie. The same precision that itched until he selected the right word demanded that he work neatly and methodically, even when he had to forge ahead on the double. Chick, on the other hand, left the devastation of a typhoon at the end of every job, even the smallest one. He'd once been busted down a step at a surprise inspection because he owned up to having created what an officer called "a bloody hellhole of a booby trap." After that, Lonnie pitched in to keep Chick out of trouble, but he didn't mind. Chick could fix anything, even the unfixable. Sam Dog said it was as if each of his long fingers had its own brain and a set of eyes.

Lonnie knew he could make a decent living off of what he'd learned from Chick, and he figured he could own his own repair shop when he got out of the Navy. Customers would like his competence and cleanliness—he saw white tiles and gleaming tools in his future—and his mama and daddy had taught him good manners. He was already making extra dough off of the officers, who liked those qualities. Once they figured out that he didn't leave clods of solder to harden on their papers or wood shavings scattered on the floor, they asked for him by name to do all kinds of repairs. Soon he graduated from minor screw tightenings and glue-and-clamp jobs on the control deck to major renos in the officers' quarters and other areas usually off-limits to the enlisted men. While in restricted areas, as his mama had instructed, he kept his brown-mouse ears wide open.

Thus he was bent over double with both hands stuck in an access panel in the officers' mess when he heard the dull clunk of trays on the table beside him. Two pairs of legs belonging to two ensigns appeared under the table. Lonnie started to rise to attention, but one of the ensigns glanced at him and said, "Carry on." Lonnie bent down again.

"Christ, did you see the chopper's gunner?" the same ensign said.

"Tanaka says the big guy looks even worse. Like his skin's gonna ooze right off."

The big guy? He couldn't be talking about the Swede. After all, there was a horde of huge Marines on board.

"Shit, man," the first voice said. "It's enough to keep you below decks when one of those things goes off."

The sheathings on some of the wires were cracked. As Lonnie listened, he pulled them and wrapped them in electrical tape for now. He'd replace them later.

"Alpha crew wasn't even supposed to be on yesterday. Whoever was should be down on their knees about now."

Sounds like there had been a problem, Lonnie thought. The big Swede was part of Alpha crew, one of the groups of Marines that manned the assault helicopters assigned to the aircraft carrier. Most of the Marines were righteous or at least kept to themselves, but some acted as if the whole carrier and everybody on it existed solely for them. Called the ship a boat, for Christ's sake. The Swede wasn't like that. He was seasoned military, older than a lot of the other guys, and his dad was a bigwig back home. He was the only Marine that got an invite to the regular Thursday night poker game. It would be trouble if he was in trouble.

" . . . some Japanese muckety-mucks and translators," one of the ensigns said.

Shoot. Lonnie had been worrying about the big Swede instead of listening, and now he didn't know what the Japanese had to do with anything.

"Japanese? You'd think they'd had enough of our A-bombs."

"The old man wants to wait until after the first dogwatch to take them off. That big fellow don't look so good, but Tanaka says he probably won't make it anyway."

Lonnie snipped and stripped a fresh end on a black wire and reattached it to a node. He'd have to find out if the big Swede was in trouble.

"Official word's come down. They were on the island during the blow-up in July."

"But anyone who knows anything about radiation would know that—"

"Yeah."

Would know what? Lonnie felt the officers' attention focus on him, so he pulled a yellow wire from the bundle and pretended to inspect its length. He'd already done so once, but the ensigns didn't know that. He waited for their conversation to resume, but when it did, they compared notes about some fueling snafu.

Lonnie already knew a few things about the Swede. One. He didn't want anyone to know his father was a general and subtly encouraged the guys to just call him the Swede or Hep, because Hepplewhite was way too long. If someone by chance asked if he was any relation, Lonnie could see him pick a dodge and use it. It worked on most people, but not on Lonnie, not with his big ears and his father stationed at the general's base. He wondered if the ensigns really knew who they were talking about.

Two. The Swede would fall for a good bluff even with the highest stakes, like the silver pocket watch. Lonnie pulled it out and caressed the HRH etched in fancy script on its cover. He felt bad about it, but he had won it fair and square. What a bluff. High card a black eight, never revealed. He longed to tell Chick or Sam Dog when they asked, but he'd learned early that reputation grew more quickly through mystery than through the fleeting satisfactions of revealing a sucker bet.

Three. The initials on the watch belonged to the big Swede's grandfather. When Lonnie first saw them, given the state the big guy was in at the time, he thought they might stand for His Royal Hangover. He played around with words like that. His daddy said quit jawing and get the thing said. His mama smiled with those pretty dimples of hers and said don't mind your father, you take after me. Two nights before, Chick asked about the Swede's grandfather. He had come to America on a ship, leaving all of his known world behind, holding only one piece of it in etched silver. Lonnie used to think that white people who had left their own countries for the hope of a new one didn't mind leaving their old lives behind. They had a choice, right?

Four. The big Swede wouldn't just accept the watch back, but he'd be willing to play again for it. Lonnie had tried to give it back the night they heard about the grandfather, but no dice. That was okay, Lonnie knew how to lose discreetly. His daddy had taught him a thing or two about cards.

Lonnie's mother was the one who taught him not to worry until he had something to worry about. Now he had something to worry about. Someone, that is. The big fellow may be about to buy the farm and here was Lonnie holding onto a piece of his history. He replaced the access panel and stood up to give the ensigns a salute. They didn't even look up at him. He left the mess deck with an automatic turn toward the machine shop. Don't listen to scuttlebutt, his daddy said. Listen for what's true, his mama countered. Lonnie did an about face before reaching the ladder and headed to the sick bay instead.

A roadblock of Marines loomed in the passageway outside of the clinic. Lonnie threaded past a few of them but a captain stopped him. "State your business," he said. None of your business, Lonnie wanted to answer, but knew that wasn't true, even if it was. His men were in there, in God knows what condition. Another Marine stationed beside the clinic's hatch stared straight through Lonnie.

He figured complaining of anything short of a heart attack would get him no further, but luckily he still had his toolbox. He held it up. "Sir, I've been ordered down to make repairs."

"To what?"

Medic Dakota Tanaka opened the hatch at that moment. He was a tall, spare bookworm who wore his belt cinched too high, but he knew his stuff and ranged outside of protocol to find treatments that actually worked. The crew swore by the hangover cures he customized for each sailor as he pocketed their fee. Lonnie had helped him sharpen his card-playing skills, and after winning a few large pots, Tanaka now considered him a buddy.

Lonnie counted on that when he jiggled his toolbox and pitched his head toward the clinic. "Phone still out?"

Tanaka caught the ball and ran with it. "About time. Been acting up all week. Come on." He grabbed Lonnie's elbow and propelled him into the clinic. "Sir," he said to the captain. The officer waved him away and turned back to his conversation.

Inside, the desk topped by the phone and charts stood to the right and the sickbay bunks stretched down the narrow room beyond. Several of the lower bunks at the far end were occupied, but neither the patients nor the two medics that slumped in the aisle said a word. The ship's engines thrummed underneath the quiet.

"What are you doing here?" Tanaka asked.

"Heard the big Swede might be sick."

Tanaka glanced at the closed door of an exam room to their left. "He doesn't look too good." His voice barely carried as far as Lonnie's ears as he glanced back at the hatch that separated them from the pod of Marines in the corridor. "None of his crew look good."

"What happened?"

"Aborted missile test."

Must of gone wrong, somehow. You don't want to be around when an A-bomb missile goes wrong. Lonnie hadn't heard anything before now but then again he didn't pay much attention anymore. He had other things to do.

"That all of them?" He flicked his chin toward the bunks.

"The old man wants to low-key it. Sent the rest of them—the ones that could walk—down to auxiliary quarters for showers and ordered them lobster dinner. Fat lot of good that will do them the way the Geiger counters were jumping."

"They taking them off today?"

Tanaka nodded.

It would be simple to leave the silver watch with Tanaka and skedaddle, but that would be taking advantage of a man when he's down. That would be cheating. Lonnie had to look the big Swede in the face to let him know that Lonnie knew he wouldn't just accept the watch back under normal circumstances.

"Can I see him?" Lonnie held up the watch. "Have to give this back to him."

Tanaka crossed his arms and massaged his bicep where a tattoo of Japanese symbols spelled "Mother," or so he claimed. "You're on your own if one of them catches you." He hooked a thumb back at the closed hatch behind them. Lonnie nodded. "Leave your stuff over there." He pointed at the desk. Lonnie dropped his toolbox beside the phone and followed Tanaka into the exam room.

The big Swede dwarfed the skinny bed and his arms glowed red against the white sheet as he lay flat on his back. Pale skin in the shape of goggles ringed his eyes and continued up under his dark hair and over his ears. The bottom of his face and his forearms oozed.

The Swede wasn't going to make it, maybe not even until the evening sunlight spread like liquid fire across the ocean.

"I thought all Swedes were blond," Lonnie said.

The Swede grunted his usual laugh, only this time it had no force. "See brown hair in Maine." His lips barely moved and the words were indistinct but

Lonnie understood the shorthand: the Swede had family up in Maine. He took a couple of short, raspy breaths.

Lonnie had seen a man die before, but not like this.

That ensign was right. Anyone who knew anything about radiation sickness would know that the big Swede couldn't possibly be suffering from exposure from a few months ago. He obviously was a victim of a recent, massive dose. Lonnie saw the lies and omissions lining up, even for a general's son.

"Why would I want to go to Maine? Snow never melts there." Lonnie leaned closer to the bed and caught the sharp stench of open wounds. He flared his nostrils but didn't withdraw. "Except maybe to beat you ass again to get this back." He extracted the watch from his pocket and rubbed his thumb over the HRH. He dangled it from the chain so the Swede could see it and just held it there while he decided where to put it. The bed was in the middle of the room, and the cupboards far enough away that someone would forget it was there, but laying anything on raw skin was unthinkable. Finally Lonnie spied a duffle bag at the foot of the bed and dropped the watch into it. "But don't think I won't hunt you down to get it back, Harold R. Hepplewhite the third."

Hep grunted in reply.

Tanaka bent over to brush fallen hair off the pillow and then looked up at Lonnie. "You ever go topside for the tests?"

"Used to. Not lately, though."

"Good. Don't."

"Geiger counters up there say—"

"There are ways of reading Geiger counters." Tanaka tipped his head toward the big fellow in the bed. "Then there are ways. Got it?"

"Aye, aye."

Tanaka pointed to his watch and drew a wind-it-up swirl in the air.

"Take it easy, huh?" Lonnie said. He wanted to touch Hep but didn't dare, not even on the pale skin of his shoulder. He turned to go but remembered the ensign's voice peddling the official story. That wasn't right, but even a general couldn't do anything about it if he didn't know the real deal. Lonnie swung back around and leaned in close. "What the hell happened, man?"

Hep's eyes fluttered open. "Had to get the nose," he said with an exhale.

In the slackness of Hep's face, Lonnie saw the edge of life where earthly duties, promises, secrets, no longer mattered. His gut clenched, and he waited until he could trust his voice to sound normal.

"So?"

Hep's eyes slid shut again. "Cap said . . . down the hole."

Lonnie looked up at Tanaka.

"Yesterday's missile," the medic said while staring at the exam room door. They could hear voices from the other side. He wound his finger again and spoke quickly. "Going off course. Blown up. These gophers pick up the nose containing the guidance system. Guess it wasn't coming in right. Someone had to go down and bring it in."

"Wouldn't it be hot?"

Tanaka stepped over to the door and opened it a sliver and then eased it shut again. He leaned a moment with his forehead resting on the door. "Yeah, real hot." He straightened up and turned. "Like my butt's gonna be if they catch you in here."

"His CO had no business telling him to go down into the hole." Lonnie gripped the railing of the bed and looked down. "Your CO had no business."

The hump of Hep's leg slid to the side under the covers. He lifted his chin, and in a stronger voice said, "Orders."

"You know what they're saying? That you all were on the island back in July. Man, that's not right."

"What does it matter? July or now. Accidents happen. Orders are orders." Tanaka waved come on let's go.

"Accident's one thing. But to deliberately send these guys. . ." to their deaths, Lonnie finished with a look. "Somebody's gotta know. That's not right."

"Come on." Tanaka moved closer and tugged on Lonnie's sleeve. "Besides, what can we do? Those papers we signed. Who could we tell?"

"His father, for one. He's base commander where my dad's stationed."

Hep rustled. "Orders," he repeated.

Lonnie reached out to touch his shoulder but stopped short. "What would your dad do about an officer who is obviously making dumbass decisions about his men? Huh? But nobody's gonna do anything if nobody knows. You want that?"

Hep exhaled and seemed to settle further into the hard exam bed. He rolled his head a few degrees from side to side. No, his lips said.

"What can you do?" Tanaka asked. "They read everything that goes off this crate."

Hep's body held the stillness of sleep.

Lonnie scanned the room as if all the tools he needed to make things right could be found in the narrow cupboards. The sweep stopped on the red lettering over a waste bin. "What if they couldn't read it?" He raised his face toward heaven. "Don't you write Japanese?"

"Yeah. They'd still read it. Or tear it up if they couldn't."

"But what if it didn't go in the mail bag?" Despite the danger of the idea, or maybe because of it, the rush of winning a big pot warmed Lonnie's face. "There's some Japanese diplomat on board."

Tanaka popped a hands-off gesture with both palms out, and shook his head. "Even I wouldn't go to the Japanese with this."

"No." Lonnie went to bang the railing of the bed but stopped just shy of jarring his friend and floated his hand down into a loose grip. "Translators. We must have one of our own. Quick. We don't have much time. I'll go topside, scout out the civilians. You write out what happened."

Tanaka drew a big breath and looked down at the big man on the exam table. He sighed and slowly nodded.

"Hep, " Lonnie said.

Hep inclined his head toward Lonnie, eyes closed.

"Make sure Tanaka gets it right."

He replied with a wisp of a nod.

"And hold onto that watch. I'm coming back for it."

Hep dropped his mouth open and grunted.

Chita
A Message from García 1

AS OUR SERVANTS took the illusion of equality seriously and departed from our employ, we blessed Mami for equipping us with solid housekeeping skills. Lupe was the last to go. Despite her rising surliness, she had been an excellent maid. When she had to add the kitchen to her other duties, she wasn't a top-drawer cook, but her meals were well received by the boys. With her gone, there was no longer a reason for Diego and me to take the first meal of the day in the dining room, so we ate in the kitchen. I had spent my girlhood playing on its tiled floor and sneaking pasteles that were left to cool on the mahogany counters. Lupe had abandoned us the day before the envelope from the country arrived.

The morning of the hand-delivered letter, the boys were already gone to school as I said goodbye to Diego. The house quieted, and again I imagined the coming time when the clatter and chaos would not return at the end of the day. If I dwelled on that sorrow too long, I would lose my will to go through with tonight's plans with my sisters. I cranked open the jalousies to catch the morning breeze. The wind bore salty, cleansing air off the bay. I opened the front door and looked toward the water. My neighbors' houses jumbled down the street away from me, and the clang of ships loading in port rang in the distance. A cousin on my mother's side marched by with her boy and two girls. Her children went to the local school, which started later than St. Sebastian, where Beto and Miguelito were already sitting in class. My cousin stopped at the gate to say hello, but she couldn't linger long. I listened to her children's subdued chatter as they paraded up the street.

I couldn't rest there all day and lament the impending absence of my family. Lupe usually swept the front walk and the sidewalk outside the gate each morning, but she was gone. My hands were sturdy and I, a Montero, was no stranger to hard work. I took the broom outside and swept.

As I finished the sidewalk, Señor Martinez, the postman, turned the corner down the street. I hurried back to the gate and latched it behind me before heading for the house. I supposed his dour wife had spelled him at the post office and at that very moment was berating some poor citizen for failing to fill out a form correctly. They were both awful, her with her disapproving glares and him with his disgusting leers. On top of it all, he freely trafficked in information not his to give away.

I continued inside to avoid any conversation with that toad. Just as I finished putting away the broom and thought the coast was clear, I heard a firm knock on the front door. I returned to the front of the house to answer. Señor Martinez waited, backlit by the early sunlight reflecting off the house across the street. He had left the gate ajar. He tipped his hat and held up an envelope, its blank side toward me. The flap had been torn and resealed with tape. "Sorry to bother you, Señora, but I bring you this official-looking letter."

"That's most generous of you." I snapped out my hand as if he had already wasted too much of my time.

He inched the letter away, the slightest gesture, but it meant he wasn't finished with his game. "Curious, the postmark is from an eastern province, and the return address is a Campo Doblase. About your brother, perhaps?"

My God! My outstretched fingers curled in and flew to my mouth unbidden. The postman knew the power of his words, of the envelope in his hand. He already knew what it contained and wanted to extract what one was willing to give in exchange for it.

My cousin's boy, the angel who had hidden shyly behind his mother a few moments earlier, whooped and dashed down the street with a rooster feather stuck in his cap. Three of his friends chased him, book bags bumping off their shoulders. They were on their way to school, or else they would've been wearing cowboy hats with chin straps. The pop of their cap guns ricocheted off the surrounding homes. One shouted, "Sal, you're dead. It's my turn to be the Indian."

Little cousin Salvador was lucky. He was not truly dead, but what of Tomasito? I must know, and this toad would not stand in my way. I pointed. "Behind you, Señor. The cavalry has arrived." He turned his head, and I snatched the letter from him. "Thank you." The boys continued their noisy play down the street. "Your kindness will be rewarded by God."

He knew he would get nothing from me. He sneered, the left side of his face crimping into the most unpleasant sight. "Condolences for your loss."

What did he mean by that? I whipped the door shut, erasing his ugly face, and turned to the cool darkness of my living room. Its neatness and the silence beyond shouted. Soon I would not have to fuss arm caps back into place on the chairs and couch or fish marbles out of the large crystal bowl on the console.

The loss would widen a fissure opened by Tomasito's abrupt disappearance. We had not seen nor heard from our brother since that night he and Selena had gone down to Liberty Square for dinner. I wondered if La Señora had directed this envelope into my hands, despite Señor Martinez and his underhanded ways, or if She was still cross with us because my youngest sister had screamed at Her in the street. Who does such a thing? Shouting at the Mother of Jesus. Did Lola think her blasphemies demanding the return of Tomasito would do anything except annoy Her and reflect poorly on our parents? I'm sure she paid for her behavior with that wrong turn in the jungle. Soon we would all pay.

Despite Lola's antics, at last I held a clue to our brother's fate. You would think I'd reopen the envelope immediately—knowing is better than not knowing, even if it is the worst kind of news. But first I had to give thanks. I knelt in front of our shrine to the Madonna of the Sacred Heart and lit a candle. I stocked her plate with tempting bright-red candies and pasteles that I never offered to the rest of the family. A small sacrifice for this answer to our prayers. The dingy envelope was addressed formally to me in typewritten letters: Señora Concepcion Montero de la Luz. I pressed it to my lips, not one care for the hands it had passed though, and whispered my thanks. La Señora put a light hand on my shoulder but said nothing. I could not bear to learn the news alone, so I hurried off to call Rosita and Lola to come right over.

As soon as they arrived, we sat in the dining room, the taped envelope a pale square on the dark top of the table. I told them what Señor Martinez had said, which sent Rosita shrinking into herself. No one reached for the letter, but prolonging our wait wouldn't rearrange the letters into hoped-for happy news. Finally I said, "Rosie, you open it. You're the oldest."

Lola nodded and sat with her hands braced against the edge of the table. Rosie covered her mouth in that little girl way she has, but she made no move to put us out of our agony, or perhaps to plunge us into a deeper one.

"No, you," she said from behind her fingers. "It's addressed to you."

The coward, as always. A surge of hot contempt for my useless older sister was enough to propel my hand to the envelope. I pulled out the enclosed paper and read the typed message aloud.

Campo Doblase
Santi Spíritus
3 September 1962

Dear Sra. Montero de la Luz:

It has come to the attention of the administration of
Campo Doblase that the effects of the late Tómas Montero,
a guest worker at our facility, includes a pocket watch
engraved with the name of the great Cuban hero, Calixto
García. We regret this oversight in our official death notice.

It is a misfortune that we have no reliable delivery
service, nor are we sure that we are writing to the correct
address. Therefore, we are retaining this family heirloom
for safekeeping. If the family wishes to retrieve it, we
have included directions to Campo Doblase below.

Since we are a closed facility, it is imperative that you
stop at the village at the foot of the mountain and ask for
David Montes. He will serve as your escort.

Viva La Revolucíon,
Humberto Eggleston
Director of Operations

I put the message on the table for all to see. Its words sent us into a
frenzy of excitement. Listen to me, we Monteros have our ways. How do
you get a message to the family across provinces when you're uncertain of
the allegiances of the carriers or unsure who may intercept it? You use code
words that you keep in the family, and you don't even share them with your
husbands. They are not Monteros, after all. This crazy letter contained the
code "Calixto García," the name of the famed patriot who worked tirelessly
for independence from Spain. It meant, "You may think that I am dead, but
I still live." Tomás alive!

"Is this a trick?" Lola wondered. "I mean, how did he get it to look so
official?"

"Look at the date," Rosita said. "It's been over a month. We must go
immediately."

"We can't go," I said. "It's too dangerous. Think about the bandit's war."
Besides the run-of-the-mill lawlessness abundant in the eastern provinces, El

Líder was rooting out former compatriots who had the nerve to disagree with his vision.

"Who else will go?" Rosie asked. "Are you going to explain to José what Calixto García means?" Like I said, we have not shared our codes with our husbands—no telling when one of them might turn on the family. We loved them, but they were not Monteros.

"It's probably a trick. Maybe they want to capture us all," Lola said. "Maybe we should call first."

I turned toward the family shrine and silently asked the Madonna if I could borrow one of her bright-red candies to shove at Lola so she would shut up her face. "Patience," the Madonna whispered back. "She, too, is anxious."

I knew that, but somehow I couldn't speak calmly. Too much was at stake. "Chica, don't be an idiot. Obviously he means for us to find this David Montes, not go arousing suspicions through the main switchboard."

"Quit squabbling," Rosita said. She leaned in to peer closely at the note and read it again under her breath. "Here." She stabbed the note. "This is the line I don't like: 'We regret this oversight in our official death notice.' What does that mean? We received no such notice." We both stared at her as she kept her finger pinned on the mysterious phrase.

"Since we didn't get it, who did?" Lola asked. "And why didn't they tell us?"

"What if it didn't get through?" I asked. I thought of bandits looking for payroll money.

"But what if it did?" Lola countered. She clasped Rosita's extended hand.

Goose bumps raised on my arms as a cold wash of air blew through the room. I knew without looking that it was the wake of the Madonna's departure. Something terrible was going on, and we were on our own. What to do? Who to trust? This was too much. My attention dashed around the room. Here to the lace cloth our grandmother carried from Catalonia. There, to the fluted columns that framed the archway between the living and dining rooms. And there, to the chessboard on the game table. I thought of the game as unfinished, although the black king lay in surrender on its side. "Mate in four," our younger boy had said to his brother the previous night.

Rosita prayed, her hands clasped, white-knuckled, against her chest. Blasts of a ship's horn in port swept me away from my sisters and out over the water. I tried to see my sons already on a far shore, laughing with new friends, but it was too hazy, and my sisters' voices called me back before the mist cleared.

"Someone has to go to him," Lola said.

Rosita interrupted her rapid supplications to ask, "What about the children?"

Tonight was the night. Everything was set. We had struggled to concoct just the right story to disguise the children's escape from the island, but when Selena mentioned the labor shortage on her family's farm, I knew their situation would provide the perfect cover. The children could miss school to join the harvest that feeds our nation. Even so, we thought it best if our husbands were physically distant during the actual departure. Ramón was to take Rosita to a patron's house at the eastern end of Varadero Beach. They would have to stay the night because of the curfews. Diego had gone to meet the cousin of El Líder and wouldn't be back until tomorrow. Only Lola's José would be in town, since the army kept him busy at all hours on any given day, but she would know how to deal with him if she had to.

Once Lola confirmed the children were launched, we could go find Tomás. Unimaginable loss echoed in the chambers of my heart, but this was no time for tears. "We do what we must with what we have," I said. "We can leave tomorrow. After . . . after tonight." I called for Lupe to bring us coffee before I remembered she no longer worked for us. I went to get it myself.

When I returned with a tray of filled cups, Rosita said, "The men won't let us go alone, and I'm not sure I want to."

"We must," Lola said. "We are Monteros, they are not. Tomás is depending on us, and we can handle ourselves."

As usual, I agreed with both my sisters. Which would prevail? Were we right to be suspicious of our husbands? I wished I could ask La Señora, but her abode was vacant. The sounds of a group of ladies twittering reached us as they traipsed down the sidewalk. What concerns were their light voices hiding? Their laughter reminded me of jaunts to Mami's cousins out in the real countryside just this side of the mountains and how my sides would hurt from laughing at all the outrageous tales we would tell to keep ourselves amused on the bumpy roads. That gave me an idea. "We can tell them we're going to see Tito Juan. Surely they would let us go there."

Lola plopped her cup on the table. "Yes, of course. Chita, sometimes I think there's hope for you."

Rosita pulled the letter closer. "This was mailed more than a month ago. Do you think he's still there?"

"That's why we have to leave right away." I can stick to my point when I have to.

"But the first twenty-four hours are the most critical," Lola said.

"First twenty-four hours of what?" I asked. Lola can be so annoying with her half-baked, half-explained ideas.

"Of a boat trip like this."

Damn La Señora's eyes, she was right. If Carlos were to turn back for any reason, it would be before the first full day died. They could also land and get word back to us in that time, if all went perfectly. At least one of us would have to stay at home, but I also knew without asking that none of us would want to be away, even for Tomás, during that hopeful, frightening time.

"So tomorrow we wait, and then we go east," I said.

"That would be best, I think." Rosita sighed and clattered her spoon into her cup. "And it gives us more time to pack."

That's Rosie, playing to her strengths—waiting and organizing things. I wondered if she had already spilled the beans about the children to that squirrelly Ramón but assumed he would be impotent to stop them if she had. There were only hours before they were to go.

Lonnie Takes it to the Bridge 2

MRS. YŪKO FUJI sat quietly in the captain's chair on the bridge of the *USS Princeton*. She was off-duty for the moment, as her assignment, a Japanese diplomat and his translator, had retired to the admiral's quarters. She should have been resting also, but the bustle of a large military operation and her unexpected access to it kept her alert and prying. When Major Caldwell had ushered her up the conning tower ladder and onto the bridge, the captain was preparing to go below. After a few minutes of chatting, he insisted that she take his place and stay there as long as she wanted. No one sat in the captain's chair unless he was taking over command of the bridge, and certainly no civilian sat in that sole built-in leather seat, especially with the old man right there. She could tell how unusual this was by the set of the shoulders of the young man next to her who was busy with the sea charts. Yet Mrs. Fuji had that effect on men, even though she didn't try.

From the conning tower's midship rise on the starboard side of the ship, Mrs. Fuji had most of a three-hundred-and-sixty-degree seascape view through the panel of windows. Swiveling toward the rear of the ship, she saw Marine helicopters lining the deck and the late afternoon sun low on the horizon. As she swung past the lineup of phone handsets and faced the dials and big red phone in front of her, she took in more choppers lining the deck. The thick glass filmed the sea and sky in the distance so the ocean formed a low lapis wall and hazed into a wide stripe of sky blue.

Humans had always wondered and worried about the horizon where sea and sky meet. Mrs. Fuji had no desire for a well-marked division between them. In fact, she preferred to dwell in the mist offered by an unsettled sea. It was her home upon waking, when she could feel the presence of her long-vanished husband beside her before her fingers reached out and touched nothing but memories. Her American granddaughter also dwelled there without knowing, as she donned her Mickey Mouse ears for her solemn performance of the tea ceremony. Mrs. Fuji should've been back in the States by now, sipping tea with her granddaughter and her teddy bear, but the A-bomb test they had come to witness had been scrubbed shortly after its launch, and the American officials promised another one shortly.

Major Caldwell entered the bridge and leaned against the wall behind Mrs. Fuji. She swiveled to face him. He was as trim and agile as a man half his age. He probably knew how to tire out the pups that leapt on board this ship with youthful notions of the romance of the sea. A thin cut striped his arm right above the wrist. Although the blood had already crusted, Mrs. Fuji noted its careless appearance on this otherwise meticulous man.

"Sorry I had to leave you alone like that." He wiped at the cut and then rubbed his hands together.

"Not to worry. I'm enjoying the vastness of the ocean."

Two young sailors in work uniforms entered the bridge, one white, one Negro. The white one passed between the major and Mrs. Fuji with a salute, but the Negro stopped just inside the hatch and said, "Sir." He waited for the major to recognize him. At the major's nod, he said, "May I check these phones, sir?" He pointed to the bank of handsets on the wall. The major nodded and moved back a pace.

The sailor picked up a handset, then ducked into a quick shallow bow to Mrs. Fuji. She automatically dipped her head.

"Excuse me, ma'am," he said. The nametag over his pocket read "Johnson." He picked up the phone closest to Mrs. Fuji and unscrewed the earpiece.

The major turned up the pale side of his wrist to look at the face of his watch. "It's about time for dinner. Do you want to wait here a few more minutes, or shall I escort you back to quarters first?"

Mrs. Fuji had already freshened up after her hours of work beside the diplomat, and although the major seemed to enjoy his assignment to her, she didn't want to take him away from his other duties more than necessary.

"I'll be fine right here," she said.

"Then I'll be back for you directly." The major rubbed his hands again. "And don't let that old sea dog steal you away just because he gave you his chair."

Mrs. Fuji smiled as he left. Although she took no advances seriously, much to her daughter's dismay, she still was charmed by men who found her attractive. Even American men.

Johnson unscrewed the phone's mouthpiece and withdrew a part. "This is the trouble." He held it up for the other sailor to see before pocketing it. "Ma'am," he said with another quick bow and moved off with his buddy.

Mrs. Fuji settled back and listened to the lullaby of numbers and directions recited by the youngster poring over the sea charts. Most of the sailors seemed like youngsters, seemed about the age her husband was when, dressed in his army uniform, he approached her about a gift for his grandfather in the men's store where she worked in Hiroshima. Her mother warned that a romance born of commerce would be barren of true deep feeling and connection. Besides, her mother had a wealthy, albeit older, distant cousin in mind as a more suitable match, but Yūko had thrilled at the ardor she felt through Masahiro's fingers as he stroked her lower back. He was not a learned man, and he could be abusive when drunk or threatened, but his devotion to her was pure and unwavering.

Several minutes later, Johnson returned. He set down a toolbox near the captain's chair and picked up the handset he had taken the piece from. Mrs. Fuji gazed through the forward windows while Johnson worked in her peripheral vision.

"Ma'am?" He didn't look at her so she didn't turn her head to reply.

"Yes?"

"Are you one of us?" He tapped his chest with the phone. "American, I mean."

Not exactly, but it was basically why she was on the ship: the United States government wanted to make sure the diplomat's translator was conveying the right messages. She nodded.

"One of my buddies is in a bad way." He unscrewed the mouthpiece again and squatted down next to his toolbox. "And it's not right. Someone should know what's happening."

"I am so sorry," Mrs. Fuji said. She wondered what that had to do with her. "Perhaps Major Caldwell can help you."

Johnson picked out a gadget from the toolbox but tossed it back. "None of these birds . . ." He stood and slipped an envelope out of his pocket. "Look. Here's the story, but it's written in Japanese. Read it. If you can, pass it on. You'll figure out where. If nothing else, you can mail it to my mom. Her address is on the envelope. It just can't go through regular channels. That's all." He palmed the envelope to her. "American, though. It has to stay American." He knelt down beside his toolbox.

Mrs. Fuji nodded. A regular civilian may have been surprised at the sudden intrigue, but her gift with languages had led her into many unorthodox governmental and military situations. She would read the notes, as she couldn't resist the appeal of a young sailor who was passing on, at great risk, a message in a foreign language. He had come to the right person. She had security clearance and could give the message to important people, if that was warranted. She could also destroy the evidence if she needed to. She would see.

She scooped up her purse and opened it. Just as she was sliding the envelope into it, Major Caldwell's hand appeared inches from hers.

"May I see that?" he asked.

Where had he come from? "I beg your pardon?"

"May I see the document this sailor just handed to you?"

Johnson twisted on the balls of his feet and peered up at her. His dark eyes were opaque and the rest of his features expressed nothing.

Mrs. Fuji retrieved the envelope and handed it over. Johnson rose and stood at attention, his gaze resting at a point far past Caldwell's shoulder. The major turned over the envelope and examined the seal. "Explain yourself, Johnson."

"Sir. Dad's being redeployed to Okinawa. Mom's learning Japanese. When I found out that Tanaka knows it, I asked him to write a letter to her in Japanese."

"Who's Tanaka?"

"Medic," Johnson shrugged but kept his arms stiff by his sides. "I just asked this nice lady to read it to make sure he did a proper job of it. For my mom, sir."

"Why's it sealed?"

"Habit."

Caldwell poised his finger under the envelope's flap. "May I?" He directed his question to Mrs. Fuji.

She understood that he had asked permission merely because he had taken the letter out of her possession. Johnson wouldn't have been given the same courtesy.

"Of course."

The hatch to the radar room opened behind the major. A murmur of voices spilled out along with a billow of stale air smelling of old coffee and cigarettes. A radar man exited the bridge through the far hatch. A burst of crisp sea air blew in after him.

Caldwell pulled out two pieces of lined paper. He turned to show them to Mrs. Fuji. "It's Japanese?"

She glanced at the black-inked characters on lined notebook paper. "Yes."

He held out the letter. "What does it say?"

She took the sheets and scanned them. After a caution about the sensitivity of the material, the letter described the critical condition of a group of Marines. It said they suffered from severe radiation sickness after being ordered to make direct contact with the nose cone of the rocket from the previous day's failed test.

Back home they called it A-bomb sickness. Her city of Hiroshima was the first to be subject to its devastating effects. She felt the blood drain from her fingers and a tremor worried them as she touched their cool tips to her throat. What a horrible mess. And according to this letter, the official story will point to an earlier accident rather than the commanding officer that chose electronics over the life of these boys. He wasn't named in the letter, and in fact the only name that appeared was that of Harold Hepplewhite III, one of the casualties. The letter suggested that his father, a general in the Air Force, would be interested in knowing what really happened.

The blistered skin, the sightless eyes. The friends that looked fine but moaned through the agony of liquid insides. The disfigured girls, forever branded with the shame of aggression and defeat. The averted eyes of other Japanese Americans if you told them that you came from Hiroshima.

She needed time to think.

Yūko looked up at the major, who was watching her closely, and forced her lips into a smile. "It's just the kind of news a mother likes to hear—lobster for dinner—although here." She pointed to the kanji characters of Hepplewhite's name. "He says that the lobster is good, but he misses her fried chicken."

Johnson widened his eyes at her in the instant before the major swung around to him. By then he was nodding in agreement.

Caldwell's gaze shifted between the two of them. "You ever meet before?"

"Just a while ago, here on the bridge," Mrs. Fuji said. "With you."

Caldwell seemed to be reviewing the first encounter. "I guess there's no harm in it."

"No, sir," Johnson said.

Mrs. Fuji quickly refolded the letter. "Your friend is very good, but his word selection is somewhat advanced for a beginner. Shall I take it and suggest simpler language?"

"Yes, ma'am, if it wouldn't be too much of a bother."

"No bother at all."

The hatch behind the major opened again and another radar man emerged. He left the hatch open and addressed his superior. "Major Caldwell, sir, you're wanted again."

Caldwell took another good look at Johnson. "You finished here, sailor?"

Johnson twisted the mouthpiece back onto the phone as the radar man retreated and let the hatch close with a thump. "Aye, sir. Should be working like a champion." He bowed to Mrs. Fuji and picked up his toolbox.

As he turned away, the major folded his arms. "Sailor."

Johnson stopped and automatically cocked his hand into salute at half-mast before the major waved it off with a shake of his head. "How are you going to get your letter back?"

"Sir?"

"Major, may I give it back to you? After I copy it over in simpler characters?" She glanced at Johnson. "That is, if you don't mind."

"I would appreciate it, ma'am." He ducked his head. "Sir?"

Caldwell shooed him away and went into the radar room. Yūko dropped the letter into her bag and snapped it shut with a click only she could hear over the rumblings of the ship. She had a painful situation to consider, and possibly a sailor's letter home to write. She figured her safest bet would be to encourage the major to forget all about the letter, maybe not even give him one unless he remembered to ask for it.

He returned a few moments later and smiled at her. She mirrored his expression with amusement. This would be easy, she thought. Even at her age.

"Shall we?" Major Caldwell offered his arm.

Mrs. Fuji rose and slipped her hand around his forearm. Her fingertips were still cool, but she would ponder the letter later. "Yes, thank you."

Lola
The Discretion of the Monteros 5

THAT NIGHT I stood in thigh-deep waves at the beach near our old family home. The sky was closed with rolling clouds, and I could barely see the tiny boat that bobbed right in front of me in the heavy darkness. It was one of the few vessels left in private hands and seemed too small to carry even a family of mice on such an important voyage. Yet it was filled with the children of the Sisters Montero. I handed a small bundle to each child, meat patties that would be devoured as soon as they were discovered. I had also packed sweets to comfort them when they lost sight of land and had only the promise of bright stars and their Cuban heritage to keep them company. I waded back to shore to retrieve the larger packages wrapped in canvas. Already my work pants were soaked dark like ink on the moonless night.

My ears strained to catch sounds of patrols or other unwelcome intruders, but I kept a calm posture. I didn't want to alarm the little ones. Our children understood the importance of silence. I heard a faint clanking from the boat but no chatter from the living cargo already on board. They were good children. I returned to the boat with the larger packages extended out to my sides over the washing sea. Their weight strained my muscles but kept my blood from rushing to burst my heart. Selena's outstretched hands greeted me at the boat. She took the bundles and arranged them around herself. She was the adult who knew what nourishment to give and when, but my Bonita, at only eight years, was the little one with the big voice and a mama's stare that kept her older cousins in line.

Bonita was the one who would let her most precious possessions go to the bottom of the sea but wouldn't remove the water bag from around her neck if the boat overturned. She would use her big voice to steer the other children to the hull. Selena was the adult in charge of the trip, but she was the hot-headed one who got too excited. Bonita and I had spoken of such things as we baked small biscuits for the bundles. She was the sensible one who would lead when she had to. She had a child's curiosity about disaster, so we had to examine all the calamities that might befall a small fishing boat that strayed out of Cuban waters. At one point, when I shuddered at one of her questions, she squeezed my chin with her small fingers and said, "Mami, you must be brave."

Now I touched each child in a silent farewell. I clasped Selena's hand as I had when she was a school girl.

"It's time," she said.

Her brother pulled his small anchor, dipped a paddle into the water, and pushed off the bottom. He wouldn't use the tiny motor until he had to. I leaned against the boat to set it on course. I hung on, my immersion deepening as the boat moved away from shore. Just as my feet left the sea floor, I lost my grip. An undeniable pull urged me to swim after them, but I merely trod water. They are going, I thought, they are going to be safe.

The pound of the surf swallowed the plop of the oar, yet I sensed when the rowing ceased momentarily. Had the vessel sprung a leak? Would the trip be over before it had begun? The boat kept moving away but a small silhouette appeared over the bow. I swam out a few strokes.

"Ay yi yi, Mami" I heard Bonita's voice on the edge of tears. "Where is my blanket? Mami, do you know?"

For all her bravado, my Bonita had only eight years. She no longer dragged around the coverlet that José's mother made when she was born, yet she still found comfort in it. I knew exactly where it lay at the foot of her bed, forgotten in our promise to remember everything. I could do nothing about it, so I pretended I didn't hear, and she didn't call out again. I turned back toward shore, soaked in saltwater.

SMALL BITS OF seaweed flecked off my pants and shirt as I sat drying on the beach. Our children, my children, had departed long minutes before. I stared in the direction the boat had gone and imagined that I was following its diminishing shape, but in truth, I saw only haze. God took his time drawing water out of my clothes. His Mother sat down beside me, but we still did not have much to say to each other. I thought I heard Bonita's voice calling faintly across the sea. I ran into the water before I could stop myself. My babies' faces would always be with me, wouldn't they? But would they know me when they return?

I retreated farther inland to sit on a low stone wall that separated the silken beach from a small turnout on the side of the road. I'd get in my Chevy soon to return to an empty house. A car approached on the road. I didn't look back as the beam from its headlights swept wide across the beach and came to rest pointing straight down the path of the departed boat. I didn't turn around immediately. It was past curfew and the other rule breakers were either soldiers or comrades with even more clandestine business than my own. The beacon of light disappeared as two car doors opened and two sets of feet crunched in the sand.

"Lola, what are you doing out after curfew?" It was José's voice. I turned in its direction and found my husband and Captain B. staring at me through the gloom.

"I came for a swim and lost track of the time."

"Why here, Señora?" Captain B.'s flat inflection reminded me of my debt to him.

José stepped closer and looked down on me. "Your clothes?"

He used the shorthand of married couples; I knew what he was really asking. Captain B.'s radio emitted a crackling voice. He went back and hunched into the car.

Without the captain's attention, José squeezed my arm and said, "Tell me quick."

"I told you . . ."

He jerked my arm, twisting my shoulder. This man I loved was a soldier of the state and loyal to his country. His wife had just committed treason without telling him first. Of course we didn't tell the men, but who of the murderous officials would believe that? I felt sorry for him, this man who attacked me because somehow he knew he'd lost a battle without a chance to fight.

The captain returned from the car as I spied a single light deep in the haze on the horizon. Was it our boat? Then I turned my head away, not wanting either man to think there might be a speck out there of any interest. Captain B. passed behind my husband and sat on the wall to my right. "Señora, it's dangerous for a woman to be out alone on such a dark night."

"It's dangerous for one who didn't grow up on the far side of that field." I tossed my head to indicate the land behind us. "My parents are back in the big house, and the older cabin—my great-grandfather's first here—still stands. It's my refuge in confusing times."

"Confusing times, indeed," Captain B. said. "I'm certainly confused. You see, your husband had information about defectors from your army trying to escape by boat tonight." He looked up at the overcast sky, as if the dark face of Sister Moon stared down in judgment. "But when we intercepted the boat, it was only a poor old fisherman." He pulled out a pack of American cigarettes and offered one to me.

"She doesn't smoke," José said from behind my aching shoulder.

Captain B. and I had entered a delicate negotiation, and I had to play my part. Russian cigarettes would've made it harder. I took what was offered and put it to my lips. The captain cupped a hand around a match, and I bent forward, despite José's protests behind me. I touched the Russian's wrist as the flame ignited the tobacco. It was the first time that I'd felt his skin, which was cool for such hot, sticky weather.

Captain B. lit his own cigarette and folded an arm across his stomach. His other arm hinged up and down as he smoked. "Now my men tell me they've detected a small vessel somewhere out there." He pointed his cigarette straight out at the spot where the ghostly light had blinked minutes before. "Perhaps the boat your husband found out about was a decoy. What do you think, Lola?"

It was. Of course it was a decoy. We had everything planned. I felt José stiffen at the veiled accusation and sound of my nickname. He dared not say anything, though.

"Maybe it's one of the ghost ships lost during a hurricane," I said.

"I see." Captain B. dropped his left hand onto my leg and brushed down the salt-stiffened cloth. His fingers encountered a small clump of seaweed. They paused before picking it off. I couldn't tell how much my husband could see, but surely he sensed an exchange taking place. "In that case, I must tell our boats not to bother giving chase. We have much work to do and shouldn't waste energy chasing phantoms."

Captain B. swung his feet to the inland side of the wall and stood next to José. I looked back, and although my eyes were accustomed to the dark, I couldn't read the look that passed between the two men. Without a word, Captain B. went to his car and leaned in. I turned back to face the sea. I could hear the captain's low voice speaking in short bursts. Not just the children, but the whole trip to find Tomás hung on this part of the operation running smoothly. Would the captain keep his side of the bargain? How could I know?

He straightened and said, "Comrade Santos, you've done good work tonight, but your car shouldn't be seen out here after curfew. My fellow officers may not be as understanding as I."

"Of course." José saluted the captain and crossed the lot to stand beside our Chevy. "Come, Dolores."

I scanned the haze again for signs of life. Later, perhaps, when the danger seeped out of our daily lives, we could dream together of a safe return of our children. "You go ahead." I twisted to look at my soldier but couldn't make out his face in the gloom. "I'll get a ride from him." My husband jerked his head once but then stood motionless, silent.

"Yes, you go ahead," the captain commanded from the far side of his car.

José opened the driver's door and stopped, his rumpled fatigues softly lit by the car's interior. I couldn't tell if he was gathering his strength to get in the car or his courage to defy the order. He seemed so isolated in the only pool of brightness, and I wanted to go to him. I didn't. I couldn't. Too much was at stake. He bent to sit in the car but stood back up.

"Where are the children?" he asked.

I looked past his hesitation and imagined I could see our family's house across the fields. I saw it through long-ago eyes, when my sisters and cousins and relatives-by-circumstance tumbled and played on the wide lawn, and the future held nothing but the possibility of love and laughter.

"The children are safe," I said.

A Glass Swan 1

THE JOURNALIST DIDN'T look like a Veronica. She was petite, had lovely legs, a pert nose, and always wrapped scarves around her neck. But she was Japanese. During her interview with the editor at the *San Diego Sun,* he asked her if "Veronica" were her real name. She said, "It's my American name. I'm an American now." He nodded his approval. She was excellent at being American. The editor gave her the job, and she was excellent at that too. She inspired a loyal following among the readers of the Women's pages but kept a low profile. Other lady journalists jockeyed to cover social functions where they met old-money scions or handsome naval officers. Veronica was content to know all about society without being in its midst.

Her prowess lay in her imagination. Once in a while, while rendering all of those recipes week after week, she loved to attribute a mundane dish to the First Lady. It gave a lift to her readers, especially the patriotic wives and esposas who hung portraits of JFK in their living rooms. Where was the harm? Those overtaxed housewives deserved relief from all of the unsettling talk of A-bomb tests and long-range missiles.

Jacqueline Kennedy glides into the kitchen of the White House. She strips off her gloves, ties an apron over her green shantung Dior suit, and fingers her pearls while pondering whether to put one egg or two in tonight's meat loaf. Understanding the significance of such a decision, she phones Laura Petrie, who answers in the kitchen of The Dick Van Dyke Show. *Rob Petrie's wife is whipping up a batch of biscuits but always has time to share a few household tips with the First Lady. After hanging up and rolling out her dough, Laura dials her favorite West Coast reporter to pass along a hot culinary tip.*

Veronica rolled a sheet of paper into her Smith-Corona and typed:

> A reliable source assures me that a certain doña
> en una casa blanca prepares this Fiesta Meat
> Loaf for her family when no heads-of-state are in
> town . . .

The finished piece sparkled in Veronica's mind as she handed it off to a passing copy boy. By then it was lunchtime. Most of the Society Page girls preferred to gather in the break room. She needed her place with them, since their meals felt familiar, like those at school back home, where everyone wanted to be exactly the same. Over homemade sandwiches wrapped in waxed paper, she gleaned tidbits from the lives of other working women, which she then used to fill up her articles and her imagined home life. None of the girls guessed that the family members who populated her lively Monday morning tales were composites of their own relations. And no one need know that Veronica spent almost every Saturday night alone at home in her tiny bungalow watching the Saturday Night Movie and eating popcorn cooked in bacon grease (a habit she picked up from a transplant from Houston).

That day she opted for the livelier atmosphere of the Sky Café and the bustle of newsmen crowded around several tables. The restaurant-bar was down the block from the paper, and a regular could get a shot in his morning coffee if his hip flask were empty after a long night. Her favorite newsman, David Wick, beckoned her over as soon as she entered the Sky. He was on the city beat, so sometimes they covered the same event from different angles. The year before, David had published exposés of the deep-pocket connections between city councilmen and the developers of the new Mill Valley Shopping Center. Meanwhile, Veronica advised her readership on outfits to wear to its grand opening. Despite their differing aims, David always had a joke and a flirtation for Veronica. He even asked her out. She didn't take his offers seriously, as much as she wanted to. She just couldn't risk it. He kept trying, though, and she appreciated that.

"Ronnie, come sit over here," David said to her, trying to shove Stan Phillips out of the seat next to him.

Stan covered sports, and although he was excitable, he wasn't easily moved. He swatted back at David but then got up. "I was just leaving, anyway. Veronica, my dear," he said and held the chair for her to sit.

Veronica smiled as she picked up the menu. Of course she would have her usual, tuna salad on white, toasted, but she needed something to hide her amusement with Stan. He was a gentleman, the sort that didn't know what to do with women, so he generally kept his distance. He was always polite and formal with her. If he only knew. She was not a woman, nor was she really American, but those were just hard, useless facts to her. They were not the truth. Look at the way men treated her. That was the truth.

After Stan left, Veronica nodded at Timmy Nichols and Tommy Thompson across the table. They did leg work for the city beat and were always together.

To many they seemed interchangeable, with their flat top haircuts and constant cigarettes, legendary even among the smokestacks of the pressroom. When one was encountered alone, often as not he would be called Timmy-Tommy. But Veronica knew that Timmy had brothers who were cops. He had the back door connections at City Hall and the courthouse. Tommy had drifted into nosing around for a large law firm after the War. He had the smarts. David gave him credit for uncovering the slimy trail that led from the shopping mall to the city council.

"Veronica Wills, will you marry me?" David said.

He had said this so often that he no longer bothered to inflect it with a question mark. He didn't wait for a reply before turning away to nod at the waitress for a refill of his coffee. His cup full, David smiled his thanks.

"The usual? Extra mayo?" the waitress said to Veronica.

"You bet, and a Coke. Thanks."

David turned the sugar container straight upside down over his coffee. He poured a long cascade and stirred. Veronica waited for him to rat-a-tat a rhythm on the side of his cup, flinging brown spots of coffee around the table, but he didn't. Instead, he laid his spoon on his plate and subsided into an unnatural quietness.

"Ronnie, seriously, I have an idea we should work on together," he said.

She didn't trust any idea that could subdue his body like that because he usually couldn't sit still. His mouth was going: chewing, talking, blowing bubbles. His fingers rattled his typewriter keys or ripped napkins into strips or pocketed small objects that didn't belong to him. His eyes scanned a room and saw what its occupants were trying to hide, but when his body was still and his brain was ticking, it was time to worry.

Veronica looked for help, but Timmy rapped Tommy on the arm and said, "We have to get down to the courthouse."

Tommy still had Boston cream pie on his plate. He scooped up a large bite and stood. Timmy joined him.

"Guys, wait," Veronica said.

Tommy shrugged, palms open. "Gotta go."

The boys took off, and David drew the pie plate over to his side of the table.

The waitress arrived with Veronica's order. She nipped at the pickle spear and, after swallowing, said to David, "What is it this time?"

"I met this Japanese lady, the wife of a lawyer, at a party at Gaujean and Fleck," he said.

"How'd you get that invitation?"

"You know our man, Tommy, used to work there." He took a bite of the pie. "Turns out our Tommy did the initial background check on the lawyer husband when the firm was looking to hire him. Only the second Japanese at G&F, but even so, he's a rising star in international business law."

"That's just absolutely fascinating, darling." Veronica picked up her sandwich. "But I don't think it'll make the Society Page."

"Very funny. Here's the interesting part. The wife, she's from Hiroshima."

White flash.

Veronica recoiled from the memory. She was good at that too. "Not interested."

"Hear me out," David said.

She bit into her sandwich and said nothing.

He slurped some coffee. "So Mrs. Kobayashi was just a kid during the War, but her mother could be a really valuable source."

"For what?"

"Civilian take on A-bombs."

Veronica shook her head. "It's been done," she said, her tone scornful. She wanted no part of this.

"There's a new angle since some of the ships from the Christmas Island tests are coming back to SD."

"Classified material, surely."

"Yeah, but look." David glanced around before he plucked an envelope from his battered brief case and slid out a photo.

A giant mushroom cloud bloomed over the ocean and filled the aerial picture. David tapped the bottom of it. There Veronica saw ships inside the bomb's shock wave. She closed her eyes briefly.

"Civilians working for the Navy, doing stuff like cleaning these ships, are being exposed to radiation," he said. "Odds are they don't know about it or what it means."

"How'd you get this?" Veronica had no taste for tuna at the moment.

He examined the picture without answering.

"You're right. I don't want to know," she said. "But how are the Hiroshima ladies going to help?"

"Get this. Mrs. Kobayashi's mother wasn't at the party because she was part of an entourage for a Japanese diplomat touring US military installations in the Pacific. I bet A-bomb tests would be on his agenda. Maybe the old lady has even witnessed one of them." David slipped the photo back into the envelope.

"But you don't know that for sure, and she wouldn't tell you if she had."

"You underestimate me. Gotta be careful about that. Anyway, Mrs. Kobayashi and her mother would love to meet Veronica Wills in the flesh. She said so."

"And?"

"Just get me in the door and soften up the old lady a bit. You know, talk about the old country."

"David, I'm from Los Angeles." City of Angels.

"You've never visited your parents' home?"

She sipped her Coke. She hadn't been back once since her crossing to California. "Too expensive."

"Come on."

Her resistance to anything related to her early life was automatic, had been for years. When she first arrived at the paper, David had asked her if her family had been interned. She borrowed the memories of a roommate in LA and told him about it in satisfying detail, but only on the condition that he wouldn't use any of it in his articles. She could extract promises like that from him. This time, it would have been easy to deny him if he had flailed around and shouted, but the heat of his crusade radiated out from his stillness.

She thought for just a second of all the people she had known, lost. Some vaporized, most burnt, others biting back their moans as their bodies melted. She shut memory's door again, but the horror lingered. He was right. No one else should suffer like that. As long as she could keep the door to the past firmly shut, maybe she could help. Veronica pushed her plate away and took out a cigarette. "You said they wanted to meet me?"

David grinned and lit her cigarette.

A Glass Swan 2

VERONICA STOOD BESIDE David on the tiny porch of Mrs. Kobayashi's angular ranch house. The husband had to be making good money as an up and comer at Gaujean and Fleck to get into that neighborhood, and Veronica guessed there was another, grander home in the family's near future.

When the door opened, David said, "Mrs. Kobayashi, may I present Miss Veronica Wills." At the last moment, he dipped his head as Veronica had instructed him.

"Mr. Wick, Miss Wells, please come in," their young hostess said.

Veronica could tell she was a modern woman. Her perfect skin glowed with the proper amount of expertly applied makeup. She wore a short, smart hairdo that would give most women a hard edge, but somehow it softened on her by framing her delicate skin and sparkling eyes. She seemed to possess the kind of natural boldness that thrives on American soil. However, David's formality wouldn't be lost on the mother lurking somewhere inside. Veronica glided through the door first. The interior matched the modern expectations raised by the design of the house. In the living room, the furniture could well have been assumed to be of Japanese origin, but Veronica recognized Jacobsen's Egg Chair and the clean, elegant lines of Danish Modern. Most of one wall was dominated by a massive fireplace built out of large horizontal stone blocks. The room had an eclectic personality but was clearly put together with an eye for beauty and harmony. Veronica approved of the design. The family's butsudan was tucked beside the fireplace. The shrine's upper doors were open and old black-and-white portrait photographs nestled in among the candles and the incense holder, as if they were there to meet a distinguished guest. She felt honored by the presence of the ancestors.

Their hostess moved to Veronica's side and said, "Mother, may I present Mr. David Wick and Miss Veronica Wills of the *San Diego Sun*. My mother, Mrs. Fuji." Modern indeed, rushing the introductions like that. David dipped his head as Veronica and Mrs. Fuji bowed. Veronica admired the mother's high-cheekboned beauty, enhanced by the creases of the years.

"We are honored to have you in our home," the mother said. The liquid melody of her voice complemented her accentless English. Suddenly Veronica wished she had family. The mother invited them to sit on the couch. It was the green of pureed broccoli and was low, without cushions, with only the slightest curve upward at each end to suggest arms. Veronica found it comfortable despite its sparseness.

Mrs. Fuji presided over the proceedings from within the curves of the Egg Chair. Her daughter perched on a smaller armchair beside her. Veronica wondered if the mother surrendered her modern throne with its high back to her son-in-law when he was home, but that wasn't the kind of query that fit into the pleasantries they traded over tea for most of the visit. They began with Veronica's admiration of a doll collection displayed along one wall and got no deeper than a lively discussion about replacing rice with potatoes in some traditional Japanese dishes. Veronica promised to publish one of the daughter's updated recipes. The young woman beamed.

David was restless with the meandering pace, and twice Veronica pulled a miniature glass swan out of his hands before he broke off the fragile wings. What he wanted would take time, more visits, and now that Veronica had met these lovely women, they reminded her of how much she had lost. She didn't know if she was up to the strain of uncovering buried memories to see it through. To her surprise, though, Mrs. Kobayashi provided a natural opening for David's coveted topic when she said, "We learned how to substitute during the rice shortages after the War."

"We don't want to bore our guests with unpleasant memories," her mother said.

"Mrs. Fuji, we want to hear your memories," David said. His hands were still. "No rice?"

Mrs. Fuji turned to Veronica. "You haven't told us where you are from."

"Los Angeles," she replied. City of the magical makeover.

The daughter said, "Really. Were you—?"

"Hiroko-san," her mother interrupted. "Will you please get more tea cakes?"

"That's all right, Mrs. Fuji. No, I'm adopted, so no, my parents were not sent away."

"I thought . . ." David said.

Veronica's imaginary family lost a house and other possessions during their confinement, according to her conversations with David, but those tales didn't fit into this scenario. She laid a hand on his arm. He got the signal. Mrs. Fuji picked up on the gesture, also. Veronica was struck by a glint of frightening shrewdness in that one look. Her studied calm evaporated along with the delicate scent of her Je Reviens perfume. She called on the Buddha of gracious conduct: give me strength and keep me from exposure, Jacqueline Bouvier Kennedy.

"You thought?" Mrs. Fuji said.

"I thought she was from Seattle." He didn't sound convincing, probably not even to himself. He reached for the swan again. Veronica let him have it. Nothing good could come of his blunders.

"Were you put up for adoption because you're only part Japanese?" the daughter asked.

Mrs. Fuji gasped and covered her mouth.

Her daughter turned to her. "Nothing to be ashamed of. Not here, anyway. But one hears tales."

Veronica expected the old sting of disgrace, but it didn't rise. The daughter was right. Here, only other Japanese could tell she had mixed blood, and they no longer filled her days with their exclusive conformity. Besides, she was American now. This was the land of immigration and mixed identities.

Mrs. Fuji shook her head. "Please pardon my forward daughter." She peered at Veronica.

Although the sharp glint was gone from the mother's eyes, under the touch of her gaze Veronica felt that she was gauging the depth of cut her daughter had inflicted. Veronica felt bereft of family and longed to tell someone, this someone, the truth about herself. Himself. Years ago, her mother's family had shunned the two of them in public because her mother had had a son with a foreign missionary. When he returned to Germany, he left behind an unwed mother and bad blood with her kin. What a mess, and the child was a living reminder of it.

"Do you have any other family here?" David asked Mrs. Fuji.

"My son, Koichi, his two boys, and his wife. They live in San Francisco." Mrs. Fuji lowered her eyes.

"The rest of the family didn't survive the War," the daughter said. "Mother had a sister, but we never heard from her, so we assume she's gone too."

"Sorry to hear that," David said.

White flash.

The smell of charred flesh pierced through Veronica's carefully constructed shield. She stood without thinking. The others started at her abrupt movement, so she tried to cover by drifting over to the glass cases filled with dolls.

"What a lovely collection," she said, returning to an earlier topic. Most of them were Japanese, but a few outsiders in European costumes were mixed in.

David again took her cue. "Please tell us more about them."

Veronica noticed a hat doll dressed in a flowered, red kimono. She wore and carried several hats shaped like the top of a pin cushion. Her aunt had given her a hat girl just like that one when she was the boy Youji. The seal melted.

BY THE TIME Youji had dug out of the rubble in the back yard after the bright flash, his mother and his friend were already dead under the toppled wall from the house next door. He could see her arm around the boy's body, as if she had tried to protect him. Youji's injured shoulder and arm were useless, so he was unable to dislodge the bodies, and his frantic neighbors didn't answer his pleas for help. At one point, as he continued to claw at sections of the wall, he whacked the smaller body on the head, furious that the boy had taken Youji's place in his mother's embrace.

Exhaustion overcame him, and he lay as close as he could to his mother's cool flesh. He wanted nothing more than to join her, but when fire swept up the street and into the yard, it forced him back to life. Escape through leaping flames was impossible, so he hid in the well behind the house. The unceasing rains followed. He hauled himself out of the damp hole but was unable to move more than that. His world had disappeared. He lost track of the minutes and hours.

Some time later he heard his aunt calling. He started to crawl but made little progress because his joints were stiff from the damp. He heard his aunt and another woman weeping in the front yard, apologizing over and over for leaving her sister and nephew behind. He tried to shout, but his voice had been taken by the smoke, and he went unheard. His aunt said prayers for the dead. "I'm alive," Youji whispered, and then a possibility grew that stopped the raindrops in midair. If his aunt thought he were dead, he could be whatever and whoever he wanted to be. Finally. He stopped crawling and lay still. The rain continued on its course. Much later, when he pulled himself into the front yard, his aunt and the bodies were gone.

After the fighting stopped, Youji drifted up to Osaka, where he experimented with the trappings of a new identity. With all of the American involvement in post-war Japan, the United States seemed a good landing place for a phoenix that had risen from an American conflagration. He learned about adult desires as he negotiated his passage across the Pacific without proper papers. Youji Toshiko landed in Los Angeles. Veronica Wills moved from there to San Diego a few years later.

VERONICA'S ATTENTION SLOWLY returned to the Kobayashi's bright living room. David was saying that he didn't realize that dolls could be so valuable. He was sorry now that he had cut all of the hair off of his sister's dolls years ago. Veronica touched the case of the hat girl. She hoped her absence hadn't been noticed.

"I had a wonderful aunt who gave me a doll just like this." She pointed to it and glanced at Mrs. Fuji. "I loved that doll, but my mother wouldn't let me play with it." There. One line of truth from the past.

"Why not?" the daughter asked. She came over to open the case and hand the doll to Veronica.

Because boys don't play with dolls. "She thought it a waste of time," Veronica answered. She brushed the cascade of hats, then handed the doll back.

"I played with this one, and now it's a collectible. Imagine that." The daughter put the doll back and they both returned to their seats.

Veronica took a last sip from her tea and with both hands placed the cup on the tray. "It's been an honor to visit your home today."

"The honor is ours. We hope you will return soon," the daughter said.

"Mrs. Fuji, weren't you recently on a Naval ship in the Pacific?" David said.

Oh David. Things had been wrapping up nicely. Now Mrs. Fuji squinted at them, as if reviewing their entire conversation in light of this one sentence. Even the bold daughter froze, her eyes bouncing to and away from her mother's face.

Veronica tapped David's knee. "Plenty of time for that later. Now we must be going." She rose with enough force to automatically bring him to his feet also. She squeezed his elbow, a warning not to utter another word outside of those common to saying goodbye. The mother and daughter also rose, with Mrs. Fuji taking Veronica's hand and looking at her intently.

Outside on the front walk Veronica asked, "What were you thinking in there?"

"Come on, she had to know something was up. I don't have all the time in the world."

Veronica shook her head.

"Besides, why did you say you were adopted?" David asked.

"Did you want to focus on my story or theirs?" Veronica was returning more fully to her current life. She took his arm. "You already know my story."

At the car he disengaged himself to open the passenger side door. "Do I?"

She sat in the car. "Of course you do. I'm a simple girl."

He shook his head as he closed the door.

Chita
A Message from García 2

THE HARDEST PART was waiting through the night in our house. Alone. Diego was in Havana to set up his special commission. That night he was probably smoking cigars and telling lies. I had promised him a haircut when he returned the next day, but I wondered if I could keep all of my own lies straight, between the children's supposed harvest adventure and our false familial visit to Tío Juan. Rosie was putting on an act for Ramón at a patron's house in Varadero Beach. At least that's what she was supposed to be doing. I still worried about that one. Lola was out at the boat, the last of us to see the children. I should have gone with her. I should have insisted, but she and Rosie convinced me that one sister in danger was better than two. How I wished to be in her skin, to lay my hand on Beto's chubby check one last time.

I tried to pack for our trip east, but it was nearly impossible with the boat operation underway. I wandered from room to quiet room, meaning to pick up something and then forgetting what. I went into the boys' room to close the curtains against the night but found the simple muslin shield they made too suffocating and had to draw them open again. At one point during the night, I looked down to find myself holding one of my flat, black shoes as I stood over Miguelito's bed. I went back to my own bedroom and let the shoe drop beside the dresser. I had no idea where the other one was. I don't think I ever found it.

I thought I would never sleep again, but I woke to Rosita's touch, butterflies trembling in her fingers. I was curled into a ball in Beto's bed with the chess set's black king cradled in my palm.

"In here," she called, and Lola soon clumped through the doorway.

"Gone," she said.

Sunlight streamed in the window and lit her tired face as she slowly crossed the room to sit on Miguelito's bed. With such an awakening by my sisters, I did not have one illusionary moment that everything was just as it had been when I woke the day before. No disorientation allowed me to wonder what to make the boys for breakfast. No. I had to move forward immediately to keep from sinking into chaotic agitation. I let the black king roll from my fingers onto the cover and squirmed to sit beside Rosie.

"No moping," I said to her. "We have too much to do to find Tomás."

"Yes," Lola said from the other bed. "So much to do." She ran her hand over the thin spread and clenched a handful of it by her thigh. "And of course I'll help with everything."

"What are you talking about?" I imagined my own clenched fist in her hair, dragging some sense out of her.

"Don't be mad," Rosie said. "It's not her fault she can't go with us. We'll be all right." She patted the hand I had unknowingly drawn into a fist.

"Mary, Mother of God, will you make some sense for once?"

"No need to shout." Rosie's taps grew into small slaps.

"Captain B. was there," Lola said.

"Where?"

"At the beach, with José, right after the launch. I think he knew about the boat, but . . ."

"But what?" If we were to live through the day it would be a miracle, I thought.

"They should be safe. They are safe. They are safe. From him, I mean. Only I can't go with you."

I lurched into the small space dividing us, intending I don't know what. It would not have been the first time that Lola and I had come to blows as adults. Rosie blocked me with her forearm, and Lola scooted away to stand against the boys' dresser.

"I have to go to another Russian camp—I can't come home every night," Lola said. "I have to go for the children. I have to go. With him."

I suddenly stopped straining against Rosie, and the force of her uncontested restraint threw me back onto the bed. Dear God, would this madness ever stop? A woman can choose to compromise her own virtue. Lola had before—we knew about her blond—but to trade against it for her own children and with uncertain outcome? Madness, that was all I could think. Rosie was talking again, but I couldn't hear her from the depths of my own discouragement.

"What?"

"I said, we were thinking that someone here needs to know, in case word comes while we're gone."

Or in case we don't return. We were all thinking it, but no one would say it aloud. Just thinking it brought it too close to reality.

"The only people we trust are in the boat or in this room," I said.

"José is a soldier, we can't compromise him," Rosie said. "And Ramón, well with the CDR and his brother's accident." She shook her head. "But Diego . . ."

No, no, no, no. No.

"And not a word about Tomás," Rosie said. "We still don't know who is with us and who is not."

You should talk with your two-faced husband, I almost blurted, but I didn't. I wished I could go after her the way I did Lola, but I didn't. Never could. There's something about that Rosie, despite her aggravations. Instead I said, "Great, I say the one thing I never dreamed of saying to my husband, but I get to lie about Tomás. I am sure we will rot in hell."

I HAD MYSELF under control by the time I left for Diego's haircut at my salon. It was on a busy street full of shops not far from the Concordia Bridge. I hurried along, greeted other shopkeepers, and waved to friends in passing cars as if that day were much the same as the one before. Diego was further up the street at the corner with several other machinists. He was rolling a cigarette but nodded in my direction as I paused in front of my shop. I unlocked the door and went inside. The white plaster walls glowed behind posters of American hairdos and recent pictures of our leaders. I had hoped to add a third chair that year, but with the rules changing every day and ownership of property constantly in question, it was prudent not to invest. Even so, my schedule called for an assistant. She would watch the shop while I was gone with Rosita. She would welcome the extra income, as little as it was.

I arranged my scissors and combs and brought out a fresh stack of hot-pink towels, but still Diego had not appeared. I went outside and stood, hands on hips, to stare down the sidewalk at the group of cronies. Diego nodded again, but I knew machismo wouldn't allow him to leave the other men until I went back inside. I sat in one of the chairs to wait, but as soon as I swiveled around to inspect the unruly patch of hair behind my left ear, the door opened. Diego brought in an aura of cigarette smoke and smooched my hand that was still playing with my hair.

"Go on now," I told him. "Over to the sink. We don't have all day."

"I would lasso the sun and tie him to the thigh of Che to have more time with you, mamacita," he said. He danced a backward rumba to lead me to the sink.

A giggle escaped me, despite my unease. "Hush your mouth and sit." This was not the moment to tell him about the boys, but soon. "Lie all the way back. That's it, just relax your shoulders." He rested his neck on the pink towel that was folded over the lip of the sink.

I waited for the water to warm, then directed the nozzle to wet Diego's hair. I'm an excellent judge of hair texture, ability to hold color, and the type of cuts that would flatter both the natural swirls in the hair and the composition of the face, but I couldn't treat this head as just another customer. Diego's straight brown hair thinned on top. I slicked it back from his high forehead. Pendants of water clumped together at the ends of his fine strands. His pale scalp peeked through. This covert nudity and the delicacy of his closed eyelids drew a rapier point from the hollow of my throat to the bowl of my breastbone.

I grabbed a slender bottle of shampoo and sniffed it. "One moment. Let me get another shampoo for you. This one is too flowery for a man."

He nodded, eyes still closed. I turned off the tap and hurried through the curtain to the tiny back room. It was a closet lined with shelves but big enough to stand in. Before the Revolution, the latest concoctions from the United States packed the shelves. Now the gels and liquids with Yanqui names ran low in their glamorous bottles and jars. I filled more and more of them with homemade mixtures that worked just as well as the originals but didn't smell as sophisticated. Should I spend a few precious drops of New York shampoo on Diego, a man? Would he appreciate it?

The Madonna's voice emanated from behind a Yanqui blue bottle on the middle shelf. "It is time to tell him about the boys."

"In a minute," I said.

"Now," the voice said.

I wished I could scream at Her the way Lola did. "Go away," I said, louder.

"What?" Diego asked.

"Nothing, papi, just worrying aloud about my supplies."

"You can do that later. Come on, Chita, it doesn't take this long at the barber shop."

"Of course," I said.

I snatched the blue bottle from the shelf and shook it. The voice remained silent as I returned to my husband's side. I nudged a place for the shampoo on the shelf above the sink, rinsed his hair again, and then lathered him up.

He inhaled deeply, the nostrils of his thin, straight nose flaring. "Wasting the good stuff on your husband? You must be feeling guilty about something." He smiled with his eyes still closed and wiped a drip from his forehead.

I forced out a laugh. Rinse and lather.

Diego tapped his fingers on his knees. "Do you think Beto and Miguelito will teach chess to those country boys?"

I rinsed a second time before I opened my mouth to answer him.

A Glass Swan 3

VERONICA HAD A deadline to meet. Fiesta ware was done. Time to revive a more subtle style. Jaqueline would certainly agree. Veronica studied the curved lips of the seaform green serving bowl that sat beside her typewriter.

Russel Wright dishes are a must for the modern family on the go. The famous designer has covered all bases for smart entertaining, from jet set living room suites to snappy bowls and platters.

She paused to read her opening, red pencil in hand, when one of the boys slumped into the chair beside her desk.

"Howdy, Tommy," she said. She was one of the few who bothered to call him by the right name. "You haven't been around much."

He checked out the green serving bowl, looked at Veronica. She pointed the pencil at her story. Tommy nodded.

"Ma's sick," he said. "Been spending time with her up near LA."

"Sorry to hear that. Hope she's getting better."

"A little."

"Good. Wish her well for me." Veronica rolled the paper up a few lines and rested her hand on top of her machine. She really had to get this piece finished.

Her colleague didn't take the hint. He chuckled and said, "She's the only one won't call me Tommy."

"Yeah? What does she call you?" Veronica asked. She red-lined "snappy" and wrote in "dashing."

"You're not getting it that easy. Anyway, I'm here about something else. A phone call I got." Tommy swiveled his head to look at her. "About you."

Veronica dropped the pencil. This didn't sound good. "Go on."

"I know a bunch of people over at Gaujean and Fleck."

"Um hmm." Oh no, that was the law firm where David had met Mrs. Fuji's daughter. Why did he have to go and blurt out the Pacific stuff?

"Sometimes they ask for help. I have to be careful, but if I can help out, I will. They do the same for me. Works out nice. Anyway, a buddy of mine there called. Said a Mrs. Fuji wanted info on our own Veronica Wills, supposedly from LA. She wanted more than the business office is willing to give out, but public stuff, like birthplace, things like that. Said she didn't want to bother you personally."

Sure she didn't. "Why's your buddy involved?"

"You know this Mrs. Fuji?" Tommy asked.

Veronica waggled her fingers. "Slightly. Nice old lady. David took me to meet her."

"She's the mother-in-law of one of the young hotshots in the firm, so what's my buddy gonna do?"

She nodded. That Mrs. Fuji was crafty—using her son's position to let Veronica know she was being checked out. Nice old lady, indeed. "Why is she asking about me? Why not David? He's the one that mentioned something he shouldn't know about."

Tommy shrugged. "Maybe she's going after David also, but we just don't know it. Anyway, thing was, I was running up to LA anyway to see Ma, so I did a little poking around. No Veronica Wills born in LA."

"I told her I was adopted."

Tommy pushed himself up straight in the chair. "You told David . . ."

"That was off the record."

"Nothing's off the record. You of all people should know that. Anyway." Tommy hooked an arm over the back of the chair and gazed past her profile. "You run across all kinds of people in this line of work. Most people who just want to be someone else, someone more than they were at first, well, they usually leave a loose trail. A trick Ma taught me is to look at references. Employment, places to live, stuff like that."

"She sounds like quite the operator." Veronica wished she could melt into the bowl's deep glaze.

"Sure enough, a reference for Veronica Wills turns out—"

"That's private. Who gave it to you?" She leaned over and jabbed Tommy's arm with the back end of her pencil. He looked down at his arm and waited. She slowly sat back, gently placed the pencil beside the bowl, and folded her arms. Thousands of times she had told a story to get the story. Tommy was no different.

He huffed out a loud breath. "Turns out to be a boarding house for Japanese immigrants. It's still there, you know."

"Sure it is." Veronica remembered the nosy parker that ran that joint.

"So I get to digging around, asking about someone who maybe was always sending off envelopes to newspapers. Sure, she remembered someone like that. Was the name Fuji, maybe? No, longer, she says. Wait a minute, she says, and goes gets her books. Youji Toshiko, she comes up with. I ask what she remembers and she gives me an odd look, suggested I might find out more at the Japanese American Center." He pauses but Veronica remains silent.

"Off I go, to the Japanese American Center. I tell the lady there my ma's sick and asking after an old friend, so she lets me into the archives. Man, the records they keep. They're very proud of them, you know. They have immigration records listing where everyone is from. Meanwhile, I keep wondering where Veronica Wills is from."

"I'm American," she says as if by rote.

"The lady looks through the Osaka list, where your family's from, maybe."

"Now look . . ."

"Hold on." Tommy sat up with a grin. "Hiya, Dave."

At the sound of David's name, Veronica put her tingling fingers on the typewriter but couldn't think of one darned thing to type except "Youji Toshiko."

"This looks like a conspiracy over here," David said. He leaned over to examine the empty serving bowl. He looked at Veronica. She pointed to the column she wasn't getting to write. "What's going on?"

"Not much, amigo. Ma's sick. I'm just looking for some womanly advice."

David stepped back, regret on his face. "Sorry, don't want to interrupt."

He hurried off and Veronica realized Tommy had said about the only thing that would send the newsman scurrying.

"Your ma's sickness seems awfully convenient," she said. "I'm beginning to suspect that you never even had a mother."

"Veronica, I'm hurt," he said. "And you're avoiding the subject. Which is, this nice lady goes down the list and bingo. She finds Youji Toshiko. Address matches the one at the boarding house."

"So?"

"Here's the thing. I tell her thanks for finding Ma's lady friend and she says I must be mistaken, Youji is a man's name. I was confused, but told her I must've misunderstood Ma." He stopped talking and hunched over with his elbows on his knees again.

Veronica listened to the clatter of the newsroom. She heard Stan's hesitant pecking and Timmy's rapid-fire business typing. She counted the rings of David's phone at the back of the room. She got to five before Tommy spoke again.

"I had that long drive back from LA to muck around with this stuff. An idea started. Impossible, right? But then, there's the famous Veronica scarves—always around your neck. And some of the things Dave's said about your coyness and all. We put it down to Oriental shyness or whatever. But." Tommy flicked a look at her chest and inspected his shoes. "Tell me I'm bowling down the wrong alley."

She could keep up the charade, only it wasn't a charade. She was Veronica Wills, born American. Trouble was, she was also Youji Toshiko. He was born in Hiroshima, and he still lived. Being born American suggested certain freedoms, but would anyone understand that a particular kind of freedom had blossomed from the heart of a disaster? That a city's worth of dead made resurrection easier?

"You're smarter than you look," Veronica said.

"Yeah." Tommy lit a cigarette and rubbed his palm with his thumb. He flicked a couple of more looks her way, at her hands, her chest, her scarf, her mouth, but he never looked her in the eye. Finally he pulled his reporter's notebook from his pocket. "My buddy told Mrs. Fuji to call me directly. She called while I was out and left a number."

"What are you going to tell her?"

Tommy wiped some dust off the tip of his shoe. "Guess I have to tell her that Veronica's original name was Youji Toshiko. Act like I don't know what that means."

"Let me talk to her first." She unearthed a scrap of paper covered with handwritten notes from her desk and pushed it over to him. He sighed and held up his notebook and copied out Mrs. Fuji's number. Then he stood and rubbed the top of his buzz cut. "Whatever you tell her, I don't want to know."

"Thanks, you're a pal."

"Tell that to Ma."

"I will," she said. "Guillermo." Some would be appalled by his Mexican heritage, the way they talked.

He raised his eyebrows. "Touché." He turned and sauntered toward the exit.

"Wait," Veronica called.

Tommy looked back at her.

She beckoned and waited until he returned to her desk. "What are you going to say to David?"

He backed up. Another quick peep at her chest. "Not my place to say anything." He turned away again.

Chita
A Message from García 3

I HAD SPENT the afternoon scurrying about, bagging and boxing black market chocolate and smoked meat, mamey sapote jelly from the fruit of our tree, American spark plugs, and other items that either we could use on a trek over the mountains or would be as good as currency for our brother if we could leave them with him. After our conversation at the shop, Diego hadn't spoken at all during dinner. When I wondered aloud about the state of the roads, he just kept his eyes on his plate and tore the crusty bread into crumbs that he didn't eat. After our silent dinner, he ran a caged construction light out from a plug in the kitchen and hung it on the trellis on the side of the house. He had brought tools home from his shop to tune the car for my journey with Rosita. I watched through the window as he raised the trunk lid and hood.

My beautiful '56 DeSoto would carry us over the mountains. It was light yellow and white, the colors of lemon sherbet and sweet cream. The government imposed heavy restrictions on gasoline, but what was it if not a government of the people? And those people—individuals—enforced the regulations as they saw fit. Our gas supply flowed more generously than most, shall we say. Don't ask questions. Earlier, before meeting Diego at the salon, I went out to the rear wall of the side yard to uncover the jugs of extra gas we would carry in the trunk. Travel was difficult, but we had Cuban inventiveness and my Diego kept my machine in perfect running condition. Surely, though, he could use some help under the hood. I went outside. Clouds were low overhead. We would have rain before morning. Would we see Tomasito before nightfall tomorrow?

Diego's head was deep in the engine compartment. I spoke to the bow of his back. "How are the belts?"

The wing nut of the fan cover and several screws nestled in his old straw hat on the fender. I peered under the hood. Diego torqued a tool deep in the compartment.

"Goddamned whore of an engine," he said.

"What's the matter?" I stooped beside him.

He threw an elbow in my direction without looking up. "Get out of my light." His voice rumbled and seemed to be magnified by the engine compartment.

Sure, I let him feel as if he was in charge, but I, too, am a mechanic, but not by profession. "I'll check the oil." I reached under the hood, but he caught my wrist and flung my arm away. My hand smacked the fender. I shook the sting in my hand.

"Leave it." Diego bent back to his work.

This car had been bought with Montero money, and I took care of it as much as he did. I hooked a finger in the dipstick's ring and pulled.

Suddenly I slammed against the trellis and felt the oily tip of Diego's screwdriver at my throat. "I said, leave it."

"This is my car." Twigs and leaves pricked my back and arms. My hands went slack and the dipstick dropped to the ground.

"If I pop a hole in your throat." Diego pushed harder, which forced my chin up. "And I go before a judge—a man—and tell him what you did. He will clap me on the shoulder and set me free to find another wife."

"Good," I said with a clenched jaw as some instinct feared impalement through my own movements. But that end to not knowing about the children was better than others. "Then do it."

A car rolled past outside the gate, the radio voice of El Líder clear in the night. Diego dropped his hands and stepped back. "But you wouldn't suffer enough for what you and your sisters did." He shook his head. I stayed pressed against the vines. "Go on." He waved the screwdriver at the door. "Go to your Monteros." He spat on my shoe.

My head floated and saliva flooded my mouth. Then I was falling, falling, falling toward the gravel and dead leaves. I saw the dipstick in the dirt. One more thing to clean. I reached for Diego to tell him, but he stepped back. At last my hands crunched on the ground.

The next second I was cradled in Diego's arms as he knelt between the car and the wall. I struggled to right myself. Fainting on cue was for manipulators, not for me.

"Rosita is supposed to be the one who faints," I said.

Surely I had only been out for a second, but in the time I was away, Diego had pulled the pins out of my bun and had unbuttoned the top of my blouse. He grabbed my hair and pulled my head back to examine my face. He'd held onto me like that during tender moments, after the boys were asleep. I had an idea.

"Take me to bed," I said.

He scooped me up and took me inside and into our room, where he laid me on the bed. He closed my suitcase with the brass buckles and moved it to the floor by the big dresser. He turned off the lamps and kept his face averted while he crossed the room to the door. I fanned my hair out on the pillow the way Rosita had taught me as a teenager.

"Diego."

He stopped with his back to me. I called his name again and waited until he turned. His face looked crumpled and old. I rolled over and allowed my skirt to hitch up to my hip.

"Wash up and come to bed." I turned my head and waited for the creak of his footsteps to either move up the hall to the bathroom or stamp away from me and back to the car. Neither happened as a muffled swish on the bedroom rug approached me.

Diego speared his fingers in my hair and bunched them into a fist. His other hand alighted on my bare hip and ran down my thigh, pressing hard and skidding on the oil and grit layered on his skin. Never before had Diego come to bed with dirty hands. His hand landed on my mother's sheet when he knelt on the bed beside me. Even in the dim light I could see the oily gray imprint it left. I would have to scrub hard to get rid of it. Diego had brought other filth into our marriage. The girls in Camagüey Province, the money he lost to those thugs in that import/export scheme.

I looked at the mirror on my dressing table. Reflected there was the yellow glow that spilled in from the hall. We were alone in the house; the door could remain open. I had brought that unspeakable emptiness into our marriage. Diego slipped his hand under my skirt and pressed a grimy finger into me. What were my grievances next to his? I folded my lip between my teeth and opened my legs.

Neither of us slept in the bed that night. Diego returned to the car while I scrubbed all but my most delicate parts with his rough soap. I took it and a brush to the grease smeared on the sheets. I didn't care if I rubbed a hole in them. I would leave them snow-white for my husband to sleep on while I was away. Then I rechecked my traveling supplies. Late into the night, when all boxes were stacked by the door and rain dripped from the eaves, I curled up on the settee in the living room. I planned an elaborate first meal in America for my boys. Eventually I fell into a light sleep.

I awoke before dawn. I had no idea where Diego had slept, if at all. As far as I knew, he hadn't reentered the house until I had gotten dressed and made coffee. He leaned against the counter.

"Sit down," I said.

Diego crossed his ankles and relaxed his arms at his waist, coffee cup cradled against his belly. His hands were clean, his cuticles scrubbed. The birds called to one another in the trees outside. "Wake up, wake up. Time to wake up!"

"Maybe you should take the truck," Diego said, his head bowed.

The truck was simpler and more reliable, but if I took it, he would be tempted to use the DeSoto in his work. To please the men from Havana, he wouldn't hesitate to load the back seat with carburetors and mufflers and such. I would never be able to get the filth out of the cream seats. He had sullied enough already.

"We'll be fine with the car." I reached out to pat his bare arm, but he slipped out of range.

If Rosita stood in my shoes, she would have had some sweet, supple words to keep her man beside her. I didn't know what they might be. "Diego. You'll stay near the phone. Or find someone to listen for it."

He swung away and stomped to the door. He stopped there and flung his cup back onto the counter. It skidded and tipped. I feared it would tumble into the sink and break, but after a precarious moment, it didn't.

Nor did I. Not that time. "And check the mail. Every day," I said to his back.

Then he was gone again. Rosita would've handled her husband better than I did mine, but she trusted neither herself nor her husband to receive the all-important message. Lola had her duties with the Russians. She always told people that she was the one to do this, she was the one to do that. But only I had the strength to be the first to know. And I was the only one with the strength to get us to Tomasito. Rosita would know what to do when we got there, but I was the one that would get us there. I resisted Diego's sly spirit that cajoled me to smash the cups in the sink. Instead, I washed and dried them and placed them carefully in the cupboard. Then it was time to go prod Rosita onto the road. With the grace of Jesus and his Mother, I would see my baby brother before that day was over.

A Glass Swan 4

VERONICA THOUGHT LONG and hard about the Mrs. Fuji situation as she sat in her silent bungalow that weekend. She could back out of David's shenanigans—too risky—which would certainly be the truth, but she didn't think that would stop Mrs. Fuji. Something in that fleeting look said there was as much at stake on her side as there was on Veronica's. What could it be? Mrs. Fuji reminded Veronica of her aunt. Despite her uncle's ban, her aunt usually stopped by every other Wednesday morning with food, clothes, and treats for young Youji. She had eagerly awaited those secret meetings, the sweets her aunt brought, and her light kiss on Youji's shoulder. The memory of the soft scent of her aunt's lilac perfume overcame her fear, and she phoned Mrs. Fuji for an appointment. She suggested the following Wednesday.

Mrs. Fuji lamented that her daughter and granddaughter would miss the visit, since they went to the other grandmother's house every week on that day. Veronica hinted that she actually preferred privacy for this matter. "As you wish," Mrs. Fuji said.

Veronica selected an Hermes scarf with crimson roses on the morning of their meeting. She believed that a lady must always dress well when discussing delicate matters. She wished that it might take her forever to arrange her scarf, but her hands proved expert even while her mind roiled. Enough procrastination, she told herself. She drove to the Kobayashi home, determined to confront the truth in whatever form the older woman sought. What might she lose? She had lost everything once, and look at her now. She could start over again if she had to, but she didn't want to. She suspected that it got harder with age.

Before she had a chance to ring the bell, Mrs. Fuji opened the door. They settled in the living room with cigarettes and coffee from a silver set. After the proper amount of light chat Veronica said, "A message came to me. By way of Gaujean and Fleck."

"My son-in-law's firm sent you a message?"

"I believe his mother-in-law did. It surprised me that she was so interested in Veronica Wills."

"It was the Hat Girl doll." Mrs. Fuji swept her hand toward the doll collection, as if presenting a lovely gift. "You knew her dress."

"Yes, of course. It was very popular."

"Only in Hiroshima. Only for a short time. You would know her only if you were . . . not from here."

"Ah." Veronica turned her attention to the crack in her facade. "Oh." As a child, she wouldn't have known the limited provenance of the toy. "Yes." She acknowledged. This Mrs. Fuji was admirable to catch such a tiny slip. But was she friend or foe? Maybe it was already too late to matter. "In that case, I must apologize for a story I told during our visit."

Mrs. Fuji folded her hands. "No apology needed. Perhaps you merely wish to correct a misperception?"

"That's a kind suggestion. Yes, I wish to clarify." She snuffed out her cigarette. "Veronica Wills was born American. It's not as good as being Japanese, but it's better than being only half in Japan. America is the country of my birth."

Mrs. Fuji nodded. "And before?"

"Youji Toshiko was born in Hiroshima."

"Youji?" Mrs. Fuji's eyes widened and she fingered her strand of perfect pearls. Frown lines marred her smooth forehead. "I am confused. This is a boy's name."

"Youji lived with his mother who didn't have a husband or an understanding family. Until the bomb fell and his mother died." Veronica remembered his aunt's singsong prayer for the dead. "Then he . . . died too."

Veronica studied her hands and waited.

Mrs. Fuji carefully poured more coffee into each cup. She picked up the creamer and stood. "Please excuse, I must refill this." She disappeared into the kitchen.

Veronica feared that she had gone too far as she shook out another cigarette but didn't light it. She tossed the pack onto the coffee table, where it came to rest against the glass swan. She wished she had let David rip the wings off the stupid thing. Look at it. Ignorant that its own thin, graceful neck could be snapped with the merest twitch of the thumb, and then what would make it beautiful? It would be nothing but dressed up sand, and its trials in the fire would be worthless.

Mrs. Fuji returned and set the creamer on the tray before composing herself in her seat, ankles crossed, hands clasped, and eyes lowered. She opened her mouth but closed it again without speaking. She nudged the cigarettes away from the swan. "My mother told me that secrets have a way of finding each other. I know this to be true, but I could not imagine that this was the secret that would find my own." She glanced at the family butsudan. Today the doors were closed.

Veronica had no idea what Mrs. Fuji's secret might be, so she kept silent. She heard the clank of the mailbox from outside and guessed that if she turned around to the window behind her she would see the receding back of the mailman's blue uniform. She wondered what it was like to move from house to house each day, carrying pieces of people's lives and dispensing hope and dismay from your heavy, government-issued satchel.

"Your young man mentioned a curious subject just as you were leaving last time." Mrs. Fuji sank back into the bowl of her chair and rested her forearms on its curved sides. She appeared to relax but her direct gaze suggested that she was as relaxed as a coiled snake.

"I'm sorry, Mrs. Fuji, but he is not my young man."

"He wants to be. Even an old grandmother could see that. You must be careful. A man who has been . . . mesmerized by a dream . . . may be perturbed if awakened." She leaned forward and gestured at the coffeepot.

Veronica shook her head to the offer. "Yes, I understand what you mean. And I apologize for his lack of refinement. He's a terrific newsman, has a razor-sharp instinct for rooting out injustice and corruption, but that means sometimes his good manners go out the window when someone is being hurt."

"Is someone being hurt?"

I am, Veronica thought. This was exactly what she feared. She had agreed to make the connection with a possible source for David, but her history had been exposed and now she was jammed between David's suspicions of nuclear contamination and Mrs. Fuji's surveillance. Did this have something to do with the secret her host had just mentioned? Veronica had so many secrets. Was it possible that Mrs. Fuji had just one?

She too leaned back, but the sofa had no real arms on which to rest her own. "I don't know. You'll have to ask him. Shall I tell him you'd like to talk?"

"What about?"

This woman was not going to let her off the hook. "I really don't know any specifics. He just wanted me to make the introductions."

"I am very busy."

Veronica had had enough. "Were you in the Pacific?"

"Sometimes my translation work takes me to different places."

"He showed me pictures. Of ships. And a cloud." That was all she was going to say. Honestly. "You were there, back home," she blurted before she could catch herself.

Mrs. Fuji stilled even more, although until that moment Veronica hadn't realized that was possible. It frightened her. She remembered her mother's stillness in the rubble. Her mind always went to the lucky friend who spent his last moments sheltered by her mother. Until now. Of course her mother had covered the boy. A mother's instinct is to protect a child, even one not her own. Veronica's anger had separated her from her mother at the critical time that day. Her mother had gathered in the nearest boy, but she must have died panicked and wondering about her own son.

Sorrow cascaded from Veronica's chest, leaving her breathless for one long moment. Finally she gulped air. As she gasped, Mrs. Fuji tilted her head slightly. She maintained the stoic facade of a Samurai, but she was a mother. She would understand.

"Everyone on the ships," Veronica said. "They all have mothers."

Mrs. Fuji covered her mouth and glanced at the butsudan. It was her first telling movement, but what did it say? Veronica may never know, but somehow she seemed to have touched something in the other woman's heart.

Her host went over to the butsudan and opened its doors. She gazed into it for a long time. These family heirlooms often had secret compartments, some which would destroy their own contents if smashed open. The grandfather clock chimed the half hour. Mrs. Fuji reached inside the shrine, causing most of her body to momentarily disappear from sight. She emerged holding a business envelope with the sealed flap outward. Veronica couldn't tell if its top had been slit, or in fact what this envelope had to do with their current standoff.

"You're right. Everyone has a mother." Mrs. Fuji came to sit on the couch. She smothered the letter to her chest. "Your mother sent you to help me, even if we never tell your young man."

"Tell him what?"

Mrs. Fuji laid the envelope on the couch between them. It was addressed in an angular hand to a Mrs. Betty Ann Johnson at a Maryland Air Force base.

"This," Mrs. Fuji said.

Chita
A Message from García 4

ROSITA AND I had planned to leave right after sunrise, but by the time she got to the last "one more thing," the morning had aged. I was to drive the entire way, as my sister didn't drive in the country, or in the rain, or during the full moon, or when she feels one of her spells coming on. How we indulged her. She made a nest for herself in the passenger seat, with food bags, the water jug, and a vanity case crowding her feet. I drove to and then southeast along the Central Highway that travels the spine of the country. Half the day passed before I turned onto the rough road that led into the Escambray Mountains. All that way we spoke of nothing of consequence, but as the tires chattered over the impotent patches in the road, Rosita finished a long tale about her neighbor's losing attempt to hang onto a large house near the water. I hadn't been listening for quite a while, so when she paused, I realized she had asked a question.

"What?" I asked.

"What did Diego say when you told him?"

How dare she ask me this. I wouldn't have had to say anything if her husband hadn't been too useless for this mission to the east.

"What did Ramón say when you told him?" I countered.

"I haven't said anything to him," Rosita said.

She stared intently out her window. She thought I didn't know about her and Ramón. She would be too weak to keep such a horrible secret from him, and he would be too cowardly to stop her from taking his children. I wished I had her penchant to spill everything. If I had told Diego before, I would still have my boys with me. He's too much of a man to be ruled by skirts, no matter how well-meaning. Oh, for a slack backbone like Rosita's.

"Come on," I said. "I'm not Lola, your worshipping acolyte." Although I had been, once, before I realized that Rosita would always get what I wanted. "I'm as sure of you telling Ramón as I am that this road is full of holes." I jutted my chin to indicate the rising road ahead.

Rosita inhaled and opened her mouth as if to retort, but instead she arrested all movement and stared straight ahead. "What's that?"

I turned my attention back to the road. A man with a donkey cart appeared just far enough ahead to look small. Since he hadn't been there a minute before, I assumed he had climbed onto the crown of the road from the brush that grew high beside it. "Just a poor old man—" In a move too agile for an old man, he swerved the cart to block the road. By this time another man, clothed in a ragged T-shirt and work pants, ran out of the bush and took a stance behind the cart. Even from this range, I could see that both men were armed with rifles.

"Boys!" I started to warn, but the mirror told me there were no children sitting among the crates in the back seat. My God, where were my boys? Rosita whipped a look at me but said nothing.

I slowed to a crawl but kept the car moving toward the blockade. I couldn't yet tell the allegiance of these campesinos. Perhaps they woke each morning and flipped a coin. Soon they would know that we were two women traveling alone, although thankfully, not entirely alone.

"Rosita, the glove compartment."

She opened it and looked at me. Her cheeks were pale but her eyes were steady. At a moment like this, we breathed as one.

"Behind the first-aid kit. Diego's pistol."

She shoved through the papers and tools and retrieved the gun, wrapped in soft white cloth.

Rosita unwrapped it as we approached the men. She checked the barrel, flicked off the safety, and then buried the gun under her purse on the seat between us. She pulled her scarf from her neck and added it to the camouflage. Despite all her girlish ways, Rosita was an expert markswoman. Papi made sure all his girls knew how to shoot. Rosita was the best of all of us. As we closed in enough to see the men's grinning faces, we rolled up the windows. Rosita then pulled an ivory-handled derringer out of her vanity case and slipped it into the crack of the seat. I had to smile, even at that tense moment. Leave it to romantic Rosita, with her Hollywood notions, to carry what we called "the lover's mouthpiece." It wouldn't stop a large animal, and it fired only two shots at a time, but it did excellent close work. I prayed that we wouldn't have to test its prowess.

We rolled to a stop. We had turned off the highway minutes before and were already elevated above its grade. In the rearview mirror, a Jeep whizzed past far behind us. It was too far away to be of any help. Even with the loudest horn a car could have, we couldn't hope to draw attention to our situation. Up ahead, the pitted road rounded a bend and disappeared into the hills. Where we had stopped, it dropped away into a ditch on both sides, and the ground leveled out into a scrub plain. To our right, a railed platform jutted across the ditch and into some thick bushes. They hid a platform from all angles of view except this one. A feed bag hung off one side. Apparently the donkey could be kept quite happy as these bandits, or government officials, or both, waited for their prey. The taller man aimed his semiautomatic at us as he circled the car and peered in all the windows. He lingered over the boxes stacked in the back seat. We had packed carefully for just this kind of situation. We stored some of our most tempting black market wares at the top of each box, ready to be uncovered and offered. If these men weren't too greedy, we could get away with our most valuable possessions.

The tall man reported back to the shorter one. A restless wind ruffled the bushes. Far overhead, buzzards circled. I hoped they weren't waiting for us. At last the short man approached my door. His hair was thick and matted with dirt. He opened his mouth and revealed bare gums where his front teeth should have been. He tapped my window, which I rolled down just enough for words to pass.

"More," the short man said. He turned a cranking motion with his hand.

Rosita leaned into me. Her hair brushed my shoulder.

"Please forgive me," I said. "I don't know you."

"I am the law," he said.

Yes, I thought. Here you are the law. You have the advantage of physical power, but we are Monteros. His companion was a long wisp of a man with a full beard that didn't hide the smoothness of his young face. His hands on the rifle, though calloused, were too small and fine-boned for a man of his height. No wonder he terrorized innocent travelers. The tall one swaggered over to the cart and picked up something I couldn't see. When he turned, he held it against his thigh. The short one stood close to my door. He didn't have formal police training, or else he wouldn't have stepped close like that. I could take him out with a hard swing of my door and a few judicious shots, but we would have to pass back this way to return home. Riling the campesinos along the only road you can travel didn't seem a good idea.

"Is this your car?" the short man asked.

"It's my husband's." No need to go into nuances.

"And where is he?"

"Back home, working a commission from El Líder."

The short man straightened up at the mention of our president. "Your husband works for him?"

"Don't we all?" Rosita said. She nudged Diego's pistol against my back. I knew exactly where it was if I needed it.

"Quit the games," the bearded one said.

He had slithered over to Rosita's side of the car. In a flash, he raised a thin strip of metal and jammed it down into the car door. The lock popped with a click. He swung the door open and blocked our exit. Rosita pressed back against me, her hand buried in the seat crack. I slipped my fingers around the butt of the pistol and prayed.

The bearded one touched the tip of his tool to Rosita's ankle and ran it slowly up her leg until it lifted her skirt. "And your husband, Señora?" He flipped her skirt with a flick of his wrist and exposed more leg than was proper.

"He's keeping the people in shoes." Rosita spoke as if we were sitting in our old social club, sipping drinks, and passing the time. Perhaps the feel of the hideaway gun kept her calm.

The short man joined the bearded one on Rosita's side of the car. They had similar cheekbones and the same pointy nose.

"He should know better than to let you out of his sight," the short man said. I decided he was the older of the two.

"Are you brothers?" I asked.

"What's it to you?" the bearded one said.

"Señor, I'm surprised at you," Rosita said. "We've been traveling all day, hardly seeing a soul, and now when my sister tries to be pleasant, you tempt us to believe the rumors about the rudeness of provincials."

"Believe what you want," the bearded one said. He would get no certificate for diplomacy.

"Of course," Rosita said as if she was in charge. "We have gifts for you and your compadres, and then we must be on our way. We're trying to get to Campo Doblase before dark."

The short man grinned and the bearded one laughed outright. "It's already dark at Campo Doblase."

"What do you mean?" Rosita snapped out of her studied lounge into a stiff formality. "What do you know about it?" I wouldn't trust any answer these two might give. We would be better off not hearing their lies.

The bearded one shook his head and put a foot up on the running board. "You're not going anywhere until we say so." He smelled of cane and hard work.

Rosita pulled her pistol hand free and leaned forward to touch the shoe on the running board. It was of Russian issue. One could tell by the sickly gray of the inferior material, whatever it was. Apparently, it had fallen apart long before, as two pieces of twine bound the sole to the upper but didn't prevent a substantial gap at the toes.

"My God. A man of your stature shouldn't be shod like this." Rosita tapped the shoe again. "Here." She hoisted an arm over the seat back and flicked open a box. The Spanish shoes sat right on top, gleaming brown even in the shadows inside the car. She grabbed them up and sat back with the shoes in her lap.

"These are for you." She tilted them as if to measure their size and leaned forward to inspect our comrade's foot. "They should fit."

Our comrade may have been an intelligent man, but his simple thought process in that moment flowed across his young face. He stared at the shoes, taking in the fancy tool work and the supple leather. They easily would've cost a year's wages for a campesino, even if he had the means to find them himself. He would be the envy of all he knew if he took them. Then his eyes wandered down Rosita's legs and up and over the seat to the parcels stashed there and on to the unknown treasures in the trunk. He broke into the smile of a man who had just surveyed a new kingdom. He could have all of it, he thought. I calculated a shot straight into his heart.

Rosita must have seen what I saw. "Señor, you can take everything from us." She swept her hand to take in the entire contents of the car. "Or you can treat us the way your mother and El Líder taught you to treat defenseless women. With honor. And take just what you need." She picked up the shoes and offered them to the bearded one.

"Don't listen to her," the short man said.

"Shut up."

The short bully pushed closer. "He may be tricked by your easy words, but what about me?"

Rosita plopped the shoes on her lap. Fast as a lizard streaking into hiding, she pulled Diego's pistol out of my grasp. As soon as she twitched, the short man reached across his shoulder for his rifle but was stunned to stillness when she flipped the pistol butt forward and offered it to him. I, too, was shocked. I knew she wanted to prove that we could have met them with fire but had not, but what if the bandits actually took Diego's gun? It wasn't hers nor mine to give away. I'd done enough damage to my husband already.

The short bandit dropped his hand and snapped back his head, mouth open. The bearded one laughed but also pulled his rifle down from his shoulder. "I see these women have a different notion of defenselessness."

"My notion is that one keep's one's gun to oneself." I gave Rosita a light shove but not too hard. The gun was loaded, after all, and the safety off, and the barrel was pointed straight at us. At this range a bullet could pass right through both of us.

The bearded one took the pistol and when shorty lunged for it, he swung it up and out of reach. He grinned. This must have been an old game for those two, but it didn't humor me. I would kill Rosita myself if they kept the pistol.

"Señora, you have daring. I like that in a woman. It was that spirit that won the Revolution." Another man had fallen under Rosita's spell. I dropped my shoulders. "It's that spirit that will keep you safe on your trip over the mountains. But you may need this." He braced the pistol, butt first, against his forearm, as if he was offering a rare bottle of wine in a fine restaurant.

"Hey, that's mine." The short man grabbed at the pistol. The bearded one shoved him back with his elbow.

"He's not as generous as I." That was a good one: him generous in letting us keep our own possessions. Come to think of it, he was more generous than the real Bearded One on that point, but we had no time for national politics. "What else might you have for my brother?"

"If Señor has no need of a handgun." Rosita took the pistol and passed it back over her shoulder to me. I slipped the safety on, since the element of surprise, for this gun at least, had perished. I laid it on her purse. She reached over the seat again and came back with a pair of cowboy boots. They, too, were of fine Spanish leather, but they had the soft dullness and creases that come from much use. They were clean, though, and worth more than the shoes because of a certain feature.

Shorty's mouth quirked. He was clearly pleased by the offer but needed to be persuaded. "Old boots, Señora?"

"Ah, but not just any boots." Rosita beckoned him closer. The bearded one crowded beside him. She traced the signature of John Wayne that was stitched along the curved seam at the top of the tongue and told them what it said.

"Brother," the bearded one said. "You've got the better deal." He glanced again at the boxes and bags on the back seat.

Rosita rummaged in a food bag at her feet and unearthed two oranges and a bottle of rum. "For your compradres."

The bearded one tucked the shoes under his arm and accepted the latest gifts with a grin. Their friends may get a sip of rum, but they wouldn't see the oranges. I was sure of it.

"Señor, the time," I said.

"Yes, I guess that's all for now." Cubans are a reasonable people, even the corrupt ones. "Try to make it out of the mountains before nightfall. And watch out for bandits."

"Yeah, watch out," Shorty said and sniggered.

He saluted us and went over to the cart. He dumped the boots into it and turned the donkey back toward the highway. The road opened before us. The bearded one closed the car door gently, as if saying goodbye to his favorite girl. Why not? He had gotten something better than he had hoped for, and we still had to pass his way again. I couldn't think of that right then. We had to get to Tomasito. I put the car into gear and drove away.

Rosita laid back and covered her eyes with a trembling hand. I wouldn't feel safe until we were out of firing range. I hoped Rosita's charm would last that long. As we bounced up the road, I flicked a look to the rearview mirror. The cart and men were still in the road. I hit an especially vicious pothole. Rosita's hand popped off her face, and clinking and clunking came from the back seat. She gave me a look but said nothing. Right before the bend in the road, I glanced in the mirror again. The men and donkey cart were once again hidden from sight.

"They're gone," I said.

"Good."

"What if they had taken Diego's gun? And used it?" Now that the immediate danger was past, I could fret. I hung on tight to the churning wheel.

"They had to see the command we have. You could see the bearded one was hoping for an easy victory. I had to discourage that hope. He had to think that I might pull a knife on him if he took his pleasure." Rosita crossed her arms. I let the point go. We had many hours in front of us, and I had to drive all the way.

Chita
A Message from García 5

LATE IN THE afternoon, we descended the rutted road that snaked over the Escambray Mountains and into the southern foothills. We had passed some trucks and a cheerful man in bright red pants on a tractor, far from any fields, but otherwise the route had been empty of traffic. My head hurt and my hands tingled from the constant vibrations of the washboard roads. Hot winds blew past us and rippled through the fields of tobacco and cane stretched across the plain below us. In the distance, a colonial mansion, a remnant of plantation days, stood among a group of outbuildings on top of a low hill. From here, the area seemed more prosperous and well-cared for than we had dared to hope for our Tomasito. I could only pray that he was alive somewhere down there.

I pulled the DeSoto over at a small turn out and stopped. My sister had slept through the many kilometers of rough terrain. How, I don't know. She slumped with her head back and knees sprawled open. Drool trickled out of the side of her mouth. If only her admirers could see her now, I thought, but then guilt wrapped my arms across my chest. I must have been tired, because I imagined her life empty of her three girls. She had not once sighed or complained since their departure. Instead of poking her awake, as I would normally, I cupped her mouth and wiped the saliva away with my thumb. She nuzzled my hand before rolling open her eyes.

"Wake up, little dove."

Rosita stretched and arched her back before sitting up, knees together, to look around. "Water?"

She retrieved the jug and cup from the floor and handed them to me. I poured a cup for us to share while she rummaged in her pocketbook.

"Don't put on lipstick before we drink," I said. It would be just like her to leave bright pink lip prints, so hard to clean, on the plastic cup. My sympathy vanished in the heat and the pressure behind my eyes.

"I won't," she said, although she did take out her compact and fuss with her headband. I swallowed a healthy gulp and gave the cup back to her. She dove into her bag again. "I was looking for this." She held up a pack of Wrigley's Spearmint gum, its white wrapping battered and tinged gray by a crowded life in the bottom of her bag.

"From Key Biscayne?" I was fascinated that she could hoard such a treat for over a year.

"Miami Beach." She whipped off the red string and popped off the top of the pack. As we had since we were girls, I pulled a stick by its waxed tin wrapper and left the white jacket with its fellows in the pack. Rosita did the same.

"Let's stretch." She got out, leaving the door wide open. She leaned against the car and looked out over the valley. Clouds crept over the mountains, portending an early evening storm. The fields nearest to us lay in the broad shadow of the mountains and the encroaching clouds, but the red-tiled roofs and white walls of the distant mansion glowed in the late afternoon sun. I scooted across the seat and through the open door to stand beside my sister. It was my turn to stretch.

I popped the stick of gum into my mouth. Instead of folding with freshness, the stick broke but quickly became pliable as I worked my jaws. Rosita puffed her cheeks to blow a bubble. We both knew it was impossible with Wrigley's, even when fresh. When her noisy exhale made no bubble, her laughter trilled into the sodden air. It was a pure sound that I hadn't heard since the children had left.

A million questions ran through my mind, but before I could voice one, Rosita said, "Campo Doblase, do you think?" She spoke with a curt nod toward the valley.

"It must be."

She pushed off the car and returned to the passenger seat. "We must be sure." She pulled out her lipstick, then wrenched the rearview mirror around to inspect her face.

"Rosita!"

"What?" She made an O with her mouth and applied bright pink to it.

"Don't do that again. The mirror is never the same."

"You're just tired," she said. "I'll drive."

She threw the lipstick and gum back into her purse and dropped it on the floor in front of her. After sliding over to the steering wheel, she turned the key. Even after kilometers of punishment, the DeSoto's engine roared to life.

"Come on," she said.

I bent down to get a good look at her. "Since when do you drive in the country?"

"I'm refreshed, you're tired. We're almost there. It's as simple as that." She twisted the mirror back to face the driver's seat, took off her headband, and tossed it on the seat beside her. "Come on, let's go."

I was tired and my head still throbbed. "You're in charge now?" Nevertheless, I climbed in the car and closed the door. I never could fit into Rosita's space. I rearranged the bags and jugs and food sacks to make space for my feet.

"A Montero girl does what she must." She shifted into gear.

I didn't like the way she yanked the gear shift. "Careful. You have to . . ."

"I know what I have to do." Her mouth worked. I thought she would try another bubble, but instead she shot the gum out the open window.

"Rosita! You spit out your gum."

She looked out the window with a slight frown. "The flavor was gone."

She wasn't aware of her misdeed. I rooted around my own mouth with my tongue. True, the stale gum didn't have much flavor after the first few chews. That's no excuse.

"Gum's essential for emergency roadside repairs," I said. "What if a stone kicks up and drills a hole in the gas tank? We may need the entire pack to fix that. Yes?" I took out my gum and groped around the seat for the waxed foil wrapper. I held both up. "This is what you do." I carefully covered the gum and put it in the glove compartment.

"You didn't even know I had it."

"But now I do."

Rosita fell forward, her forehead banging on the steering wheel. She slammed her hand on the horn for one long blast that pulsed in my temples and startled a flock of finches out of the bushes below us. Such drama.

"Mary, Mother of God, please keep me from strangling this woman before we see our Tomasito again." She was silent a moment before she sat up again. The finches resettled and the wind blew stronger.

"I don't know what you're going on about."

She looked at me with her patient face, the one she reserved for a slurring husband who wants to drive home after having too much fun at a party. I hate it, and I hate it more when she uses it on me.

"Querida, please close your eyes," she said. "We'll be there in no time."

I would have given her a verbal backhand, but the wind brought no reprieve from the steamy heat and my vision blurred with pain. I took some aspirin with water from the jug and settled back in my seat. Maybe I was exhausted. A few minutes of quiet would do me good. After all, we must stick together and be strong for Tomasito's sake.

I HAD CLOSED my eyes for just a moment, or so I thought, but when I opened them, the mountains had receded to the horizon, and the sky had filled with racing clouds. We were idling in a dirt clearing at the center of a small cluster of bohios. The main plantation house we'd seen earlier was hidden from sight, but perhaps we had come to the small settlement the letter had referred to. Dust swirled in the freshening wind. Although space opened in the center of the cluster, a short end of every rectangular, thatch-roofed bohio faced the dirt road. Neighbors, yes, but each also looked outward in the hopes of witnessing something of the passing world.

"Where are we?" I asked as I peered at the tidy huts through the growing dusk.

"Here," Rosita said. She turned off the ignition.

Woman Waving to the Future 2

"COME HELP ME," Sonny Saunders whispered in the late night darkness.

Lucy turned her head on the pillow into a bouquet of Dial soap and Old Spice. The few times her husband had needed to leave like this before, he'd always awakened her as soon as he'd started to get ready. He liked the company, him in the shower and her making coffee and heating leftovers in the kitchen. Something was different this night. The weight of him sitting on her side of the bed pitched her toward him. In the spill-over glow of the bathroom light, she could see the perfect crease of his midnight-blue pants and the sheen of his spotless black shoes.

"Come on," he said. His touch glanced her shoulder before he stood and walked toward the door.

"What?"

"I have to go in," was all he said before leaving the room.

Lucy got up and slipped into the fuzz of her chenille robe. Two years before, she and Sonny had been proud to announce to their families his assignment to a base right outside of Washington. It was a plum Air Force post. President Kennedy had just moved into the White House, and Jackie was showing America how to dress and entertain. Lucy wrote letters to her friends, boasting of day trips to monuments and flying kites on the Mall. With the new threat, though, being posted to these ex-tobacco fields near DC had lost their charm, and she would've welcomed the arid safety of the old assignment in California.

She shuffled into the kitchen as she looped the pink belt of her robe and pulled it tight. Sonny had taken out the can of coffee and was holding the basket from the percolator. She took them from him and filled the pot with water. He went to the living room and came back with a pack of cigarettes and a brass ash tray he had gotten in Tokyo. Neither of them spoke. She opened the fridge and took out the makings for ham sandwiches while he tapped out two cigarettes and lit both.

Everyone had noticed the extra flights that moved through their base and had felt the unspoken frenzy. The wives had made their own escape plans. They were ready, but was it time already? Lucy wanted Sonny to say something but couldn't pause in her duties to draw it out of him. She spread Miracle Whip on four slices of bread and opened the mustard jar.

"Is this it? The Big One?" she asked.

"No, of course not. I told you already about the exercises coming up. I'm sure I'll be back for dinner tomorrow. Or the next day. There'll still be plenty of ham, right?" Lucy wondered how routine exercises could pull him out of bed in the middle of the night, but she didn't ask. Sonny tried to give her a reassuring smile, but they knew each other too well, and he didn't get it right until she gave him her own false face. He moved closer to her as her hands stayed busy with the sandwiches. He held out a cigarette and she took a drag.

She didn't even smoke, really, and had never touched a cigarette before she met Sonny. Her life had changed so much.

He poured the coffee and took a sip. "You going to be all right?"

"Don't worry about us."

He nodded that tight little shake of his that meant there was more to say but he wasn't going to say it. She took out his lunch box as he launched into his final preparations. What she meant was, don't worry about me. With the temperament of an artist, Lucy felt unqualified to be a top-notch military wife, but Sonny loved her and never gave up on her. Not when they had scrambled eggs for dinner or hot dogs for breakfast. And not that time after Erica was born eight years prior, when they had just moved, and Lucy had stopped talking.

He had greeted her silence as a joke at first. Then he yelled, just once, and upset the baby. None of that mattered to Lucy. She just sat in his recliner. Though they were newly posted to the West Coast and didn't know any folks yet, some wife must've recognized the desperation of a man looking for emergency care for a toddler and a newborn. Lucy didn't know where he took the babies that day, but at some point the air pressure changed and the small noises of other inhabitants ceased. Finally she had no burden of taking care. After a while, Sonny returned and sat on the ottoman in front of her.

"Talk to me," he said.

She didn't bother to look at him.

"I'm listening now. You can say whatever you want."

She wasn't even there.

He left the room and someone with her eyes watched a rectangle of sunlight move across the floor.

When Lucy noticed her husband again, the ottoman bore a tray of pastel sticks and a large tablet of drawing paper that she had bought early in the pregnancy but had never used. He set a cup of tea on the side table. After standing over her a moment, he knelt and picked up the red pastel stick. She returned her attention to the light that crawled across the beige carpet.

He picked up her hand and put the pastel on her palm. "It'd be nice to have a picture. Maybe you could draw the house across the road." When she didn't reply, he stood and left. She reached for the cooled tea some time later and realized that she still cradled the bright red stick in her hand.

Sonny was a good man, but his request felt like one more order: draw a house. The glare of the California sun bounced off the flat-top duplex across the street, the twin of her own and the duplicate of quarters that lined streets with unrelenting regularity on military bases all over the world. You can let their monotony overwhelm you into neglect, but when Lucy glanced across the street, she noticed that the wife had recently planted asters in a handmade window box. It was the wife's handiwork because the husband didn't do anything outside; he didn't even mow the lawn. The flowers stood out against the pale green aluminum siding. Red asters, a standard cheap decoration. Of course they weren't the pure red of the pastel. There was blue and orange and maybe a little brown to muddy it. By the end of the thought Lucy had started to sketch.

She never told anyone about that day, so the other wife across the way never knew how her simple flowers had saved a marriage. Sarah was her name. Lucy gave her the drawing when she finished it. Her neighbor giggled and protested, but her delight was evident. She invited Lucy over for coffee with a bunch of other wives the following week. She had mounted the drawing in a used gold frame that made it look substantial, even to Lucy. They all admired what Sarah called her house portrait. One woman asked if Lucy could do a picture of her living room with a Japanese chest and a red wedding kimono on the wall. Of course she could. Other women wanted to place orders also. Sarah stepped in and said, "Lucy has two little ones to take care of. We all know about stretching an Air Force paycheck."

"I'll pay," the woman with the kimono said. "It can't be much, but I'll pay. And I'll babysit while she's doing it."

Right there, a new business was born. Sonny had his wife back, and they had extra cash to boot. Her mom had said that her artistic life would die if she married a military man. It almost had, but Sonny wouldn't let it. When little Erica joined her brother full-time at school, Lucy was able to take more serious commissions and work in oil. She always obliged the military wives, though, in whatever medium they desired. Her art documented their efforts to beautify their uncertain stays in the mobile world of the military.

Now with Sonny about to go in after midnight, Lucy tidied up, carrying a stack of *Ebony* magazines into the unlit living room and dumping them on her work table. As she went back to the brightness of the kitchen, she passed him frozen in the hallway between the children's rooms. She left him to his moment, continuing on to sit at the kitchen table. Soon he joined her for one last shared cigarette.

"I've been thinking," he said. "Since I'm going to be extra busy on base the next few days, maybe you want to take the kids to see your mother."

Lucy knew more than her husband thought she did. Sure, she could've said, I can be on the road in twenty minutes, but she didn't. She answered the way she thought he expected. "What are you talking crazy, Sonny-boy? The kids can't miss school."

"Yeah, I guess you're right." He held up the cigarette again. Coffee drunk, sandwiches made, clothes packed into a flight bag, too many butts in the ash tray for too short a time to say goodbye. A soft knock sounded from the back door.

"Must be Ray," Sonny said. They both stood. He pecked her goodbye, as always, then squeezed her until it hurt. "Stay by the phone."

"Why?"

He pressed his forehead against hers and walked the pads of his fingers down her face, as if for the first time. She inhaled his coffee breath and the stink of cigarettes. The sharpness of his after-shave cut through it all.

"Just stay by the phone."

He picked up his gear and reached for the door. A list of names tacked to the message board halted him.

"New car pool?" he asked.

The key to deception is honesty. "Some of the mothers don't drive yet. Thought I'd help out."

"Good," he said. "Glad I'm not taking the car." He opened the door and left without another backward glance.

Lucy wandered into the living room. There she turned on lights and sought out a distraction. She turned on the jumbo goose-neck lamp on her work table and flipped open the box of pastels. The red was missing. She wondered if Erica had gotten into the box again, because she liked to use what she called Mommy's crayons. None of the mothers of her friends had their own colors. Lucy scanned the room and spied the missing pastel. Moving closer, she discovered the phone bill's envelope underneath it, covered in big, red block letters. "LOVE YOU, S." she read. He hadn't said those words out loud before he left. She folded the rough paper into the pocket of her robe and crept back to her worktable.

Lucy woke again five hours and seventeen minutes after Sonny had left in the middle of the night. She had fallen asleep at her worktable and now found her latest drawing pushed to one side. The living room was lucent in the dawn as she looked out the front window. The early morning street was empty but for a few yellow leaves gliding through the crisp air. Her mind lit on the emergency evacuation plan that was disguised as a car pool schedule. The camouflage was brilliant—Sonny had seen nothing unusual about the roster of mothers, but then, he had other lists on his mind.

She opened the door onto the bright promise of her tree-lined street to retrieve their two glass bottles of milk. She carried them into the kitchen. Sonny's cup sat in the drain alone and the percolator still held the dregs of the coffee she had made the previous night. She emptied the overflowing ashtray. The aluminum canisters with copper tops needed to be wiped down and filled, but she didn't have time for that yet. She took out two peanut butter and jelly sandwiches wrapped in wax paper from the fridge and put in the milk. She checked the ketchup bottle and noted that she would need more for that evening's meatloaf. Housework sometimes made her want to hurt someone, but now she appreciated her mundane tasks.

Then it was her turn to check 31L. She wouldn't have to wait like a good military wife for a phone call or a telegram. That day she was the messenger. She would gather the children with Betty Ann and run, flat out, if it came to that. She checked the kids one more time. If all went well, they wouldn't miss her for the few moments she would be away. She donned a red sweater as she walked into the living room. She reached for her pocketbook but drew back. *Stay near the phone,* Sonny had said. The phone's mute presence and the quiet comfort of the armchair invited her to stay, to obey. The drive to the end of Cedar Street would take two minutes, but so much can happen in no time at all. What if Sonny called, the phone ringing and ringing, her sleepy-eyed son bewildered by its unanswered insistence? Betty Ann could take a risk like that. She could cover the assignment. Lucy knew her number by heart.

No.

Lucy reached past the phone and picked up her pocketbook. She went out to the carport and got in the Rambler station wagon. Even though the day would warm up, the cool night had left a chill inside the car. As she settled into the driver's seat, her breathing slowed and her shoulders dropped. She was ready for this, whatever it was. Her mission took her along the fence at the end of 31L. Three choppers huddled as if for warmth. A truck sped away from them, but the blades remained still. The threat still existed but it hadn't come to blows. Not yet, anyway.

As she looped back onto her street and rounded the bend at the far end, Betty Ann's porch light went on, then Gladys' and Debbie's. Lucy stuck her arm straight up out the window and waved broad sweeps. The lights went off, one by one. She imagined a snapshot of her mission, her brown hand sweeping above the white top of the Rambler. She decided to sketch out a painting of it after the kids left for school. The title of the piece would be "Woman Waving to the Future."

After returning home and parking, she went inside to the hall. "Tony! Erica! Time to get up."

She knocked on her daughter's door and waited until she passed, trailing her blue blanket. It wasn't a security blanket—she was too old for that—but she used it as a pillow because, she said, a regular pillow got too hot. The blanket slipped to the floor but she didn't seem to notice. This girl was not a morning person.

Lucy went to the blue heap and pointed down at it. "Hey. Come pick this up."

Erica turned at the bathroom door and gave her a look of pure annoyance. "Mommy, can't you pick it up? You're right there."

Lucy didn't move. Her daughter stomped over and swiped the blanket away with her foot. She hobbled down the hall, sweeping the blanket.

"I said pick it up."

"Okay." At the entrance to the living room, Erica kicked her foot and sent the blanket sailing into the air. "It's up."

Chita
A Message from García 6

ROSITA AND I waited in the car to be approached, as one does when one stops at a dwelling in the countryside. No one seemed to be out and about in the hazy gloom. An old mutt curled in front of the closest bohio, his muzzle bristled with gray. It took him long seconds to struggle to his feet. He howled a sound that died away in his throat, then he circled twice around himself. He plunked down in the same spot, as if he had done his duty and wouldn't trouble himself to do more. While we waited, we brushed the dust from our hair and touched up our lipstick. Rosita replaced the scarf around her neck with a fresh one.

Presently, a line of women materialized at the far end of the clearing. At the same time, a short old man with gigantic ears and black-rimmed glasses emerged from the nearest hut carrying a kerosene lamp. He stepped over the dog, which didn't bother to raise its head. Just then, a gang of children exploded into the clearing, scattering squawking chickens. An elderly woman peeked out from the old man's hut at the commotion but quickly withdrew.

"Stop!" a woman shouted at the children, her arms akimbo. They ignored her, much like children anywhere would. They bunched around the man.

His admiring gaze swept from the DeSoto's tail fins to the sleek lady on the hood before he greeted us. He stretched to set the lantern on the car as Rosita rolled down her window. The lantern hovered just inches from the hood.

"May I?" he asked.

"Of course," Rosita said. She would. It wasn't her lemon-yellow paint job that might blister under a poorly made lantern. The wick threw black smoke into the leaden air.

The old man stepped back, and the children moved with him as if he was the body of a many-legged beetle. "I am Pedro Ramírez, at your service. I am known as Paco."

The mothers drifted back into their bohios. They would hear all from Paco's old wife, who would pull every single detail from him with practiced ease. I was sure of it. Rosita leaned her forearms on the car door and tilted her head at a pretty angle. She led with her charm from a window sill, as she had thousands of times before at home, at friends' houses, and in cars.

"I'm sorry to trouble you, Compadre Paco."

Paco moved closer with the clump of children following. He was even older than I first thought. "It's no trouble to assist two beautiful ladies in a magnificent automobile. To what do we owe such an honor at this late hour?" Apparently he wasn't too old to flirt and probe with the skill of an expert.

"My name is Rosita, and this is my sister, Chita." How causal she was way out here in the bush. Yet I sensed a strategy in her use of first names. The car already shouted our status by its very presence. No need to say more with last names. For once Rosita was thinking like I would. "We have business at Campo Doblase."

"I see." The old man rubbed a hand across his ribs. "It's a pity you've arrived so late in the day." The kids inched closer and eyed the crates in the back seat. I worried the unlocked door would invite pilfering hands, but it was too late to reach back and plunge down the locking button without insulting our host.

"Will they not receive us at this hour?" Rosita asked. I hoped she wouldn't expose our ignorance of the operations of the camp.

Paco slowly sunk into a crouch and peered into the car. "Are you seeking a guest worker there?"

What did that mean? An inmate? A rebel in need of rehabilitation? A patriot lending a much needed hand to the provinces? I knuckled Rosita in the back, telling her to be careful.

"Compadre Paco, are we not all workers for the people?" She could be clever when she wanted to be.

Paco nodded. "I myself do some modest work at Doblase. Perhaps I can be of some help, if I knew something of the nature of your business."

Careful. We knew nothing more of this place or its intentions than when we had started over the mountains. I knuckled Rosita again. She rolled her shoulder back at me but didn't turn around.

"Actually, we have a letter saying to ask for an escort in a nearby village," Rosita said. "David Montes. Does he live here?"

Paco's smile faded. He straightened as much as he could and stepped back. He almost knocked over a girl that lurked behind him. "When did you receive this letter?"

I didn't like his darkening tone and didn't understand why he thought our letter was his business. "Just recently, but the post is slow. It was mailed a while ago. Is Señor Montes still available?"

"Is something the matter?" Rosita asked.

"No, Señora." Paco swatted at a skinny little boy who had dared to touch the car. The children giggled. The old man raised his nose to the sky like a dog sniffing a passing scent. "The rains will come soon and the road to Doblase will be difficult in the dark. Besides, the top officials are off duty now, and you might have troubles with some evening underling who might seize a chance to act purely on his own authority."

I shifted closer to my sister, the better to see and to judge. "We are familiar with the ways of underlings. We mustn't delay our journey further."

Paco nodded. "I understand the pressure to continue when you're so close. But really, it's best if you stop here for the night. I would hate to see this beauty stuck in the mud. Our home is humble, but we would be honored to share its roof with you." Lightning lit the sky in the direction of the colonial buildings we had seen. At least I thought it was in that direction. It was clear that there would be no getting there in the dark without a guide.

Rosita opened the door and got out. Paco and the children scuttled back. Now what was she doing? Her hands were free, although I couldn't tell if her lover's mouthpiece lurked in the pocket of her skirt. I had no choice but to follow her out. As I stood, I felt my distance from the pistol behind me in the glove compartment.

"If Señor Montes is not available, might someone else guide us?" Rosita asked.

Just then headlights brightened the small clearing. All faces turned toward the incoming vehicle. I squinted as my head throbbed with the sudden light. A Ford step-side truck, a '51 or '52, raced up to a halt behind our car. Its body was a faded red, but the engine ticked like a champion. I myself couldn't have gained as pure a sound without specialty parts. The lights and engine died, and a young man jumped out. He had Paco's proud shoulders and gigantic ears. Two midsize mutts bounded out of the truck after him. They wagged and barked their arrival.

Two of the boys broke away and ran over to the newcomer. The bigger one shouted, "Look Papa. A very pretty car. And beautiful ladies, as well."

Not too young to flirt, so much like my own. I wrapped myself in my arms and fatigue weighed on my chest. It would be good to see Tomasito.

"My youngest grandson, Chucho." Paco swept his hand as if introducing a famous son balladeer.

Chucho stepped into the lantern's circle of light. The old dog wandered over, sniffed the other two mutts, and wagged his whole ancient back half. Chucho's grin and deep bow to me made up for the big ears and a snaggle tooth. One couldn't help but notice the sinuous muscles of his arms and chest that were poorly covered by a T-shirt full of holes. He seemed a man who knew how to use his assets, not to mention tune an engine, maybe. He turned to

Rosita and bowed even deeper while holding her gaze. His eyes didn't stray as he straightened. Rosita would call this Chucho handsome, as she did any man who worshipped her so quickly. In fact, I bet she already had a fond memory of the tall, bearded gunman who had harassed us.

"The sisters . . ." Paco said.

"Rosita and Chita." Rosita pointed to herself and me in turn. I nodded.

"What brings you and this gorgeous machine to our corner of paradise?" Chucho asked.

"They're going to Doblase. They stopped for an escort," Paco said.

"Whoever escorts you is a lucky man." Chucho grinned, his snaggle tooth gleaming.

"David Montes," Paco said.

Chucho's lip hooded his tooth and his whole body sobered. Again, an unhappy reaction to this escort's name. Did Rosita notice? A chill born deep inside me raised goose bumps on my arms. Chucho dropped a casual hand on his small son's shoulder. The other children now lounged against the car, two with their noses pressed against the back window. None had yet tried the door handle, but I slipped down the side of the car to guard against possible attempts.

"Do you know David Montes?" Rosita asked.

Chucho raised his chin and snuffled like a bird dog, the same way his grandfather had. The fresh smell of rain infused the air. "The roads will flood with this rain. You don't want to get stuck tonight. The runoff will disappear by morning. Abuelo, shall we offer these two beautiful ladies, as Paquito so rightly called them, our humble hospitality for the night?"

I couldn't help but glance at the cluster of dwellings in dismay. True, from what I could see in the failing light, the simple huts were well cared for and the open areas free of trash and excrement, but still.

Paco must have read my mind. "This is no three-star hotel, but we're proud to offer safe haven for weary travelers."

"Do you know anything about this Señor Montes?" Rosita asked again. We could be here all night sparring politely about two possibly related subjects.

Just as I was about to demand an answer to Rosita's question, Chucho's oldest tugged at his hand. "Papa, can the pretty ladies stay with us? Please, Papa?"

"I would like nothing better. But all the noisy breathing of you kids will keep them awake all night."

"Please, Papa. We'll breathe quietly. We promise."

Chucho glanced at his grandfather, who must've given him a signal that was invisible in the twilight. He shook his head, but his wayward tooth poked out of his small smile. "No. They'll stay with Abuelo."

"But Abuelo snores." The boy giggled.

Chucho pulled him into a playful hug and rubbed his head. "Hush now and take your brother in to supper."

"Please, Papa, can we . . ."

"No. Go on now, hurry."

A scene so familiar I almost promised them a treat if the ate all their supper. I wondered if Rosita felt the same.

"How about some gum before you go?" she said.

"Yes, yes!" The children crowded around Rosita as she ducked into the car to get her purse. I poked her—giving away valuable repair supplies—but she ignored me.

However, Paco said, "Señora, you must keep your gum. You may need it for your car, as the roads are rough."

She laughed. "What's with the gum and the cars? Are you a mechanic too?"

Paco squared back his shoulders. "I know a thing or two about cars."

Rosita opened her purse and the kids jumped up and down with a burst of cheers.

"Hush, children," Chucho said. He went over to the old man and clapped him on the shoulder. "Abuelo is being modest. He drove the first automobiles ever to enter the province and raced in Havana in his younger days."

"Really?" I said. "What name did you race under?"

"Pepi Ramírez," Paco said.

"He once drove a Bugatti owned by an American playboy."

"Of course," I said. "I know of your career. My husband is of the La Luz family. He is called El Mechanico de la Playa."

"What a lucky woman you are." Chucho flicked his eyes and beamed a knowing smile.

The Beach Mechanic had other, less savory connotations, but Diego inherited the nickname from his father, so what was I to do? I lifted a shoulder in a lazy shrug.

"Do you machine your own parts?" I asked.

"Yes, up at Doblase."

"Perhaps you will show me the shop if we have time before we leave?"

"Me too." Rosita's voice was high and girlish. Of course. She wouldn't want Chucho's attention to stray.

He clicked his heels and bowed as if he were wearing the finest linen. "My deepest pleasure," he said to her. Of course.

"Gum." His youngest reminded us of the real matter at hand.

"Abuelo said no gum for you," Rosita said. The children protested as she snapped her purse shut.

I felt bad for them. "We cannot disobey Abuelo, but . . ." I ducked into the car and pulled out a box tied with a string. The children's anticipation rippled in the saturated air. Drops would condense right out of the air any minute. I held up the box. "How about chocolate?"

"Yes! Yes! Please!" the children yelled.

One might have thought me even more foolish to give away precious chocolate, but I didn't care. For the first time in days I was a happy mother again, if only for a moment.

"Just one, then off with you. All of you," Chucho said.

I opened the box and held it out as the children jostled each other. Chucho's youngest was the last to choose a candy. He hugged me, and I let him, even though his arms were grimy and his face was caked with dirt. I held him close even after the other kids had run off and he tugged to go.

After releasing him, I laid a hand on Rosita's arm and looked her in the eye. "Let's press on. Alone, if we must."

She shot a glance at Chucho. All these looks passed more or less with head movements, since few nuances could be deciphered in the dusk. Still, he answered her.

"Please, Señora. Your stay here will not go unrewarded."

A big, fat raindrop plopped on my forehead.

I looked around for Paco, but he must have slipped off to warn the old woman about her visitors. The next moment rain fell in curtains, straight down, and quickly soaked us all. Without another word, we scrambled to pull our suitcases out of the car and allowed Chucho to carry them all to his grandfather's hut. Rosita scurried after Chucho, but I draped a jacket over my head while I made sure that every window of the car was closed tight and each door was locked. I carried the box of chocolates with me as an offering to our hosts. Anything more practical would be an insult to their hospitality.

Woman Waving to the Future 3

AFTER THE CHILDREN hustled off to catch the bus, Lucy returned to the kitchen to tidy up. The phone rang, and she immediately pictured Sonny, ignoring his own safety to talk with her one last time. Her pulse quickened, but she was not surprised to hear Betty Ann's voice when she plucked the receiver from its base on the kitchen wall.

"Lucy, hon?" Her friend sounded puzzled. "Something strange is going on."

Leave it to Betty Ann to state the obvious. Lucy watched through the kitchen window while a blue jay swooped across her back yard and landed on her clothesline. The cord swayed back and forth under its weight. Two squirrels chased up the trunk of the young maple at the back of the yard. Local life continued, heedless of any national crisis. "We knew that when we set up our operations. Didn't Ray lie about routine exercises also?"

"Not that. Something about Lonnie. I'm scared."

Oh Lord. Didn't they have enough to worry about with the possible end of the world? Lucy promised to come right over as soon as she finished the breakfast dishes. She bustled around the kitchen and then dragged on her sweater and gathered up her pocketbook. She had the front door open and her car keys dangling from her hand before she remembered the idea of "Woman Waving to the Future." Whatever news Betty Ann received might well knock the idea right out of her head, so even though she was rushing, she left the door ajar and went back in to find a scrap of paper. She scooped up the red pastel to scrawl the title and a bare bones sketch of her imagined action self-portrait. That would have to hold her until she could get back to it, who knew when.

Betty Ann lived just up the street, but since Ray had left her with the old, somewhat unreliable Pontiac, Lucy took her own car in case they needed wheels to deal with this latest development. The Johnsons lived on the same side of the street but in the B duplex, so their layout was the same, only reversed left to right. Betty Ann had slices of a poppy seed coffee cake and a full pot ready when she arrived. Her friend looked calm but more subdued than usual. A thick, ecru business envelope with her address typed out was propped against the sugar bowl on the kitchen table. Clearly it was not from the military— the paper was way too good. It looked like the kind of stationery that you might use to invite a business associate to lunch at the Ritz. The mystery of its connection to Betty Ann's son weighed, but neither remarked on it until their plates and cups were full.

"Okay, spill it," Lucy said. No need for preliminaries.

"This envelope arrived in yesterday's mail. I set it aside, but with all of the commotion getting Ray ready and everything, I forgot it until after he left." She tipped out its contents: two pieces of paper that matched the envelope, and two pieces of plain notebook paper covered in handwritten Japanese characters. The letter was in standard form and covered both pages of the fine stationery; if it was an invitation to the Ritz, it was a long one. Betty Ann pushed the letter over. "Read it."

201123 La Bonita Drive
San Diego, California
September 30, 1962

Dear Mrs. Johnson,

I hope this letter finds you well. I had the great fortune to meet your son, Private Lonnie Johnson, while on diplomatic duty on the U.S.S. Princeton when it was patrolling the Bikini atolls. He is a lovely young man who reflects well on his upbringing. You must be very proud of him.

When Private Johnson learned that I am a translator and can read and write Japanese, he asked me to review the enclosed letter that a fellow sailor wrote for him to send to his mother. I understand that you are studying Japanese in anticipation of living in Okinawa when your husband is stationed there.

I applaud your ambition! Not many Americans would undertake the study of a language that is so much unlike their own. Private Johnson was very proud of your determination to learn as much as you can about another culture. The enclosed letter may be somewhat advanced for a beginner, but I think you will find much value in it. I assume that you may seek aide in understanding what is written. In looking for such assistance, I only ask that you seek someone that you trust to give you an accurate reading, as nuances can easily be lost in translation. Just

imagine that the precious lives of all of the sailors on
the U.S.S. Princeton depend on an accurate rendition, for
instance, and you will surely do the right thing.

I wish you the best of luck in your endeavors. May your
diligence be rewarded.

Very truly yours,
Yūko Fuji (Mrs.)

P.S. Any commanding officer of a U.S. military base
would be interested in your success.
Y.F.

The handwritten signature was in both English and Japanese.

"Is this a joke?" Lucy said.

Betty Ann shrugged. "And what is this bizarre reference to a base
commander?" Neither of them had touched their coffee.

Betty Ann looked miserable. It was definitely time to worry if her son was
involved in these shenanigans. "The only thing I can think of is the Hepplewhite
boy. The obit said something about an accident in the line of duty in the Pacific.
Kind of vague, but it did mention that his marine troop had also been stationed
on the *Princeton*."

"Oh sweet Jesus." Lucy reared back from the papers as if they were on fire
before taking into account the turmoil her friend was feeling. She scooted in
close to the table and considered Betty Ann.

"What if Lonnie's next?" Tears slipped down Betty Ann's face, which she
swiped away with her fingers. She was tough, but the unknown could kill you.

The knock on the door can come for anyone. Even Mrs. Hepplewhite, as
they recently found out. Of course they had sent condolence notes. As difficult
as Mrs. Hepplewhite had been to deal with, she was still a mother who had
lost a son. Each wife knew she may be called to stand in the shoes next to the
grieving wife or mother or daughter.

"We need to get this translated, quick-quick," Lucy said.

"How? How in hell did he come up with Japanese?"

Lucy tried not to smile, despite the seriousness of the situation. "He was
always the creative one, you said." She took a healthy bite of her coffee cake
and chewed with a finger over her mouth. "Wait a minute." She swallowed and
snapped her fingers. "How about that librarian?"

"What librarian? Girl, I haven't been back to the library since the Grayson
House."

"The one that works in the children's corner and wrote the book about a unicorn. I bought one for Erica. She loves it. She's kind of grown out of it, but she reads it to the littler kids when they play school."

"What about a unicorn suggests she knows Japanese?"

"Not that. Don't be silly. She has a small, stone Buddha statue on her desk in the children's section. Erica asked her about what she called the smiling man doll and the librarian replied that she got it growing up in Japan. It reminded her of home."

"I don't know. We can't trust just anyone."

"She's not just anyone. Her name is Beth Willom. I tell you, this woman has a good heart. You should see how the kids flock to her. God love her, I could never do that all day. Anyway, we both have good radar. Let's go sound her out. You want to know ASAP, right?"

Betty Ann pushed away her plate, her slice of cake untouched. The scent of fresh bread lingered in the air, and two loaves cooled on the counter. She got up to wipe and straighten her already spotless and neat-as-a-pin counter. "All right. We have to solve this thing. Let's go before I change my mind." She refolded the papers and slipped them back into the envelope. She tucked it into her purse, and they headed out the door.

Lucy steered her over to the far corner of the main room, where half-height wooden shelves surrounded low, round tables and kid's chairs painted either red or black. A colorful poster of the Cat in the Hat adorned the far wall. Beside it was a drawing of Peter Rabbit and his friends clustered around a toadstool table with their little bunny noses buried in open books.

A slender woman with chestnut hair and soft brown eyes behind round glasses sat at a nearby desk. She was reading a catalog with great concentration, yet looked up immediately with a welcoming smile when Betty Ann and Lucy neared.

"Hello, ladies. May I help you with something today?" She placed a bookmark in the catalog and closed it without looking down. Buddha offered his infinite smile from the front of her desk.

Lucy introduced Betty Ann and then herself as Erica's mother.

"Yes, of course. Erica is one of our best readers. I wouldn't be surprised if she announces she has read every book in our section, even the ones supposedly for boys. She keeps me on my toes—luckily I have a few dollars to spend." She tapped the catalog.

Lucy beamed. She praised the unicorn book and related her story about her daughter reading it to the younger children in the neighborhood. Not wanting to lose Miss Willom's attention to another patron, as nicely and as quickly as she could, Lucy turned the conversation to the request at hand.

"Of course I speak and write Japanese. I'm flattered that you would remember such a thing."

Betty Ann took out the envelope and retrieved the two pages of notebook paper. She handed them to Lucy.

"We think this message may be of a sensitive nature," Lucy said. "May we rely on your discretion?"

Miss Willom gently laid a hand flat on her upper chest. She drew a long breath in and exhaled, settling her body as if for meditation and relaxing her face into a somber expression. She nodded, and Lucy gave her the pages. Miss Willom pushed aside the catalog and squared the pages on her desk. She ran her fingers lightly down the paper as she read, and then pressed her fingertips against her lips when she finished. Her expression had melted from somber to sad, and her liquid glance up pulled Lucy and Betty Ann closer. Miss Willom surveyed the room. No one approached her corner, and all of the children's chairs remained empty and neatly pushed up against the tables. It was early yet for the reading circle crowd.

"Oh dear. This is not good news at all," she said.

"Is it about Lonnie? My son?"

"Oh no. This says he's fine."

Betty Ann leaned over the desk. "Are you sure?"

"Yes. But he sent this to you because it's about the Hepplewhite boy. The one who died." Miss Willom shook her head and looked out the window. Lucy followed her gaze. Trees shaded this side of the library. Their branches swayed slightly in a light breeze.

"What about him?" Lucy also bent over the desk.

"This says he didn't die from an accident. Or rather, there was an accident, but he was ordered into a hot zone."

Betty Ann reared back and Lucy stopped breathing for a moment, knowing how soldiers are taught to disregard their own personal safety to follow orders.

"What?" Betty Ann asked. "Why?"

"They were ordered to make sure the nose of the rocket was secured. I guess it was very hot. The marines received massive radiation doses. Several died, including the Hepplewhite boy. The note says this is what really happened, but the truth will be buried unless someone like General Hepplewhite hears the real story."

Betty Ann and Lucy looked at each other. Taking something like this straight to General Hepplewhite was strictly out of the question. They didn't even have to say it aloud to agree.

"We have to do something," Betty Ann said.

Miss Willom watched them. Somehow her calmness steadied Lucy and made an idea seem plausible.

"We don't *have* to do anything," Lucy said. "Officers can take care of their own. But you're right. We should do something anyway. After all, you would want to know if it were Lonnie, right?" Betty Ann nodded. "So let's take it to Mrs. Hepplewhite."

"Oh no, too much is at stake. Lonnie. Ray."

"But she loved the dress, despite herself. And she even paid you double, like she said she would."

"Sure, but she made such a big deal about it that I almost didn't want to take her money. And when she handed the check over, she said something about Ray leaving base at a time like this. How'd she know about that? No, thank you." Betty Ann gave Miss Willom a polite smile of gratitude as she picked up the pages and refolded them. As she did, she brushed the catalogue, as if by accident, but her touch left it perfectly aligned with the side of the desk.

"Look," Lucy said. "Lonnie already took a big risk just getting this to you. Don't you think you owe him something? As his mother?" She pivoted away and shook her head.

"Then there's that other thing, you know, the ring. She mentioned that, also. No. Think what might happen to Ray."

Miss Willom stood up, not to send them on their way but to bring their swirling attention to a focus. Lucy turned back to face her.

"Ladies. I have no idea what you're talking about," Miss Willom said. "But consider this. Is any of what you're referring to worth more than this boy's life?"

Chita
A Message from García 7

INSIDE, TWO OVERSIZED, ornately carved mahogany chairs finished with plush red cushions crowded the front room. The family shrine rose between them. All the other necessities of the family's public room—a table, some kitchen chairs, the family radio, and the like—were squeezed into the rest of the small space. A roof leak near the table seeped through the thatch and dripped into a pan crusted with rings from earlier rains.

The old woman we had seen earlier emerged from a back room, and Paco introduced her as his wife. She wore a simple white apron and carried towels for us. As we dried off, Chucho pushed past her with our luggage, turning sideways. Rosita and I sidled over next to the fancy carved chairs to make room as he disappeared through the doorway toward the back of the house. My sister admired the chairs, and she went on so you would think they were carved from gold. Even so, you could tell from the prim set of the wife's mouth that it was the right thing to do. Marisol was her name, but Rosita called her Señora Ramírez and Abuela. There was no equality of the Revolution just then. Again, it was the right thing to do, I suppose.

"They're from the big house at Doblase," Abuela Marisol said. "As a little girl, I had to dust them carefully with a polish cloth, but I was never allowed to sit on them. Now, thanks to El Líder, I own them." She finished with a proud shake of her head. Chucho returned empty-handed. With the five of us together, there was barely enough room to stand without touching. As it was, I was pressed up against my sister.

"Tell us about Campo Doblase," Rosita said.

"Paco, where are your manners?" Abuela said. "Please invite our guests to sit. I must get back to my stew."

Would we never find out anything about this place called Doblase? It appeared as if we would have to discover it ourselves without the armor of foreknowledge. Paco swept his arm to indicate the ornate chairs for us, and although we made polite protests, we quickly landed in the seats of honor. As I suspected, they possessed more beauty than comfort, but one could hardly complain under the circumstances.

As soon as we sat down, Chucho moved back over to the front door.

"Please excuse us," Paco said. "We will go tell David that you have arrived."

He donned a straw hat and a jacket from a peg by the door and, after a nod to us, followed Chucho out into the rain. What was going on? I looked my complaint at Rosita. She nodded. No words needed to be said, so for once I didn't conjure them. The one lit kerosene lamp flickered and smoked on the table, throwing the edges of the room into gloom and worsening my sore head. My neck ached and the chair dug into the back of my thighs. I wanted to stretch my legs but couldn't in the tight quarters.

After a few moments of silence, a figure entered and stood in the gloom at the door. At first I thought Chucho had returned, but when he didn't speak, I wasn't sure. Was this someone sent to guard us while the car was pillaged? Anything was possible in this crazy province. I squirmed to the edge of my seat, preparing for I didn't know what.

"I am David Montes," the figure said.

I knew that voice.

"Tomasito!" Rosita and I exclaimed together.

Only then did he move into the light. We jumped up, but he held up a hand to ward us off. He had always been thin, a high metabolism, Mami always said, but now his cheekbones made sharp planes on his face and emphasized the depth of his large eye sockets. He was dressed, as Chucho had been, in a worn T-shirt and plain work pants. He was wet with rain but not soaked as we had been. This was not the urbane Tomasito that had left Matanzas over two months before. Where did he come from? Then I noticed a heavy bandage on his right arm. It ended in a club where his hand should be. My God! What's happened to him? Why is he holding us off?

"Not so easy to get rid of me, is it, dear sisters. Where's the other one?"

"Where have you been? What is Doblase? Who are Paco and Chucho?" Rosita said. "What happened to your arm? I'm not going to utter another word until someone tells me what's going on." She shook her finger and spoke in her big mama's voice, the one that Tomasito always obeyed. Suddenly we were teenagers again and he was a little boy standing over a mess to be explained. I prayed, not for the first time, that it wasn't his fault.

Tomasito dropped his hand and breathed a sigh. "I never thought the Sisters Montero would give in so easily to the craziness of the Revolution. And turn in your own brother."

"What are you talking about?" I asked. "We didn't even know of the existence of this Doblase place until we got the Calixto García letter."

"Oh come off it, hermana. Ramón described the family meeting."

Rosita stiffened at the mention of her husband. "When did you speak to Ramón?"

"I didn't. But Chucho's wife, she lived for a while in Sancti Spíritus. She learned to read there, so she works in the office sometimes. She logs in the guest workers. People like me."

As I thought, the polite term for prisoner.

"She saw the letter from Ramón—she was too scared to take it—but she copied it word for word for me."

"What letter?" I asked.

"The one that listed all of my offenses and said how my behavior alarmed the *entire family*." With each of those two shouts, he thumped his thigh with his good hand. I wondered if Marisol would come in to see what all the shouting was about.

"What on earth are you talking about?" Rosita asked.

"You know you all signed it. Even Mami and Papi."

"We signed no such letter. I swear to you." Rosita crept closer to our brother, but he retreated until he bumped up against the table.

"Wait a minute," I said. "Remember those petitions Ramón asks us to sign? They're always two pages, one for the petition and one for the signatures. Maybe he switched out the second page of a petition we freely signed and married it to this despicable lie. But why?"

"Ramón?" Tomasito rubbed his thumb back and forth across his fingers. "Money."

Rosita covered her mouth with both hands. Her eyes shone in the dull light from the lantern. "He couldn't have. He doesn't need money."

"He doesn't need blow jobs from poor women who want to feed their kids, but believe me, he takes advantage of them." Tomasito hunkered into his shoulders. His jaw muscles bulged as he clinched his teeth, and his left leg quivered. He seemed ready to explode with anger, but I knew that leg tremor also helped him hold back tears. Poor little one. Left all alone in the world because of that bastard Ramón. Rosita should've never brought him into our lives.

"But we tell each other everything," Rosita said.

"Did you tell him about the children?" I asked.

"What about the children? Where's Lola?"

So many questions. "Let me get this straight," I said. "You thought all the Monteros had turned against you." Tomasito nodded. "Then why did you send the Calixto García letter?"

Tomasito held up his bandaged arm. "This was an accident. At least I think it was. You all wouldn't want anything like this to happen to me, right? Then I died, so I thought I would go to the States. But I wanted to let you all know that I wasn't really dead, just headed to the States, but no way was I going to let Ramón know that he hadn't really gotten rid of me, because then no telling what he would do. As long as I was letting you know I wasn't really dead, I thought maybe I could see you one more time before leaving. Even if you had signed that stupid letter." His voice trailed off, and he cradled his bandaged arm in front of his chest.

Rosita went to stand directly in front of him. She touched his good arm but looked at the other. "Hermanito, your arm." Her voice was as soft as her touch. He drew her in and let her hug him. Her husband sent him away to a hellhole, but still he sheltered her. Meanwhile, I remained with empty arms at the other end of the tiny room. The injustice of it.

"It's nothing. Good thing I'm left-handed, eh?" He waggled the fingers of his left hand as he had so many times before as he took off on boyish adventures. The smell of frying food filled my nose, and my empty stomach responded with a rumble. Usually a headache takes my appetite, but I was famished. There was still so much to hear from Tomasito, yet here I was thinking of food. I felt like a wicked stepsister. Yes, clearly I didn't deserve to be embraced by my baby brother. Rosita's tears flowed.

"Don't cry now." Tomasito pulled her closer with his good arm. "I told you, it's nothing."

I always must be the practical one, and much more needed to be said before I too succumbed. I was glad I had kept my distance while soft Rosita let her emotions overcome her. My stomach gurgled.

"Wait, go back," I said. "You died, but you didn't die? What does that mean?"

"It started with the accident on the machine that crushes cane. It's old. The guard gave way. The teeth grabbed me."

"Mary, Mother of God! Our Tomasito could've been killed!" Rosita's sobs escalated.

Tomasito stroked her hair and rocked her back and forth. I, too, wanted to release the tensions of those uncertain months, but I didn't. I couldn't afford to yet.

"But I wasn't. Not really," he said. "Only two fingers lost."

Rosita gasped and went silent. I covered my mouth to keep in any sound. My eyes remained dry.

"Chucho says I was lucky that a campesino was there to stop the machine and pull me out. It's eaten up more than one man, he says."

Tomasito appealed to me with his large, dark eyes. Despite my resolve, my tears brimmed but didn't fall. He shook his head and rolled his eyes at them. His muscles had softened and the leg tremor was gone. He was enjoying the attention.

"Go on," I said.

"Look at it this way," he said. "It got me out of Doblase."

"How?" I asked. Thunder rumbled and rain dripping from the roof pinged faster in the pan.

"An infection set in . . ."

"Oh no," Rosita said. She mumbled into his chest. Although I couldn't hear clearly, I assumed she was saying some Hail Marys.

"Stop that." Tomasito held her away from him with his strong left arm. She assented with rapid shakes of her head, then turned to grope for the purse that she'd left on the colonial chair. She took out a handkerchief and carefully dabbed at her eyes. I thought again that no woman looked prettier when crying than Rosita. Maybe that's why she did it so much.

"You finished?" Tomasito asked.

Rosita sniffed and nodded. She tucked the hankie into her pocket and grabbed my hand. Her palm was damp, but her grip was strong.

"As I was saying, I was in the infirmary when an infection set in. The doctor was away in a remote part of the plantation and couldn't get back right away because the roads were rivers. Abuela Marisol was in charge of the infirmary while he was away."

"Her?" I pointed toward the other room.

"Um hm. She never went to school, but she was the main doctor around here for years. Many still prefer her to the new man with the fancy degree. You should see her medicine chest."

"Go on," Rosita urged in a calm voice.

"Two red tracks ran up my arm. Abuela piled all the blankets in the infirmary on me and still I froze. She showed the tracks to the assistant director and told him, right in front of me, that I may not make it through the night." Rosita squeezed my hand harder, if that was possible, but said nothing.

"She put a poultice on my hand and gave me some pills, and then left me completely alone some time during the night. You three, you used to read to me and do skits to make me laugh when I was sick. Remember? Just thinking of your elaborate plots helped me through that night. My sisters were all with me, so I wasn't afraid."

I squeezed Rosita's hand harder. He thought we had betrayed him, yet he turned to us in his hour of need. I saw him, a man prepared to die alone. How hard-hearted this Marisol must be, to leave our Tomás like that. Why were we accepting her hospitality?

"When she returned, Chucho and his father were with her. She gave me a horrid brew, which I immediately puked up. Chucho laughed. 'You're going to live, my friend,' he said, 'but we've got to get you out of here.' Abuela wrapped a blanket tight around me, and Chucho and his father carried me out into the night. I've been in his father's hut ever since, only going out after dark."

"Wait a minute," I said. "What did the officials do when you disappeared?"

"Ah, Now you will see Abuela Marisol's true genius." Tomasito cradled his bound arm with his good one. "They had an old goat that had stopped giving milk. Time for the pot, so they killed her, took the tail and some steaks, and wrapped her in sheets. I died that night. Of course, without preservatives, a body has to be buried right away out here. The next morning, Chucho and his father volunteered to bury me, and the goat went into the ground."

The kerosene lamp threw Tomasito's looming shadow onto the wall. It bobbed with the flame's flicker.

Abuela Marisol stopped in the doorway. "Dinner's almost ready."

Reprise
The Man with the Spanish Shoes

"DID YOU KNOW about it? What they did with my boys?" Diego's voice purrs and his open gaze invites confidences. He, Ramón, and José sit in the kitchen of Ramón's house with a bottle of rum on the table. They each have already emptied several glasses before addressing this subject.

Ramón wants to avoid talking about it. The others have always seen him as weak. He knows this. But what if they knew that he had killed to save their children? They would think him a man then.

"Look at the position they've put me in. I could kill Lola." José squeezes his hand shut and open several times before taking another gulp of his drink. *"The Russians. When they find out, they won't trust me. Then what?"*

"And you?" Diego again levels his gaze at Ramón.

Ramón had started drinking long before the other two arrived. Since Guillermo's death at the tannery, he seemed to have taken over his brother's fondness for the rum. His plaid shirt is damp with sweat. He knows he stinks.

"How did they get the money they needed?" Diego asks. Ramón sees in his eyes an avenging angel who has come to punish him for murdering his own brother. He wants to confess, but all he does is shake his head. Helping the women with the money was nothing.

"Women," José says. *"I slapped that bitch around when she told me."*

"Me too," Ramón says. *"Rosita, I mean."*

The other two look at each other, bemusement on their faces. *"Sure you did, hombre,"* Diego says.

They don't believe him. They don't believe him! He is a man. Strong. His wife does what he tells her to. *"I killed him,"* Ramón blurts.

"Who?" José asks, his voice dull. He doesn't look up from the table.

"Guillermo."

"Ah, hermano." Diego sits back and passes his hand over his eyes. *"The Monteros killed him. The way they're trying to kill us by stealing our boys."*

I have girls, Ramón thinks.

Diego rises and pulls Ramón from his chair. Here he comes, the avenging angel.

"You must be tired after such a long day at the tannery," Diego says. His hand slips on the slickness of Ramón's arm until it finds purchase at his elbow.

"*I did. Rolled him over,*" Ramón says.

"*Sure, hombre.*" Diego tugs at him to get him moving. "*Come, go to bed. We'll close up here.*" He leads Ramón to the hall and gently pushes him toward the bedroom.

Do they not hear him? He sways in the dark hallway, confused. Maybe he hasn't spoken aloud. That happens sometimes to him. Or maybe . . . He stumbles to the closet in the bedroom. Guillermo's Spanish shoes are gone. Perhaps they had never been. That's it.

All is normal. Thank God.

Ramón returns to the hall and stops outside the bedrooms of his daughters. "*Virginia,*" he calls softly. "*Alma, Margo, Papi's here.*" There is no answer.

Chita
A Message from García 8

ROSITA FLOATED THE short distance over to Abuela Marisol and grabbed her hands. "Tomasito tells us a fantastical tale." She almost hopped with delight. You would've thought she was nine years old again and without a care for all our current complications. How does she do that? I still had too many questions. "You're a miracle worker?"

"It was nothing. He's too saucy for God to want him yet." Abuela untangled a hand to pat my sister on the arm.

Meanwhile, something had struck me as odd. "Why haven't the authorities notified us of your death?"

"What?" Tomasito said, and Rosita echoed a second later.

"If he's dead, why haven't they told us?" The lack of logic in those around me kills me sometimes.

Abuela propped herself up with a hand on the door frame. I realized again how many years she had, yet she moved like a much younger woman. "I don't know, Señora. The doctor no longer questions my judgment, so he just signed the death certificate. We filled out all the proper forms." She straightened up. "Maybe they have reasons of their own for saying nothing." She shrugged. "Tomasito, will you move the table so we can eat, please?"

"Of course." He pulled back a chair from the table with his good hand, and Rosita pulled out the one at the other end, as if all was well. Together they dragged the table over to the colonial seats. Rosita went back for the chairs, while Tomasito ducked through the doorway and returned with a third chair, unlike the other two.

"They didn't tell us he was here in the first place," Rosita said. "Maybe they're content to let us think of him as one of the disappeared ones."

I conceded that she may well have been right. "Then he has to go the States. He can't come home with us."

"Oh dear." Rosita sank into one of the kitchen chairs.

Abuela brought in a stack of bowls and set them on the table. She considered Rosita and shooed her into one of the ornate chairs. I dropped into the other one without complaint, although I knew it would be a task worthy of Che to reach the table from it in a dainty manner. Abuelo Paco returned, as if on cue, shedding his wet hat and jacket. He took off his glasses and wiped them with a red calico scarf as he sat in the chair nearest the front door.

"That was what I was planning anyway." Tomasito distributed the bowls on the table. What a change in him. I had never known him to set a table in his life as long as a woman was around. Perhaps he *was* dead. "Now that I've seen you. It's longer from here, but it's easier to get a vessel out of one of these provinces."

"What about the Russians and the Americans?" Rosita asked.

"These are our waters," Tomasito replied. "We don't have to worry about them. It'll be the Cubans that we'll have to dodge. Besides, I've been in a rehab camp. What better credentials for the Americans?" He rested his hands on the back of the chair opposite us. "But where's Lola?"

I shifted in the stiff chair and looked at Abuela. This was a family matter. She understood and inclined her head to tell her husband to join her in the back room.

After they left, I said, "She's off feeding the Russians."

"The Russians are more important than her hermanito?"

I shrugged.

"Sit down. We have our own tale to tell," Rosita said.

Tomasito pulled out a seat and moved the dinner bowl aside after sitting. He propped his elbows on the table. Rosita turned to me, but I was as tired as I was hungry and had no desire to explain things. She waited, but I can be patient if I have to be.

"Well?" Tomasito switched his eyes between us.

Finally Rosita started. She spoke of the Russians and their secrets and their threats to the family. Our brother's eyes grew wide when she finally got to the children.

"You didn't tell your husbands?" he asked, wonder slowing his words.

"Calixto García," Rosita said.

Tomasito scanned the room as he took in the family code that he himself had used. He brought his attention back to us and nodded. "I will join them. In Miami. I will look after them." He picked up the bowl and carefully placed it back as part of the dinner setting.

"Of course you will," Rosita said.

They were both liars. We had no idea where the children were or where they would land, and Tomasito could barely take care of himself, let alone motherless children. I could have pointed that out but decided to let them have their little moment of fantasy. After all, it was my fantasy, also.

"Well, then. Nothing we can do right now. Let's eat," Tomasito said. "Abuela!"

She immediately appeared in the doorway. How much she may have heard, I couldn't say. And at that moment, I no longer cared.

"I can eat a goat," he said.

"Oh, you," she said with a swoosh of her hand.

You could tell she held much affection for our hermanito. She disappeared and returned with a big pot of stew. Paco followed on her heels. Something about this moment made me suspect I might never see this charming brother of mine again. My heart thumped but strangely was calmed by the smell of Abuela's stew. She heaped a spoonful of yucca and goat-tail bones in his bowl and moved on to Rosita. After serving all of us, she went out back again and returned to set a cup of steaming brown liquid beside my bowl. No one else received one.

"Pardon me, Abuela, but what's this?" I asked.

"For your headache." How did she know?

She frowned at me and pointed to the ridges between her eyes.

Tomasito laughed. "Careful. I told you what happened to me when I drank one of her concoctions."

"You turned into a goat?" I asked, and everyone laughed. I sipped the sweet tisane. We were in expert hands.

After dinner, Chucho brought in his wife to meet us. Her yellow shift was faded but clean. Spots of rain darkened the hem where it had hung below her jacket. She had a habit of bunching the dress at the waist and smoothing it out again. Her hair was pulled back into a ponytail and had the brassy look of a bad henna job. What I could've done for her if I had the time. Our brother rose to offer his seat to her, but Abuela insisted that he sit and rest his injured arm. Chucho's wife, Berta was her name, stood by the door, as it was the only place for her in the crowded room. She hardly spoke until I thought to ask her whether a notice had been sent out immediately when Tomasito was declared dead.

Berta glanced at her husband as if asking for permission to speak. He nodded once. "Oh yes, Señora. All our guests are accounted for at all times." Her hands were pressed flat at her sides, as if she were reciting her catechism.

"We received no notice," Rosita said. "Did it go to our parents?"

"No, Señora. They told me to send it to the gentleman who signed the original papers."

A fire burned near my heart, but I had to be sure of my suspicions. "Do you remember the name?"

Berta's eyes searched the thatch roof above for her answer.

"Was it Ramón Fernandez?" I asked.

"Señora, that's it. I remember now because our youngest is also named Ramón and he makes his R big like a balloon like this gentleman did. Of course, our Ramón had only seven years, but already . . ." Her voice trailed off as she stared at Rosita.

My sister had blanched whiter than a christening dress. I thought she was going to faint. I reached out to her, prepared to catch her if she flopped out of her chair. This was certainly the limit: not only had Ramón sent our hermanito away, he then kept silent about his supposed death, even when he knew we were frantic for information.

"I'll kill him," I said.

My words seemed to revive Rosita. She put a hand to her throat, closed her eyes, and lifted her face to the sky beyond the low thatched roof. We call this her martyr pose.

"I'll handle him," she said.

Please. As if she would do anything to him that really mattered.

"You know this Señor Fernandez?" Chucho asked.

I glanced at Tomasito, who was watching Rosita closely without expression. How mature he looked. He had become his own man in those two short months. He must've also learned some lessons about trust, because Chucho's question made clear that he had never revealed Ramón's connection to him and our family.

"Intimately," Rosita said.

She lowered her chin and opened her eyes but didn't say anything more. That was all right. We had a long ride back over the mountains to address the subject of her traitorous husband.

Chucho soon escorted his wife home, leaving behind a promise to return to help with whatever needed to be done. In a household that probably retired soon after dusk, we kept the front room alive with family chatter late into the night. We quickly decided that we would leave all our provisions with the Ramírez family, either for their own use or to help speed Tomasito on his way. As much as we wanted to linger with our precious brother, those other absences and uncertainties tugged at us. We would leave for home in the morning.

My DeSoto had drawn notice when we arrived, which added to my concern for our brother's safety. He assured us that everyone in the batey knew about him and his hiding place. It was only a passing official or a nosy campesino from another settlement that might cause upset. In any case, late at night, after the storm had passed and the singing night insects were joined by the steady drip of back country vegetation shedding its shower, Chucho returned to unload our car. A few provisions, such as the American dollars, were stashed in compartments hidden in the DeSoto's body. I retrieved those goods myself. Our hosts admired the ingenuity and extent of our resources.

I offered Diego's pistol to my brother. My husband liked him and wouldn't begrudge him the gun. He, though, was concerned with our safety, especially after he heard the tale of the bandit brothers. Rosita showed off her Derringer, which evoked snickers from the men. Tomasito decided that we would need the protection of the pistol more than he would. Besides, two of the authentic ration books for the Havana province would pay for adequate, and more modern, firepower for his needs.

Every time I thought of leaving Tomasito behind I could scarcely breathe, but Rosita seemed to be her old animated self. Tomasito spoke so cheerfully of joining our kids in Miami that we were happy to let the uncertainty of their exact whereabouts slide. He waved his injured hand around as if it were whole, and his face glowed when he spoke of living out in the light again. We continued to drink our fill of our brother. Our hearts tugged toward home and the fate of our children, but that night we had eyes only for Tomasito.

After a miniscule amount of sleep on pallets in Abuelo's front room, we clumped together out in the last night shadows in the valley and hugged and cried and hugged again. The light of dawn struck the mountains with its golden rays. Clouds gathered on their crowns and wisps of mist danced among their lower heights. At last the sun peeped into our bowl of shadows and we knew we must go. We would return home with one question answered but many more to ask. Tomasito agreed to wait for word from us before taking off for his new land, but I could see in his eyes that he would jump into the first seaworthy vessel he found with the first set of men he hoped he could trust. That Tomasito was always reckless as a boy, but he had made it that far. He worked his angels overtime, I thought as we finally got in the car.

He closed my door, and I took his hand before starting the DeSoto and turning it around in the small clearing. I stopped in front of him so Rosita could also clasp our little brother one last time. She took his good hand in both of hers and pulled him quickly toward the car.

"What are you doing?" My voice was harsh with surprise.

"Come with us." Her fingers clutched Tomasito, and her voice came out equally harsh, but with something else. "We can hide you. I will take care of Ramón, and then you can be free again. Come. Now." She tried to hang onto him with one hand while reaching for the door handle with the other. Tomasito snapped his hand out of her grasp and jumped back.

"Drive," he commanded.

Rosita reached out to him as I floored it. The wheels spun in the mud and the rear fishtailed twice, but both Tomasito and I knew that Rosita was capable of all kinds of romantic foolishness at a time like this. A quick getaway was our only hope of leaving without more antics. She hung out the window, her arm stretched back toward the batey long after it disappeared from view.

After that, our journey home was uneventful except for a punctured tire in the mountains, which I fixed. Please. That was child's play, even with little room between the road and the rocks that rose high above our heads. We found our bandit friends' platform empty, the feed bag gone, when we passed it in the late morning. Given my sister's last minute histrionics, I thought it best to leave any discussion about Ramón to after our return. Look what had happened to our family. I had every right to run down that worthless slug and her, too, for bringing him into our lives. Despite my resolve, I would have pounced if she had brought him up, but she didn't mention her husband. Not once. When she broke her quiet, it was usually with a memory of Tomasito, the wave in his hair, his impish smile, his infectious laugh.

Back on the highway, just as we were again feeling comfortable with our surroundings, I had to crawl for a while behind a truck laden with tobacco leaves, a harvest that smelled like the cigars the leaves would be rolled into. Suddenly a rock shot into the windshield. Rosita jumped and yelped, and her breath immediately turned into sobs. Virgin of Charity, you would've thought it was a real gunshot straight into her heart, the way she carried on. It was only a stone. It left a small nick that didn't even craze, although we would have to watch it.

As we returned deeper into familiar territory on the northern coast, we again passed the man dressed in a straw hat and red pants on the tractor. He now had a passenger on the fender and was heading toward Havana. I honked. We waved as we sped past. A few more kilometers, and I turned off the highway and headed across town to my home.

Woman Waving to the Future 4

PLANE ENGINES RUMBLED overhead as Lucy sat at her dressing table and filed her nails. The radio on Sonny's side of the bed played Top Forty hits. The station would suspend the music for President Kennedy's speech, which would begin in about an hour. Would he confirm the wives' intel about a crisis in Cuba? She wanted to be on the right track, yet she hated its inevitable destination. She had been Tony's age when she and her family had listened in stunned silence to the radio set in the living room as President Roosevelt described the attack on Pearl Harbor.

Now she was the mother. Now she had to stay calm and reassure her children that they would be all right regardless of the news from the president. She waited for Erica to finish her shower. Her daughter should have been in the tub in the main bathroom, but she was convinced that the incessant throttling up and down of takeoffs and landings at the air base meant that planes were falling straight toward their house. She believed this despite Tony's repeated explanations of engine mechanics and the illusions of the Doppler effect. Lucy didn't blame her. With an evening shift in the winds, the planes tacked to a new compass point and sounded as if they might leave tire marks on the flat roof of their house. Ordinarily, huge blocks of quiet separated the roar of the Air Force aloft, but now the caravan of craft arrived and departed in intervals of less than a minute. Lucy knew, because she had finished her nails and was watching the second hand spurt around the alarm clock.

The shower stopped. "Mommy?"

"Still here."

"Mommy?" Erica's voice pitched higher. She was so close to hiccup-weeping all the time now.

"Still here," Lucy said louder. She clicked off the radio and went to slide the bathroom's pocket door a little wider. "Here I am."

Her daughter jumped at the sound of her voice and draped the towel in front of her. She still wore the purple shower cap. Her stance suggested that easy panic warred with the newly acquired and fierce desire for privacy.

"Hurry up, missy. Put your pj's on."

Tony was at the dining room table, constructing sentences with the week's spelling words. He had showered right after supper. Lucy wished Sonny was home and getting ready to watch the speech with them, but he had been gone more than forty-eight hours without a call. She and Betty Ann had assumed they would get together for the big announcement, but as they scrabbled back and forth about who would host, it became clear that each wanted to be near her own phone. Each imagined her husband wrangling a moment at a phone, and each wanted to be home to receive the call. The wives could talk with each other afterward. And since no formal officers or leaders had been elected by the other wives, they would look to Lucy and Betty Ann to devise the course of action once the president had spoken. Another plane screamed overhead. The crescendo and diminuendo of engines signaled the efficient movements of the US Air Force. Crescendo? God, she was thinking the way Betty Ann's husband talked.

Erica struggled with the arm holes of her pajama top. She had fit into the baby doll top just two months ago, but it was already too small. The ruffles on the sleeves made her arms look scrawnier than they were. Time for that fall necessities shopping trip. Lucy imagined shopping for underwear as a nuclear mushroom bloomed on the horizon. She shook off the thought as Erica scooted past her. She had left the damp towel heaped on the floor and the shower cap on the toilet seat. Lucy called to her as she rounded the corner into the hallway. Her daughter either didn't hear her—yet another jet roared overhead—or she pretended not to and disappeared. Lucy let her go. She didn't have to engage in every skirmish. A sigh escaped her as she picked up the towel. She would have to watch that in front of the children. She would have to appear stronger than she felt.

After tidying the bathroom, Lucy settled down with the kids in the living room. Tony's long limbs folded into his father's recliner, and Erica sat cross-legged with a deck of cards on the floor. She pleaded with her brother to play War with her, but he was absorbed in a new Fantastic Four comic book and ignored her. Lucy shook her head when appealed to, so Erica bent over and laid out the seven piles of solitaire. In this way they would listen to the president and, God willing and with no more interruptions by the network, would continue on with the regular routine of *To Tell the Truth* and *I've Got a Secret*. At that point, Lucy would argue Erica into bed. God willing.

At Tony's age, Lucy knew that the attack on Pearl Harbor was terrible but had no idea how much it would change everyone's lives. Sonny's crew still had to stagger the planes so they couldn't all be easily targeted like the ones that had been parked in straight rows on that December day. Our nation was outraged at the cowardice of the preemptive strike by the Japanese, but would the president consider it a loss of honor if he used the same tactics? She prayed he would. She prayed again that the fiasco at the Bay of Pigs had pointed him and his advisers to a third way.

At Tony's age, she had dreamed of the drama and spontaneity of an artist's loft in Greenwich Village. What did her children dream of? Would they have the chance to see them come true?

Walter Cronkite announced President Kennedy. The president sat at a desk, his face drawn into a mask of deep seriousness, and addressed the nation.

Good evening, my fellow citizens:

This Government, as promised, has maintained the closest surveillance of the Soviet military buildup on the island of Cuba. Within the past week, unmistakable evidence has established the fact that a series of offensive missile sites is now in preparation on that imprisoned land. The purpose of these bases can be none other than to provide a nuclear strike capability against the Western Hemisphere.

Upon receiving the first preliminary hard information of this nature last Tuesday morning at 9 a.m., I directed that our surveillance be stepped up. And having now confirmed and completed our evaluation of the evidence and our decision on a course of action, this Government feels obliged to report this new crisis to you in fullest detail.

The characteristics of these new missile sites indicate two distinct types of installations. Several of them include medium range ballistic missiles, capable of carrying a nuclear warhead for a distance of more than 1,000 nautical miles. Each of these missiles, in short, is capable of striking Washington, DC, the Panama Canal, Cape Canaveral, Mexico City, or any other city in the southeastern part of the United States, in Central America, or in the Caribbean area.

Additional sites not yet completed appear to be designed for intermediate range ballistic missiles—capable of traveling more than twice as far—and thus capable of striking most of the major cities in the Western Hemisphere, ranging as far north as Hudson Bay, Canada, and as far south as Lima, Peru. In addition, jet bombers, capable of carrying nuclear weapons, are now being uncrated and assembled in Cuba, while the necessary air bases are being prepared.

This urgent transformation of Cuba into an important strategic base— by the presence of these large, long-range, and clearly offensive weapons of sudden mass destruction—constitutes an explicit threat to the peace and security of all the Americas . . .

There, he had said it. It was out in the open now. She and the other wives were no longer alone with this terrible knowledge. The president was precise in his evidence through quoting words from Soviet officials that directly contradicted the photographic images from the spy planes. He didn't use that phrase—he called it "surveillance"—but Lucy was married to the Air Force and knew how we surveyed our foes. Friends too.

Tony's comic book laid open on his lap but his attention was directed to the television. Erica flipped over the played out cards and messed them about in a pile.

> *. . . Our policy has been one of patience and restraint, as befits a peaceful and powerful nation which leads a worldwide alliance. We have been determined not to be diverted from our central concerns by mere irritants and fanatics. But now further action is required, and it is underway, and these actions may only be the beginning. We will not prematurely or unnecessarily risk the costs of worldwide nuclear war in which even the fruits of victory would be ashes in our mouth; but neither will we shrink from that risk at any time it must be faced.*

Ashes and afterimages. That's all nuclear war would bring. What was the sense in that? What was worth that?

> *. . . Finally, I want to say a few words to the captive people of Cuba, to whom this speech is being directly carried by special radio facilities. I speak to you as a friend, as one who knows of your deep attachment to your fatherland, as one who shares your aspirations for liberty and justice for all. And I have watched and the American people have watched with deep sorrow how your nationalist revolution was betrayed—and how your fatherland fell under foreign domination. Now your leaders are no longer Cuban leaders inspired by Cuban ideals. They are puppets and agents of an international conspiracy, which has turned Cuba against your friends and neighbors in the Americas, and turned it into the first Latin American country to become a target for nuclear war—the first Latin American country to have these weapons on its soil.*
>
> *These new weapons are not in your interest. They contribute nothing to your peace and well-being. They can only undermine it. But this country has no wish to cause you to suffer or to impose any system upon you. We know that your lives and land are being used as pawns by those who deny your freedom. Many times in the past, the Cuban people have risen to*

throw out tyrants who destroyed their liberty. And I have no doubt that most Cubans today look forward to the time when they will be truly free—free from foreign domination, free to choose their own leaders, free to select their own system, free to own their own land, free to speak and write and worship without fear or degradation. And then shall Cuba be welcomed back to the society of free nations and to the associations of this hemisphere . . .

Three hundred eighty-seven miles. That's how far it was from Lucy's house to her mother's. That's how far she would have to travel with the kids if they activated their plan on her watch. Most of it was on interstate highways that were built to move the very weapons they would be trying to escape. How big was Cuba? Would a woman on the coast run out of land if she tried to flee the same distance? Would she wind up standing hip-deep in the ocean, watching its indifferent surf wash away her chances of survival? Would a mere three hundred eighty-seven miles be far enough for safety in either place? Lucy couldn't afford to think that way.

> *. . . Our goal is not the victory of might, but the vindication of right; not peace at the expense of freedom, but both peace and freedom, here in this hemisphere, and, we hope, around the world. God willing, that goal will be achieved.*
> *Thank you and good night.*

Kennedy had just confirmed what Lucy and her friends had guessed from keeping their eyes and ears open on the Maryland base where they lived. The nuclear phantom had just become flesh. Lucy wondered if they should activate the plan now, before any missiles flew. She would consult Betty Ann. She would know what to do.

Lucy shooed Tony and Erica down the hall for teeth brushing before their other shows came on. She had just settled into the old, faded pink armchair when the phone rang. The first call was from her mother. She asked Lucy if what Kennedy said about Russian missiles in America's backyard was true. What a strange position to be in, to have a crisis elevate her authority above that of the president, in her mother's eyes. But then, you always trusted the people you knew, the ones who loaded the planes and cooked for the officers. Then her mother complained that Lucy's letters lacked detail, especially about the daily lives of her grandchildren.

She insisted on talking to Tony and Erica, although precious long-distance minutes were not usually wasted on the children's awkward silences. They were at each other more than usual and didn't respond well to this odd Monday night call from their grandmother, whom they called Dee Dee. They mumbled, "Yes . . . no . . . good . . . me too . . ." and so on before Dee Dee let them off the hook.

Lucy retrieved the phone from her oldest, and of course, her mother brought up her usual lament. "You never visit."

"Maybe next summer," Lucy said automatically. This rote answer didn't seem to strike the right note this time, not with so many dangerous unknowns just acknowledged. "Or maybe Thanksgiving."

"Come now."

The rest of Lucy's family was still in Cleveland. They didn't like to travel, especially her mother. To her, a car trip to Pittsburgh in the next state east was a major undertaking and entailed a level of planning worthy of a transatlantic voyage. "We can't. The kids are in school. Why don't you come here?"

"All right."

"All right, what?"

"All right, I'll come there."

"Are you sure?" Lucy wondered if she had surprised herself as much as she had her daughter with her sudden willingness to travel. Her mother had never visited their assignments, even when the children were born. They always had to trek back to home base to see her.

"Miles can bring me."

"Okay, that's great. You and Miles work out the details and let me know." Lucy was unsure whether her mother would actually have the nerve to see this through, but perhaps, under the influence of this nuclear dream, she would.

"Don't say okay. You know better than that." Her mother hated slang.

"Yes, ma'am." Lucy was ten again and safe in her mother's rules, if only for a moment.

"Oh my Lord," her mother said. "Look how long we've been talking." Apparently she just awoke from one level of the dream. "This will cost me a fortune. I won't be able to eat for a month."

They signed off. Instead of returning the handset to its cradle, Lucy pinched it between her shoulder and neck and pushed down the plunger. She held it while she retrieved the address book and flipped it open to her brother's number in Toledo. The phone's bell buzzed against her thighs and startled her. It was her sister. The call to her brother came next. Everyone mentioned the president's speech, but no one asked what it might mean for Lucy or her Air Force husband.

Sonny slipped in a call. Said he might not be home for a while.

She knew he couldn't really say anything, but she had to ask. "Are you going to be reassigned . . . anyplace?"

There was a pause. "No," he said. "At least not right now." She had to be satisfied with that. "Let me talk to Tony."

She called her son and put him on the phone. He didn't say much at all and sometimes just nodded without speaking. When he was finished, Lucy asked what his father had said to him.

"Nothing. Just, you know, be a good kid."

To him, the adults must have been acting strange. He slumped back into the recliner and turned his attention to the television.

Woman Waving to the Future 5

LUCY'S DOORBELL RANG. She opened the door to Betty Ann sheltering from a downpour. They had work to do.

"Now what?" Lucy asked.

Betty Ann made no reply as she unwound her rain bonnet and headed for the kitchen with a paper bag. Lucy told the kids to stay in the living room. Tony nodded, eyes still trained on the television. Lucy put on water for tea while Betty Ann took her usual place at the table. In the light of the kitchen, Betty Ann looked older, drained, not her usual perky self. Her eyes were dull and puffy. The lateness of the hour couldn't have been the sole explanation for her pallor. She could dance until four in the morning and then make a breakfast for ten and still have the energy to sing in the choir at the church on base. Had she been crying? Lucy pushed a cigarette pack across the table. Betty Ann shook her head, so she didn't light up either. Smoking was one activity that Lucy didn't do by herself.

"What's up?" Lucy asked.

Betty Ann would know what she meant. The larger crisis could hold a few seconds longer.

"I thought Lonnie was safe," Betty Ann said.

"He's not?"

"Lonnie's on the *Princeton*."

"In the Pacific, right?"

"It's an aircraft carrier. They're probably steaming for the Caribbean right now."

"Come on, Betty Ann. We can't leave the entire rest of the world unprotected."

"Then he's continuing to get radiated in the Pacific." Betty Ann covered her heart and turned her dull gaze on Lucy. A mother knows, her eyes seemed to be saying. There was none of her usual dramatics.

Erica pushed open the swing door.

"What?" Lucy bit the word short.

"I'm hungry."

"Here." Lucy rummaged in the paper bag and pulled out two chocolate-covered doughnuts. "Get a paper towel." Erica ran to the counter and jumped back to her mother. "Give one to your brother." Lucy handed over the doughnuts. "What do you say?"

"Thank you." Erica backed through the swing door.

"And don't bother us again."

"Yes, ma'am." Her daughter disappeared as Lucy turned back to Betty Ann. "Where were we?"

"Lonnie in harm's way."

"Calm down, now. What's your rule? Don't worry 'til you have something to worry about. Right?" Lucy didn't feel as confident as she sounded. She peered into the paper bag, then dumped the rest of the doughnuts onto the plate. She set the tea steeping and brought the plate and napkins to the table. Now was not the time for diets. She and Betty Ann sat silent, listening to the rain.

"When he got vague, I thought it was because they were in some trouble spot. Now this." Betty Ann slumped further into her chair.

Her air of defeat unnerved Lucy. You could grab up the younger kids and run if you had to. Lucy was sure she could even carry her son after the flash of a bomb. But Betty Ann couldn't carry Lonnie—he was already out in the world on his own. Already in a danger zone, maybe, or heading to one. She felt the fierce pull from her gut, the one that she felt the first time she held Tony. No one was going to harm her children. Not while she was alive.

"Let's activate the plan," she said.

"What?"

Lucy swept to her feet, which forced Betty Ann's head and eyes up. She tilted her head at a familiar angle and looked almost like her usual self. That look gave Lucy a surge of energy. She paced to the other end of the kitchen and back again, then prepared the tea before answering. She put the mugs on the table but remained standing.

"Send the kids away." Lucy plunked a finger on her chest. "We're a target." She turned the finger out into the air. "Cleveland's not. We send them."

"For how long?"

"For as long as it takes."

Betty Ann shook her head. She pulled the cigarettes closer and shook one out of the pack. "Nothing's changed. It's just that the whole nation now knows what we already knew."

"No. Before tonight, we assumed we knew what was going on. The ships steaming south, all the ordinance moving through the base, Rosie's story about the choppers, the rumor of the downed plane. We put two and two together. The president just confirmed that it indeed adds up to four. And that four could explode at any minute. I don't care about me, but Tony and Erica . . ." Lucy couldn't say it. She covered her eyes.

"Sit down." Betty Ann held the cigarette between her fingers but didn't light it as she leaned on her elbows on the table. Lucy slipped into her chair. "Panicking will get us nowhere."

She was right. That was the whole point of making a plan in the first place: to avoid irrational behavior based on fear during a crisis. Lucy's mother love battled mightily with the reason of it all. She never thought parenthood would include this particular impossible situation. She wondered how Sonny felt.

"We stick to the plan," Betty Ann said.

"Okay, but what if the White House has changed its plans?"

"What do you mean?"

Lucy shrugged. "What if, now that everybody knows, they move the choppers to National or something?"

"Then let's go check. Right now." Betty Ann gulped her tea and roused to stand.

Lucy looked into the living room and gauged her children's well-being through the subtle pressures only a mother can feel. She had left them alone for a while in the daytime, but never at night. This, however, was no ordinary night.

"Right. Let's go," she said.

She put Tony in charge and headed into the night with Betty Ann.

The helicopters still sat on the apron of runway 31L. An MP Jeep stood in their shadows, but the women couldn't see anybody, neither in the vehicle nor on the ground. But they were still there, and the president was still in the White House. No panicking for him. Or for Betty Ann and Lucy, now that they knew they could stick to their plan. They divvied up the list of mothers who were in on it. Although the hour was late, they decided to make the calls before morning. Surely no one was actually asleep. A phone call would startle but wouldn't alarm as much as a knock on the door would. All of the worst news always arrived in person.

Betty Ann dropped Lucy and went home to make her calls. After Lucy finished her own calls, she sat for a long time in the pink arm chair, listening to the clock ticking and the refrigerator running. The rain had stopped but started again before she finally dragged herself to bed in the early morning hours.

Break
Back in the USSR

YOU THINK I don't belong here, but I do. Wouldn't it be convenient for all of you to forget that I'm here, but my voice floats across the waves and soars over alien land. Follow the vapors of its trail and look at the wife he left behind. Look at me. Look.

The papers don't write about women like me, standing with tots in arms, watching the ships bear our men away. You think ours is not a noble fight, or you tolerate our men because they serve your ends. Can you hear me?

What about me and my small son? That one, the officer that left on the ship. He loves the army and has already infected our son with his passions. The little one, too, wants to board a godless ship and sail away to where the nights are hot long after our feeble memory of heat is buried under layers of old wool.

You have no image of me. The cameras are banned and the writer too busy sharpening political points.

CAN YOU HEAR ME?

You think I'm . . . no, that's right, you don't think of me at all. You should.

I am the world to him.

I am who he wants to protect with his harsh commands and certain destruction. Me. Me and my son. I am what my officer seeks in the sultry night with dark legs around his waist. You think he wants the exotic, but I know he repeats the familiar. Smell his sweat, and you will know my wifely labors.

You think you cannot know me, standing faceless behind your iron curtains. Stare into the metallic sheen of your mirror. You will see my eyes, the eyes of a mother, frightened.

Lola
Gathering Time 1

I HAD PONDERED how to open the subject of our children on my ride with the captain into the back country. Although I had been intimate with this Russian officer, that was not enough to soothe my apprehension about mentioning the children. Too much danger. I saw how easily he had dispensed of his own; I couldn't afford to be one of his casualties. The family needed me. Even so, the shortest wait to hear of the children's fate proved too much to stand, and my reluctance to speak ended that night as I sat with him on his cot. He spoke of the Yanqui president's speech and the big Russian and American ships that were on a collision course in our waters. Yet another unforeseen danger. I did not feel like my usual daring self, and yet I had to speak. "I worry about those poor crafts carrying disillusioned Cubans to other countries."

He pinched his cigarette from his mouth and examined it. "What about them?"

"They just want what's best for their families."

"The wisdom of the Revolution is what's best for their families." He took one final drag and stubbed out the cigarette in the tin can on the ground beside the cot.

I dropped my chest to my knees and stared down. "Do you think those big ships can see the little boats to avoid them?" I felt as defenseless as a tiny mouse caught running across an open floor.

"Nope." Captain B. stood to put on his shirt and button it. I bent over and stared at my bare feet while he drew on his trousers. "A collision's unlikely, though, the wakes would be much more dangerous. Those ships? Steaming full speed ahead. The wakes are easily taller than any building in your city."

I rocked back and forth, my feet pulsing against the ground with each stroke. He dangled my blouse in front of me, but I couldn't stop rocking.

"Honestly. They're fine," he said. I dared not ask for confirmation of the people he was talking about. "That storm probably blew them off course." He shook my blouse in front of me, but I still didn't look up. "Come on, darling he said in a softer voice.

He hadn't called me that before, even in the heat of passion. Its soft edges did nothing to blunt the sharp reports that reverberated from Karl the driver's execution. I wondered if anything would ever quiet them.

We had driven all the way out to the new camp, just to find that Kennedy's speech the previous evening had changed the Russians' plans: they wouldn't start the new camp until the standoff was resolved. Under the circumstances, Captain B. could have easily detained me for as long as he wanted, doing whatever he wanted. Instead, he dropped his bulk onto the cot beside me and laid my blouse between us. He patted me on the shoulder.

"Go home," he said.

I gathered my things, and we left the tent. He put me in a truck and pointed the driver back to Matanzas. There would be no mistaken turns on this ride.

As we approached the city, I automatically directed the driver to our bungalow on the western edge of town, which I truly didn't remember would be stripped of life until we pulled into the empty driveway. The dark, blank windows discouraged entry. I stayed in the truck and instructed the driver to take me to the café. The streets popped with activity in the late afternoon heat. Snatches of El Líder's broadcast admonished us to prepare to defend the country to the death. Yes, of course I would fight. Gladly. Just as soon as I heard that Bonita and Chalo were safe.

My café was also closed up tight, but there I unlocked the door. I carried in my large pots and deposited them on the stove. The Russian driver followed with the box of spices and condiments, then went out and returned with my vanity case. Although twilight had come early inside my small shop, I didn't turn on any lights. I depended on the late afternoon sunlight filtering in from the open door.

Ernesto stuck in his grizzled head. "Have you heard?"

"Of course." I raised a fist, wondering where I found the strength to do so. "To the death!" My neighbor returned the salute and disappeared down the walk.

The Russian driver reappeared and asked if I needed anything else. I thanked him for getting me home safely and cracked a cold cola for him. For the first time since we had started out, I dared to examine his flat brown eyes and the hairy knuckles on the paw that held the cola. Suddenly, I was sick of them. All of them. These Russians brought nothing but their inferior shoes, hunger for satisfactions beyond a simple meal of chicken and rice, and the renewed fury of the North. Their so-called protection would rain ruin from above while a swamp of self-righteousness in the name of equality surged from below. It *had* been the right time to send the children, I reassured myself.

Still, I wondered. This one, this driver, had the looks of an ox, but would he have had enough animal sense to avoid the captain's lethal jungle clearing? Without that unfortunate encounter, I would've still had my children close to me.

I demurred when the driver thanked me for the drink. He left as I loaded bags of hot spices into a large stew pot. They were flavors that Chita never stocked at home. Of course I was going to the Montero House. Where else would I go? I checked my hair and makeup, picked up my pot and parcels, and closed and locked the café door. As I made my way to our family home, friends, distant cousins, and even strangers stopped me to discuss the latest developments. Trucks filled with soldiers drove past, Russians in some, Cubans in others. Most headed toward the port. The Russians rumbled by in military silence. A solder, one that resembled the late Karl the driver, flicked away a cigarette butt that landed on a wheeled cart an old black woman dragged behind her. I scurried forward to swat off the burning stub. The old woman never turned around.

The Cuban soldiers wore a kaleidoscope of clothing, usually finished with a bandana around the neck or head. They commanded rickety trucks or rode on the fenders, hoods, trunks, and sideboards of Chevys, Oldsmobiles, and other proletarian American cars. Several of these groups headed against the general flow of traffic to the port. These would patrol the plentiful coves west of the city where the enemy might sneak ashore undeterred by Russian might. Occasionally a patriot unleashed a cheer and a barrage of bullets to the sky. Although the Cuban men were clearly serious and proudly carried their new Kalashnikovs, they still attended to their women, young and old, who paused to wave and cheer. One soldier called, "Hey, mamacita! You! With the big pot and the juicy red lips. C'mere, mamacita, and cook for *me*!"

I waved but kept moving toward the Montero House. All of the commotion failed to keep me tethered to my body striding toward home. Again and again, I flew across the choppy bay waters and beyond, searching, searching.

The Montero House was as serene as ever as I approached it. I sought out the window of the second-story bedroom I had occupied by myself as my older sisters had moved on. The louvered window let through not a speck of light or movement from the inside. I walked along the front fence and steadied my burdens against the driveway's big gate while I fished out my key. As I did, José pulled up in the Chevy. I opened the gate wide and stepped aside.

"You're back early," he said. He pointed to the pot I embraced with both arms. "Did the good captain find another cook?"

He drove past me before I could fire off an answer. I noticed Ramón sitting in his car at the curb, so I waved at him and left the gate open for him to drive through. I didn't wait for him but followed José's car up the driveway.

Ramón
Gathering Time 2

RAMÓN HAD BEEN at the Montero House for a while. In fact, he had been the first to arrive. He waited for the others and sipped from a bottle of clear, homemade liquor he had confiscated from a worker at the tannery. He rubbed the stubble on his chin with satisfaction, as it was a sign that he had gotten up long before dawn to secure his neighborhood. He had worked hard that day as an important member of the Committee for the Defense of the Revolution. He had attended two meetings, one at the community center, the other at a grade school, where his voice rang out in confident tones as he handed out mandatory assignments. His compañeros listened to him with what he took to be a respectful silence. None dared to contradict his ideas. Everyone knew at least one person who had unfortunate dealings with the authorities after a run-in with Ramón. Now they were beginning to whisper about his brother's death.

Without robust debate, the meetings broke up more quickly than others held in the province. Soon he would be honored by the authorities for his efficiency and the general orderliness of his watch area. After the meetings, he arrived at the tannery with an uncustomary air of command. It dissipated as soon as he stepped out of the bright sun and into the rank darkness of the main room. He found fewer than half of his men at work. The others would claim defense assignments, as sure as bullets shot into the sky fall to earth.

A peak of tangled hides rose from the lime bath. His brother's replacement ignored it as he lay on the catwalk and read a newspaper. Soon after beginning this job, he had discovered his manager wouldn't venture out onto this particular catwalk. Taking advantage of Ramón's reluctance, the oaf camped out there, working when he felt like it and feigning deafness when Ramón yelled at him from the safety of the floor. Let him rot, Ramón thought. Although the loafer had been assigned to the factory as a reward for his hard work during the last sugarcane harvest, his position was not assured. Ramón could contrive a way to send him to the swamp around Playa Girón, where the Americans had made a mess of their earlier invasion. The thought cheered him. He slipped off to his office and closed the door. The bottle of clear liquid and a bag of mints waited for him there. He left the factory before quitting time, at an hour that he sometimes had left to pick up his girls at school. No such errand detained him that day, and so he drove directly over to the Montero House to wait.

Just as he was closing the gate behind his car, Diego drove up with a tap on his horn. Ramón swung the gate wide to admit Diego's truck. After parking in the side yard, the men settled in the courtyard with plantain chips and drinks while Lola kept her own company in the kitchen. She was not particularly welcomed outside.

A man with a bullhorn rode by with a nonstop line of patter. His amplified voice crested the house and fell on the gathering in the courtyard. "Stay inside if not on duty. Don't open the door to strangers. The enemy comes in many guises."

Ramón listened intently and nodded as the patter repeated. "That was my idea."

"It's a stupid one." Diego snapped the last fried plantain strip in two and shoved both pieces into his mouth.

José leaned his elbows on the cast-iron table. "I don't think so. Some of the worms that landed at the Playa Girón had been my friends."

"Not that part," Diego said. "I mean the part about not letting in strangers."

He leaned back. The sapote tree rustled with the evening breeze as Lola came out to check on the snacks. The tree towering over the front of the house shook and dropped a mango on the roof. It thumped, rolled off, and splattered on the pavement of the courtyard. Lola went over to clean it up. Diego watched with crossed arms.

"Look here," he said. "As far as I'm concerned, the devil is locked inside here with us."

Mango juice dripped from Lola's hands. She dumped the pulpy mess into the snack bowl. "Look, mister big-shot mechanic . . ."

"Woman, enough!" José's voice rumbled. Lola rounded on him as if to land a verbal or physical blow, but she stopped herself. Plenty of time for arguing later. When she went back inside without a word, José's chest expanded.

Chita
Gathering Time 3

WE ARRIVED AT the Montero House at the end of the sun's time in the sky. Our house didn't reveal any interior activity, as the front windows were already shuttered. Yet I could already sense the energy of our family gathering. Normally the street would have been lousy with Montero children, but only the boys of Luisa and Big Beto, who lived at the end of the street and were not Monteros, could be seen yanking and twisting a branch of a neighbor's bush. The wood gate was slightly ajar as I pulled into the foot of the driveway.

"Open the gate," I said to Rosita.

"Can you believe it? At the beginning of this day we held Tomasito in our arms." She wiped away a tear.

"Please do me a favor. Save your tears and open the gate."

The boys abandoned the bush and ran over to the car. They shouted greetings at us and peered into the back seat. I grabbed at them through my open window, but they were too quick for me as they jumped back out of reach with shrieks of laughter. How like my boys they were! But I couldn't dwell on that thought without sinking into a well, yet I couldn't let them see anything was wrong.

I stuck out my tongue at them. "Open the gate. Hurry now."

The oldest did as he was told, then he slugged his brother and they both ran off while I drove in. Light from the kitchen fell on the drive, and the screen door banged as Lola came out onto the stoop. She immediately shook her head, "No." No word of the children. This was information too important to be left until after "hellos" and "how are yous" and "how was your trips." My resolve faltered, and I slumped over the steering wheel. Yet the conversation was not finished. Lola volleyed a question back with a jut of chin. Rosita nodded a vigorous "Yes!" The message had gotten through to García.

Despite the fatigue of the long drive, we barely stretched the cramps out of our legs before snatching up some of the trip's bits and pieces and crowding past Lola into the kitchen. Her stock pot simmered on the stove, and I could hear animated chatter through the window opened to the courtyard. Lola always over-seasoned her stews. I knew this. She followed us but stopped at the stove to stir her brew.

"So?" she said.

"Who's here?" I asked. Tomasito's safety couldn't be trusted to just anyone, even a family member. Especially a family member, as we had found out.

"Just husbands," Lola replied. "So did you find him?"

"Yes!" Rosita went to the stove and hugged our sister.

Lola shrieked and I hushed her with a glance toward the courtyard window. My throat constricted at the thought of Ramón's treachery.

"Remember, he's supposed to be dead. To everyone," I said in a strained whisper.

My sisters ignored me. "Thank God. Thank you, San Judas. Is he all right? Where is he?" Lola gazed at the door, as if expecting our brother to spring through it. "Is he all right?"

"That place Doblase is a rehabilitation farm. Mostly cane," Rosita said. She drew Lola over to the kitchen table, sat her down, and clasped her hands.

Lola tugged at the pause. "And?"

"And these wonderful people helped Tomasito escape. You would like them, I know. Abuelo Paco and Abuela Marisol. She has the best remedies. She even rid her of one of her headaches." She nodded at me. I rolled my eyes at this digression. Rosita could never tell a straight tale. "I asked her for a package of her headache medicine for myself, stronger than Chita's. You know I suffer more than she does."

Right. I inspected Lola's unnecessary additions to the spices with squinty eyes and a sniff. I left off fiddling around at the counter and dipped a spoon into the steaming pot on the stove. I sampled the hot broth. Just as I had suspected. "Too much cumin."

Lola turned to me and took the spoon away. "But is he all right?"

"Mostly," I said.

"Of course he is." Rosita spoke rapidly from her seat at the table.

I had dumped my purse and some bags on the kitchen table and now was sorting through them. No use wasting time while Rosita wandered down her meandering paths to the truth.

"The things this girl leaves out," I said.

"Like what?" Rosita asked.

I waved my right hand and fluttered my fingers the way Tomasito would have without the bandages. Rosita shrugged.

"What is she flapping about for?" Lola asked, swinging her gaze between me and our sister.

"Imagine our Tomasito farming," Rosita said.

"Why should I do that?" A burst of male laughter rolled in through the courtyard window. How could they joke at a time like this? Men.

Rosita had yet to unpack, unbag, or move anything in the kitchen. So like her. She drifted over to the stove and sniffed the steam rising from the pot. "He got hurt by some farm machinery. An injury to the hand. It is nothing."

I snapped my purse shut. "Nothing?"

Again, Rosita had left the hard work to me. I thought this for the thousandth time since we had left together the previous morning. Would she ever shoulder her share of the family burden?

"He lost two fingers," I said.

"Mother of God preserve us," Lola said. "You call this nothing? What are we going to tell Mami? She'll want to go to him." She dropped the large spoon into the pot and turned as if she were going to go herself right away.

"She can't." Rosita stopped Lola's flight by grabbing her shoulders. "Abuela takes good care of him, thanks be to God. I promise you. And remember, he's dead, according to the officials. It's best he stays that way."

"As soon as he's better, he's going across the water," I added.

"Isn't that wonderful?" Rosita tried on a smile, but sadness clouded her eyes. I felt they mirrored my own. Still, she plowed on. "He can look after our little ones until they return."

There was so much longing for happy endings for all in that hopeful statement that I found myself not wanting to puncture her fragile hope. It buoyed me, but we had to get on with the evening. I opened a lower cupboard and peered inside.

"What are you doing here, anyway?" I said as I looked for the yucca flour. "What happened to the all-important Russians?"

"Plans changed." Lola didn't elaborate. She shook some salt into the pot.

I plucked the flour from the cupboard and stood up. "What do you mean, plans changed? I went through all of that with Diego for nothing?" That was the limit. I slammed the cupboard shut and slapped the flour on the counter.

"I don't see Ramón," Rosita said, looking out into the courtyard.

That traitor. It had all started with him. Now we were at a stalemate. So much to say and do, yet none of it would change the fate of our children.

Music from the radio outside grew louder. The swing of Sinatra's "Let's Face the Music and Dance" bounced around the kitchen. The smell of cigars seeped in with it.

"I love that song." Lola tuned the kitchen radio to the same station.

"There he is." Rosita left the window.

"So what happened?" Lola asked. "Why were we told nothing?"

"They did tell us," I said.

"Not yet," Rosita cautioned. "I want to talk with Ramón first."

"What does he have to do with it?" Lola turned up the flame under the stew pot.

I settled in to tell the damning tale, but Rosita preempted me. "Chita, not another word until I talk to Ramón."

I imagined the scene—her tears, always, her tears, his blustering. Spare me. "Go then." I could wait until she went out into the courtyard.

"Promise me."

What was a few minutes? I nodded. I wouldn't tell yet, but I could hint.

"I'll be back to help unpack in a moment."

"Sure you will," I said.

Rosita wouldn't be back. Chances were, she wouldn't do the main unpacking at her own house, either. That was one thing Ramón was good for, or had been before he started drinking so heavily.

Woman Waving to the Future 6

LUCY STOOD IN the hallway between her children's bedrooms. "Tony! Erica! Time to get up."

She waited until she heard stirring on both sides. It had been a long night without much sleep. She reached into Erica's room and flipped the switch for the overhead light. A grunt rose from the lump in the bed, but Lucy felt no remorse. That girl was worse than the extinct volcanoes that were her current obsession; she could lie inert for a millennium, it seemed, if not prodded to action. A millennium. The president's speech suggested they may not have a week.

"Get up," Lucy said.

Erica raised up on her elbows and looked over her shoulder with narrowed eyes. Sonny said their daughter had gotten this look from her mother and had already perfected it when she was only two. The thick rope of a braid fell across her cheek, and a halo of escaped hairs fuzzed at the top of her head.

"Cut out the light." Erica's voice was raspy with the night's accumulations.

Lucy ignored her cross daughter. She'd have to come back, and as likely as not, would find Erica still buried under her blankets. Tony passed in his pilot pj's on his way to the bathroom. At the age of ten, he already reached Lucy's shoulders. He didn't speak, but at least he had gotten up.

The hallway remained dark, but as Lucy went into the living room, she emerged into the gray light of a cloudy day. One glance outside confirmed that rain showers had come and gone again. The trees shed drops of water, and the streets and sidewalks were still darkly wet. She continued on into the kitchen. She followed her routine of making Cream of Wheat and toast for the kids. No way could she eat.

She eventually got both kids to the table.

Erica picked up her spoon and eyed the yellow puddle of margarine in the middle of her hot cereal. "Why do the Russians hate us?"

I don't know, Lucy thought. "They don't hate us."

Tony snicked his tongue. "Of course they do." He looked up at the ceiling, as if he were reciting the obvious. "We stand for freedom. They hate freedom. Everybody knows that."

It wasn't that simple. Lucy wished she could confide in Tony, tell him her fears and what she and the other women had planned in case of an emergency, but her son needed her certainty, and the school bus would swing by in fifteen minutes.

"Hurry up and finish your breakfast," Lucy said. "No lollygagging. The bus will be here before you know it, and Mr. Farley said he wouldn't wait for you anymore."

Her two children passed a look. She could tell they had cooked up something.

"Do we have to go to school?" Tony asked. He had cleaned his bowl and was holding a last bite of toast.

"Is it Tuesday? Of course you have to go to school."

Lucy scooped up Tony's empty bowl and plate and took them to the sink. She looked out the window but saw nothing of the scuttling clouds and the trees bending to the will of the wind. What if she died but the children survived in the basement of their school? What if it were the other way round? What if they never saw each other again? What if? Lucy turned to face her son and daughter. She could read real fear on Erica's face but detected a note of cunning, too, in her wide, staring eyes.

"President Kennedy went to work today. Daddy is at work today. I'm going to paint after you leave." She leveled a finger at her children. "You two are going to school."

Erica lowered her gaze to her bowl. After a moment, she picked up her spoon and ate the last ring of buttery, yellow-tinged cereal. She then dug a curve in the remainder and left the spoon there. Usually Lucy would insist on a few more bites, fighting with her youngest over mush hardening into a crust, but not today.

"Go brush your teeth," she said.

The usual last-minute scramble followed. Books, a Barbie lunch box for Erica and a plain brown lunch bag for her sophisticated son, a quick change of barrettes from yellow to purple for Erica, a notebook retrieved from under Tony's bed, and finally they were ready. Lucy stood at the door as the school bus rolled to a stop at their corner. Erica looked so defenseless with her jacket hanging off her shoulder and her bangs already starting their rise to a straight up salute.

What if, what if, what if? She tugged Erica's jacket up onto her shoulder and pecked her on the forehead. What if she kept her children home, just for today?

"Do you have your dog tags on?"

She didn't like calling them that but the kids did. They thought it was neat to have the same ID tags as the soldiers did. The usefulness of the stamped bits of metal in identifying dead bodies didn't cross their minds. No child should have to wear them for that reason, Lucy thought, but they all did. She reached for Tony and aimed a kiss at his cheek. He squirmed but let her land one on his ear.

"Be extra good today," she said.

"Yes, ma'am," the children replied as they hurried out the door.

She watched them run to the bus, then pushed open the screen door and stepped out onto the porch to watch the bus until it disappeared around the bend at the far end of the street. What if? She went back inside and felt the silence of the house as if it were a cascade of muck pressing down on her. She needed to talk with someone to tell them what she had just done, sending her Tony and Erica away from her. Someone who would understand. Betty Ann. They had done most of their talking last night, but hearing her voice would soothe her. She would call, but first she needed to do the breakfast dishes. She would not leave a dirty house if she needed to evacuate.

Lucy cleared the rest of the dishes and ran water in the sink. She reached for the radio perched on the counter, but the phone interrupted her. Maybe Betty Ann was calling her, although it could've been anyone. The whole nation had reason to panic, even if they did so quietly so as not to disturb the concentration of the people who might get them out of this mess. She answered the kitchen phone.

"I can't sit on this any longer," Betty Ann said.

Lucy knew she meant the Hepplewhite thing. Even though they had agreed to take it to Mrs. Hepplewhite, they hadn't decided just how to approach her. Miss Willom had promptly written out a translation of the Japanese note sent via Mrs. Fuji and had refused any compensation for doing so. Just doing my job, she had said with a jaunty salute when they went to pick it up. Next Betty Ann copied out a version that left Lonnie and everyone else out of it. It would be hard to convince Mrs. Hepplewhite of the note's legitimacy without its provenance, but they would have to find a way. It wouldn't take much to connect it to Lonnie as the link between the *Princeton* and Betty Ann, but she was not about to make it for them.

"How are we going to get an appointment with her? Once I delivered the dress, that was it," Betty Ann said.

"Let's just go over there."

"We can't just show up on the general's doorstep."

"Why not? Things are all out of whack. And besides, we may not have another chance. Do you want that on your conscience?"

"No, of course not."

Lucy twirled the phone cord around her finger. She would rather get on with her own life, but they needed to see this thing through. She wouldn't dream of making Betty Ann go it alone.

"Let's just go over there," she repeated. "If she's not home, we go back later. If she refuses to see us, we tried, and then it's on her."

They went back and forth for a few minutes until Betty Ann agreed to the plan. They signed off after she decided she would pick up Lucy shortly before ten. That was a civilized hour to be visiting. That also gave Lucy time to finish the dishes and do some picking up and light dusting. One of the best antidotes to uncontrollable chaos in the world was a neat and tidy home. Her mother had taught her that, and although the artist in her naturally rebelled, when the situation got this severe, she reverted to basics. Painting would have to wait. Again.

Betty Ann was right on time. She didn't say much as they made their way over to the main part of the base.

"You know what?" she said, while waiting for a red light. Her voice slid along in a monotone.

Lucy worried about Betty Ann. "What?"

"They pick up astronauts too."

What was she talking about? "Who?"

"Lonnie. On his ship." The light turned green. "Imagine surviving space just to be picked up by a contaminated ship." She shook her head and moved on.

"Imagine a bunch of housewives as your main line of defense," Lucy said.

They didn't speak much after that. They drove to Officer's Row, which lined the parade grounds.

Betty Ann parked the Impala in a small lot in front of a Nike missile monument. They got out of the car, and Lucy buttoned her cardigan against the breeze. High clouds striated the sky and occasionally blurred the sun. Puddles from the earlier rain lingered along the curb and sidewalks. Leaves skittered along the pavement and caught in the pooled water. The American flag at the center of the parade grounds snapped in the post-storm wind. Only maintenance personnel dotted the wide flat expanse of grass. It was hours since reveille, and hours still until the recording of "Taps" would halt both pedestrians and cars in their evening journeys home.

They crossed the road and made their way up Officer's Row toward General Hepplewhite's house. As at many military bases, the base commander's residence wasn't exceptionally grand, but it was the most prominent on the row. Each house they passed had a generous porch flanked by Doric columns and the occupant's name clearly displayed in no-nonsense black block letters. Major D. Ostertag, Captain R. Aborn, Captain M. Wilbraham. The sidewalk cracks were free of weeds. Lively decorations, all in patriotic themes, graced most of the porches. Even among the autumnal color of potted asters and chrysanthemums, officers' wives had placed wooden country folk figures dressed in red, white, and blue and had accessorized wicker porch chairs with pillows covered in the stars and stripes.

"Captain Wilbraham must be a bachelor," Lucy said.

"Why?" Betty Ann had been staring straight down the sidewalk, seemingly oblivious to the riot of patriotic decorations they passed.

Lucy put a hand on Betty Ann's arm to stop her in front of Captain Wilbraham's. She wanted to shake Betty Ann out of her funk before they reached the general's house. Betty Ann would need all of her innate bravado to get through the meeting with Mrs. H.

"Because his porch is bare. Look." Lucy nodded toward the unadorned entryway, not wanting to point. Two rattan chairs that had seen better days sat alone.

Betty Ann followed her glance, then swept a look up and down the street at the other colorful displays. She smiled. She loved speculating. Lucy counted on that.

"Maybe they just moved in," Betty Ann said.

"You think? No . . . he's a bachelor, but he's messing up the perfect look of Officers' Row. Mrs. H. probably demanded that he marry one of three candidates she's picked for him." Lucy pictured Mrs. H., clipboard in hand, ticking off a lady's attributes to poor, hangdog Captain Wilbraham.

Betty Ann laughed. "She'd better hurry up, before Mrs. Ostertag offers to help with more than the front porch." She linked her arm with Lucy's. "Come on. Let's go see if Mrs. H. will have enough sense to see us." They marched up the sidewalk. "You know, she doesn't have an A-bomb. Somehow the Russians have gotten one up on her."

"Mrs. H. doesn't have an A-bomb *yet*." Lucy giggled. A-bomb jokes had become the norm on base.

Betty Ann opened the wrought-iron gate at the foot of the front walk. Lucy took a few steps beyond to the driveway, which led to the back door. Betty Ann kept her hand planted on the gate.

"Lucy. May I remind you? This is not a service call." She tugged lightly at the scarf that covered her curls and stepped through the gate, then she tossed her head toward the house.

Lucy returned and followed her up the front walk.

A white maid answered the door. They could tell she wanted to ask the nature of their business, but Betty Ann's tone when she announced their names preempted any misplaced queries. The maid left them on the porch and closed the door before retreating back into the house. Neither spoke as they waited.

Mutually Assured Destruction 1

AS ROSITA ENTERED the courtyard of the Montero House, the men debated the top three first basemen on the island. A suitable topic for a group of men who were avoiding so many others. Next would come the ranking of major league players.

Diego stopped ticking off attributes on his fingers when he saw Rosita. "There's one of the traitors now."

"They'll think we're all worms. Who will believe we didn't know?" José asked.

Rosita ignored their remarks as she launched into an account of their trip. She focused on the condition of the roads and the heat and sudden rain. About Tío Juan, who they allegedly went to visit, she said nothing, since they hadn't seen him. She did say that everyone they saw was fine, which was the truth. As she was talking, Ramón continued to drink, seated on a concrete bench in the shadow of the vines on the guest house wall.

Rosita crept over to her husband, who rested his drink on his thigh and leaned back to look up at her. She twitched her fine nose, but he had stopped thinking that he stank, so he missed her cue. He lifted a butt cheek to make room for her, but she shook her head. Before, she would have squeezed into a place that didn't really exist by leaning her gardenia-scented bodice into her husband and encircling him with the strength of her arms. Now she remained standing but gave Ramón her sweet Virgin of Charity smile. A woman who could offer a smile like that could surely forgive any transgression. His shoulders relaxed, and he returned her smile with one loosened by rum and showing the front teeth that had begun to yellow. She could absolve him of anything.

"Ramón, my heart," she murmured smoothly. Her voice was soothing. "We need to talk."

"Of course," Ramón said. "You had a good trip, eh?"

He raised his glass in a toast and drank off the rest of the clear liquid. Now his family gave him the cheap stuff that had once been reserved for his brother. Rosita crossed her arms but he didn't notice, as his eyes were closed over the last drops from his glass. He set it on the bench and followed Rosita to the door.

"Hey, hermano," Diego called. His voice sounded harsh and loud. "I warn you. You're not safe alone with a Montero woman." He raised a bottle of rum.

It was amber, the good kind. "You need reinforcements." José snickered at Diego's comments.

"One moment," Ramón said to Rosita's back.

She paused as if he had waylaid her with a touch but then continued inside. Ramón backtracked for his glass and held it for Diego to fill to the brim before joining Rosita in the cool, dark corridor.

"Let's go up on the roof," Rosita said.

He smiled as he followed her upstairs and to the steep, ladder-like roof steps. A little privacy right after a separation was always welcome. He took a big gulp of his drink to prevent it from spilling. Rum sloshed over his hand anyway as he ascended.

She sat on a bench against a wall of the widow's walk. This crowning enclosure looked over the roofs of the surrounding houses and offered a perfect view of the harbor and the river. It, too had solid stucco walls.

"Sit." She patted the bench beside her.

He complied and kissed her, but as soon as their lips touched, she slipped away from him and stood with her back to the light still lingering in the western sky.

"Honey, you never told me. Why didn't you ever tell me?" She stared at him.

"You know about Guillermo?"

"Guillermo? I'm talking about Tomasito. Why did you send him away?"

Ramón looked down at his drink. "I didn't."

"Don't lie to me."

"I didn't. I swear to you."

Rosita crossed her arms. "I know about the letter," she said in a softer voice.

Her husband shrugged. "What letter?"

"You know what letter. The one you doctored. Don't lie to me."

"How do you know about that?"

"We went to Campo Doblase."

Ramón stared at her, then drained off the rest of his drink. "You were supposed to be at Tío Juan's. You can't trust anybody these days."

"That's not the point." Rosita slumped onto the bench beside Ramón.

The evening birds chattered in the trees below them and rapid gunfire popped in the distance. The undersides of towering clouds glowed pink in the last rays of the sun, but inside the half-walls, Rosita and Ramón sat in the deeper shades of night already come.

"You could have told me," she said quietly.

"No, I couldn't." Ramón slammed down his glass. "That idiot brother of yours was so foolish. He ran with the wrong sort and made my CDR work impossible. I tried to talk to him, but he wouldn't listen. I checked out the different camps, made sure he went to the most lenient one. You should thank me for saving him from certain arrest and prosecution."

"But now he can't come home. He's dead."

"He was going to leave anyway. That Carlos—he smuggles out money too, you know. It's true. Tomasito would've left us all to answer to the authorities. It's best this way."

"We were running around, praying to La Señora." Rosita sat up and stared at Ramón. "You could have told me."

Ramón tipped his glass to his mouth, although not a drop was left. He got up and leaned on the top of the wall to look toward the bay. The stiff breeze ruffled his shirt and caused him to squint. With his back to Rosita, he said, "You don't get it. You Monteros. If I had told you anything, the whole damn family would've been in an uproar until you got him killed." He shook his head. "It's not my fault he had an accident."

A car door slammed on the next street over. The wind roiled in their enclosure and swirled the crackling dead leaves at their feet. A silence grew between them.

Rosita put her hand in her pocket. "My family thinks you're worthless, and I get tired of defending you. Now this. Tell me one thing you've done for us."

Ramón whipped around and stabbed a finger at her. "I'll tell you." His lips barely moved. "I killed my brother."

"No."

"Yes. He wasn't to be trusted, but Quique trusted him. Carlos did too. *Your* daughters were at stake. So I drugged him." He slid down to a sitting position against the wall and bowed his head. "I rolled him over." He put a hand to his forehead. "Into the lime." He dropped his hand like a boom lowering.

"Really." Rosita's tone was flat, disbelieving.

"You don't believe me?" Ramón looked up at her. Sweat bathed his face.

"You never said anything." She withdrew a handkerchief from her pocket and offered it to him. He didn't respond, so she returned it out of sight. "After we find out what you did to Tomasito, suddenly it was you who did in your brother." She shook her head. "What's happened, Ramón? We used to tell each other everything."

He stretched both hands to her. "Please forgive me."

"My poor, dear one," she said. "You've always taken care of your own, haven't you? That's one thing I'll always love about you." She knelt and gazed at him for a long time.

"Rosita, my love." Again his hands went out to her.

"I forgive you, but I can no longer trust you."

She took the Derringer out of her pocket. It wasn't very powerful, but it did excellent close work. She laid it on the concrete between them. Ramón furrowed his brow as he glanced from her face, to the pistol, and back again.

She rose and stepped back. "I'm going to see about dinner. You stay and rest." She turned and descended the steep stairs into the life of the Montero House.

Appointment with Mrs. H. 5

MRS. HEPPLEWHITE'S MAID eventually returned to the front door, ushered Betty Ann and Lucy into the sun room off the library, and indicated a floral couch. Lucy sat, but Betty Ann had never made it into this room when she had worked on Mrs. H.'s dress, so she took a quick look around. In front of the windows facing the backyard, two white wicker chairs faced the couch, their cushions a soft yellow pulled from the couch's floral pattern. A knitting basket snugged beside one of the chairs with an unfinished baby's sweater peeking out. This was clearly Mrs. H.'s room.

A painted demilune cabinet stood against the brick chimney back of the library's fireplace. On it sat a portrait of Harry in his Marine dress uniform with a silver watch hung from a chain draped over its frame. Betty Ann understood something about the Hepplewhite household from this location of their late son's photo. In the homes of her friends, a formal portrait of a son in uniform who had given the ultimate sacrifice for his country would have been public property in the living room, a shrine and patriotic statement for all to see.

Harry's picture and its watch told a different story, the way she saw it. His death was automatically public property by virtue of his being the son of a base commander. Visitors who mattered already knew about the family's loss. But the general was the head of a larger family, one that extended off the base in whichever direction his people were deployed. His orders could lead to the loss of whole squadrons or more; his people had to think that he cared about them as if they were his own sons and daughters. The whole base had turned out for Harry's funeral, yet the general's personal grief was to remain private, tucked away and ably presided over by Mrs. H. The portrayal of Harry's military crispness was in sharp contrast with the easy lines of the classical scenes painted on the cabinet's door, yet this memory of a beloved son fit right into this woman's world.

Betty Ann reached out to adjust the position of the picture but stopped when she realized it was angled perfectly for optimal viewing from Mrs. H.'s wicker chair. Mrs. H. entered the room just as Betty Ann returned to the couch. Lucy rose beside her. Mrs. H. wore a lavender day dress and a diamond-shaped gold locket and chatted with her guests as if she had expected them.

This surprised Betty Ann, but she figured that Mrs. H., as a Southern lady, was observing the niceties of polite society, much like she imagined Lucifer's civility as he welcomed his denizens to Hell. Mrs. H. eventually waved for her guests to sit and sat herself in her wicker chair near the windows.

"Thank you both for your kind sympathy cards. There has been so much to do, I haven't had a chance to acknowledge them all. You know Harry was so very popular," Mrs. H. said.

Betty Ann wondered if she actually remembered their cards or just assumed they had done the right thing.

The maid brought in a coffee set and served them. Betty Ann and Lucy waited for their host to pick up her cup before they reached for theirs. Mrs. H. took a sip and glanced at Harry's picture.

"To what do I owe this unexpected pleasure?" She did not look particularly pleased.

Betty Ann wished to be anywhere but here, yet she had a job to do. She resolved to do right by Lonnie and Harry and all the other boys in uniform, so she scooched forward on the couch and put her coffee on the table. "Believe me, we would not dream of bothering you at a time like this if we could see any other course of action."

"Yes?"

"Some information has come to our attention. I would rather not say how, but it concerns your son, Harry."

"Go on."

Betty Ann drew an audible breath and let it out again. "What happened out there. It wasn't just an accident. Someone gave bad orders. Men died."

Silence.

"Including your son."

Silence.

"I'm sorry to have to tell you this, and believe me, if there were any other way—"

"How do you know this?" Mrs. H. guided her coffee onto the table, without looking down, while staring at Betty Ann. Her motionless friend might as well have been invisible.

Betty Ann fumbled in her pocketbook and drew out the scrubbed version of the Japanese translation. She handed it over. As hard as this was for her, and as much as she disliked Mrs. H.'s treatment of her, she couldn't imagine being in the other woman's place and having to maintain her composure while a subordinate delivered even more bad news about your son.

Mrs. H. held the edges of the page, as if it might be contaminated, and read down through its contents. Twice. She looked up with steady, steely eyes. "Where did you get this?"

"We can't say," Lucy said. "But, Mrs. Hepplewhite, we would not be here if we didn't know it was true."

Betty Ann was glad for the cover, as Mrs. H. turned her scrutiny on Lucy.

"You know how it is. There's an accident, which is unfortunate, but in recovering someone makes a mistake. That's unfortunate too." Lucy paused and shook her head. "But to put the fortune of electronics over the precious lives of our sons. And then to cover it up?" She pounded a fist on her lap. "That's unforgiveable." Mrs. H. continued to stare. "In our book, anyway." She slumped back in the couch.

Betty Ann was surprised by Lucy's obvious anger—she had no sons in the military. Of course, her Tony was a few short years from eligibility and the possibility of orders from some idiot officer. Betty Ann patted her hand.

"Why should I believe you?"

"Mrs. H., I may be reckless, but I'm not stupid." Betty Ann snapped, proving her first point, at least. "This is no time for games, even for me. And this," she indicated the letter, "is no joke."

Lucy squeezed Betty Ann's hand.

Mrs. H. let the paper fall from her fingers onto the table. She rose and went to inspect an ivy topiary on a table near the French doors to the patio. She picked off a few dried leaves and dropped them onto the soil below.

"My boy is dead," she said with her back to them. "I know what people say about me. Maybe you think I would want revenge." She turned to them. "No amount of revenge can bring my boy back." She narrowed her eyes. "But we can keep some son of a bitch from killing more of our own people."

"Yes, ma'am." Both Lucy and Betty Ann sat up straight.

"What do you propose to do?" Betty Ann asked.

Mrs. H. fingered the locket at her throat and turned back to the glass doors. Betty Ann noticed that she hadn't looked at her son's picture. Not once. Betty Ann wondered if the locket held her son's photo or a lock of his hair.

Mrs. H. watched a gardener push past with a wheelbarrow full of branches. "You have your secrets, I have mine."

"As you wish," Betty Ann said. She rustled as if preparing to leave.

"Of course, if you want to keep secrets, you shouldn't tell that pretty little Clara Menendez."

"Ma'am?" Betty Ann gave her a pleasantly quizzical look with eyebrows slightly raised. It was the look she used when a cop stopped her for speeding.

"Little Clara does the Officers' Wives Club books for me." Mrs. H.'s mouth pursed into a little smile. "Knowing you, Betty Ann, all I had to do was mention you and her husband in the same sentence and she was sniffling and complaining and spilling all the plans your crowd has hatched." She glanced between Betty Ann and Lucy. "Why did you invite her? She thinks she's one of us."

In a world divided into black and white, if you were neither, you would want to be on the team that seemed to be winning. Betty Ann knew that including Clara in their scheme had been a bad idea. Sure, she'd contributed intel about the copters, but they could've come up with something else. Meanwhile, Mrs. H. claimed herself free of vengeance, but here she was already torturing the bearers of bad news.

Mrs. H. came back and stood looking down at them. "Did you seriously think your plan wouldn't be discovered?" She laughed. "I had half a mind to tell the general to move the copters just to watch you all scramble like chickens. In fact—"

A siren sounded three short blasts.

Attention!

A pause.

The sound came from the tower near the parade grounds. It was loud here, much louder than in their neighborhood to the west of the main base. It reminded Betty Ann of the signals back home in southern Illinois. They lived in town, but her grandparents owned land outside of town where they kept chickens, goats, and a sheep or two. There the signals had been for the volunteer firemen. Her grandfather would stop mid-stride when the signal sounded, then run to the house and his car. He responded every time. You never knew when the blast might be for you. Betty Ann slipped her hand into Lucy's. Mrs. H. covered the locket at her throat and looked outside.

Two long blasts, two short. Pause. Repeat.

Betty Ann let out a sigh. A fire someplace on base, not good news, but better than the cycle of four short blasts that would send them dashing, pell-mell, to fallout shelters, all the while wondering if they would get in.

Lucy released her hand. They waited for Mrs. H. to speak. The air in the sun room was still, the perfect temperature. Mrs. H. stood motionless at the French doors, her steep nose outlined against the light from outside. The silence lengthened as she held this pose, her face pale.

"You were saying?" Betty Ann's words seemed to send ripples through the air, but the waves broke against the shield of silence that surrounded their hostess.

She and Lucy glanced at each other. In a similar situation, they might smother Mrs. H. in feminine concern, Betty Ann patting and cooing, Lucy fetching a glass of water or sending the maid for a cold compress. But this was the general's wife, and they sat in her house. She was grieving, yes, but not so much that she couldn't play her power games. Still, Betty Ann felt sorry for her. There was no larger loss of power than to be genuinely pitied by your underlings.

"Mrs. Hepplewhite." Betty Ann shifted as if to rise, which brought Mrs. H. back to life.

"Yes, quite," Mrs. H. said. She started back to the seating area but caught sight of the gardener. "Don't leave yet."

She opened the door and stepped out onto the brick patio. The light there, though not direct, was bright enough to wash out her features. She seemed an ordinary woman with an ordinary household to run. She called to the gardener, who set down the wheelbarrow and bowed his head to listen to her. Her guests could hear only the lilt of her voice.

"Now what?" Lucy asked.

Betty Ann shrugged and shook her head. "No telling." She swirled the cooled coffee in her cup.

The gardener's dark hair glistened as he nodded and walked away, leaving the wheelbarrow. He disappeared around the back corner of the house as Mrs. H. returned to the sun room. She perched on the other wicker chair facing the couch again and appeared composed. However, she kept up a light tapping with her little finger.

"I normally wouldn't do this." Mrs. H. patted her auburn hair and lowered her voice. "But you have brought me some very valuable information, and I do appreciate that. And I remember you gals did right by me. I wasn't going to let anything stop me from having the best dress Jackie Kennedy has ever seen on anyone except herself." She tilted her chin up, lengthened her neck, and pulled her ribs up out of her waist as if she were a prima ballerina. She stared at them with triumph in her tired eyes. On another day, her look may have terrorized. At that moment, though, with certainty stripped away from the world, she just looked ridiculous. She sank back into her waist and her fingers pressed against the crepey skin of her neck. "Besides, I appreciate initiative and loyalty. You two can keep a secret. Not like that Clara."

"Thank you for the vote of confidence. But we have work to do." Betty Ann pointed at the paper. "We'll leave that with you." She snapped her purse shut and sat forward on the couch to rise.

"Wait." The resonance in Mrs. H.'s voice seemed to stop time itself. It certainly arrested her guests.

Despite Betty Ann's shallow breaths and tightening throat, she admired Mrs. H.'s command. That's a main reason why the general married her, she mused in the instant after that one insistent word.

Mrs. H. rose and closed the door. She returned to stand in front of her guests. "This is something I haven't even given our maid." She pulled two blue cards from her dress pocket. "There's a fallout shelter. It's not on the maps. It's at the rear of the yard behind the Grayson House. I don't think even your captain knows about it. Anyway, with one of these cards, you can get in with three other people." She held out the cards, and Betty Ann and Lucy took them.

    FOR EMERGENCY USE ONLY
    Special Admittance, Four (4) Persons, 6 Maple Street

    Issued by _____

"There's no signature," Betty Ann said.

"Oh bother." Mrs. H. took back the cards and got a pen from the cabinet. She signed both and returned them.

"This is quite a surprise," Lucy said. "I don't mean to sound ungrateful, but why?"

Mrs. H. backed away and opened the door. She remained beside it, signaling the end of their meeting. "I take care of my people."

"But why us of all your people?" Betty Ann asked. Just a few minutes before, she had been torturing them. Now this.

"You could have kept your mouth shut about Harry. Probably would have been prudent to do so. But you didn't." She glanced at Harry's photo, then swiveled her head to look from one to the other. "I appreciate that."

"Thank you. Thank you very much." Betty Ann thought maybe she wouldn't have to worry about being exposed, but you could never tell. She stowed her blue card in her bag.

"Let's just hope that none of us ever has to use them," Mrs. H. said.

Lucy nodded and Betty Ann said, "Amen."

Mrs. H. shook their hands as they passed and the maid ushered them to the front door.

Neither of them spoke. Post-storm winds snatched at their skirts and pushed them across the road. Betty Ann grappled with the feeling that she had just been cut from the herd. For once, they were among the privileged. Of course, their privilege depended on the mercy of the person at the door. As always. She stuck the key in the ignition but didn't turn it.

"Not even her maid. Just think of all the crap that woman has to put up with, and she doesn't even rate."

"No telling if we would actually get in." Lucy echoed her own thoughts.

Betty Ann felt the new weight of the blue card in her purse as it lay on the seat beside her. The other wives carried no such burden. Instead, they bore their promises to each other and to their children. Gusts buffeted the car. The snap of the grand American flag and the slap of its tether filled Betty Ann's heart. She felt lighter.

"Listen. Anything happens, whoever has the kids tries to get as many of them into the shelter as possible. Otherwise, we stick to the plan."

Whatever the coming days would bring, Betty Ann would not face it alone. Neither would Lucy. And whether Mrs. H. wanted them there or not, they also had her back. Betty Ann started the car. They had work to do.

Mutually Assured Destruction 2

THE STEW WAS ready and the table set. Rosita stood in the archway to the courtyard. "Come eat dinner."

Diego and José continued to argue about baseball as if she hadn't spoken.

"Come on in," she said louder.

Diego stayed her with a finger as if she had interrupted tense negotiations at the United Nations. "We'll eat out here."

"Don't be difficult. Your wife has set the table inside. Come on now." She let the screen door bang. Eventually chairs scraped on the flagstone, and the two men made their way into the dining room.

The Sisters bunched around Rosita at one end of the table, while their husbands sat on either side of Ramón's empty chair at the other. The glass doors to the courtyard stood ajar, emitting fresh air and the distant noises of an unsettled city.

"Let's say grace," Rosita said.

"Where's the little manager?" Chita asked. Her hands were clasped for prayer, but her head remained unbowed.

Rosita stared at her husband's place. "Up on the widow's walk."

"What's he doing up there?" Chita asked.

"He wanted to check it out for a possible observation post. He has to decide who to assign to it when Chita and Diego are away."

Diego swore. "That pip-squeak isn't going to have his little buddies traipsing around my house."

"It's not your house," Lola said.

"Shut up, woman. You've done more than enough damage already," Diego said.

A single report of a gun burst through the open doors. Rosita and Lola flinched.

"Oh my God, what was that?" Chita said.

Lola relaxed into a shrug. "You know how the sound bounces. It could've come from anywhere."

"It was some patriot, happy to have a chance to shoot his gun," Diego said. He picked up his fork, but after glancing at his wife and Rosita, who had tears in her eyes, he set it down again. His voice was subdued. "It's another shell case for Beto's collection. That's all."

Rosita paled and took a deep breath with pursed lips. "Let's say grace." She reached for the hands of her sisters, who in turn reached for their husbands. They were united for a moment.

Then the moment was gone. The bickering resumed as soon as the first bite was taken. No one ate much, which left plenty of space for accusations and counter-assertions. Chita complained that Ramón's food was getting cold. The food she had helped to cook after driving all day and fixing a puncture in the wilderness.

"He'll be down," Rosita said. She hadn't touched her plate.

Diego glared at his wife. "I should turn you all in."

"Sure," Chita said. "Of course, I'd have to tell them about the shipments of petrol that never reach their intended destinations that supply the soldiers of our great country."

"You wouldn't dare. You've used too much of it yourself."

"I won't need it anymore in prison. Or in heaven."

Lola slapped the table. The dishes rattled. "Enough! No one here is going to tell anyone anything about anyone else here. Agreed?" She looked into the faces around the table.

"What about Ramón?" Chita asked.

All attention settled on Rosita.

"He won't talk," Rosita said. She shook her head with her lips pressed firmly in a straight line.

"Ha!" Diego said. "Where is he, anyway? He should be here. The weakest link and, as always, off someplace else. I want to hear from his own mealy mouth that his loyalty is to us."

"I don't know if I would believe him." Chita glared at Rosita, who still hadn't told Lola everything that happened over the mountains.

Rosita took another deep breath. "I'll get him." She stood and walked away from the table.

The phone rang.

"I'll get it." Chita jumped up and pushed past Rosita and out into the hallway. Diego continued to throw words at Lola, and José refused to defend her.

"Quiet!" Chita shouted.

She carried the heavy black phone on its long cord to the dining room and stopped beside Rosita. She held the handset to her heart as the angry words swirling around the table died away.

"They're in Texas. A place called Galveston. All of them." At last, Chita could cry.

Photo by Justine Martin, Dinner Geeks

Brenda Sparks Prescott lives and writes in eastern Massachusetts and southern Vermont. Her writing has appeared in publications such as *The Louisville Review*, *Crab Orchard Review*, *Portland Magazine*, and the anthology *Soap Opera Confidential*.

Brenda is co-chief editor of *Solstice Literary Magazine*, an advisory board member for the Solstice MFA in creative writing program, and a founding member of Simply Not Done, a women's writing collaborative. Brenda's family has a long history of military service, with records stretching back to the Civil War.

CPSIA information can be obtained
at www.ICGtesting.com
Printed in the USA
LVHW021159160321
681670LV00007B/234